Mike Robbins is a journalist turned development worker. He is also the author of *Even the Dead are Coming* (2009), a memoir of Sudan; *Crops and Carbon* (2011), on agriculture and climate change; a novel, *The Lost Baggage of Silvia Guzmán* (2014); and *The Nine Horizons* (2014), a pen-portrait of some of the countries in which he has worked and travelled since 1987.
He is currently in New York.

THREE SEASONS

THREE STORIES FROM ENGLAND IN THE EIGHTIES

MIKE ROBBINS

THE MORAL RIGHT OF THE AUTHOR HAS BEEN ASSERTED

NO PART OF THIS BOOK MAY BE USED OR REPRODUCED IN ANY MANNER WHATSOEVER WITHOUT WRITTEN PERMISSION FROM THE PUBLISHER EXCEPT IN THE CASE OF BRIEF QUOTATIONS EMBODIED IN CRITICAL ARTICLES OR REVIEWS.

© MIKE ROBBINS 2014

THIRDRAILBOOKS@GMAIL.COM

Cover design by Jasiek Krzysztofiak/www.jasiek.co.uk
Front cover picture by Dylan L. Spangler
Back cover picture by the author

First published in the United States

Publisher's Cataloging-in-Publication data

Robbins, Mike, 1957-
Three seasons: Three stories of England in the eighties / Mike Robbins. - 1st ed.
p. cm.
ISBN 978-0-9914374-5-0 (paperback)
I. Robbins, Mike, 1957- II. Three Seasons.
PR6118.O23256 T47 2014
823.92--dc23

Acknowledgements

THERE are a number of people without whom this book would not exist, or would be less than whatever it is. I would particularly like to thank Tim Oliver, for whom I worked at *Fishing News* in the 1980s. The first of these stories, *Spring*, was inspired in part by Tim's stories of the deep-sea fishing industry, recounted in the City Pride pub next to our London office. Many years on, he has been kind enough to review the fishing-related parts of the text (but any errors that remain are mine).

Christina Harlow gave invaluable help with preparation of the manuscript for publication. Several people provided useful advice on the draft text; I would especially like to thank Lindsay Davies. Others whose comments were helpful include Samuel Astbury, Stephanie Jelks, Peter Jason Payne and Katharine Vincent.

Last but not least, as the project neared completion, Sandrine Ligabue and Hazel Marsh provided moral support. Writers need that.

Three Seasons

Spring 9

Summer 81

Autumn 151

I   SPRING

WHEN the door of the pub opened it let in a wave of cool air, touching the faces of the drinkers in the saloon bar who had been there since half-past seven and reminding them that it was half-past ten. In fact, it was not that cold outside; a blustery, slightly muggy spring night, and the bar was warm. Every figure was spectrally wreathed in cigarette smoke, their outlines further blurred by the seven or eight pints of Old Nick that Skip had drunk.

Old Nick was right, he reckoned, for it was the very devil to keep down. Not his thing, this Real Ale, with its flat, smooth texture. He missed the slight fizz and clean white head of the beer in the North, dispensed from normal electric pumps instead of these handpumps with their pretentious decorated ceramic handles. Not for the first time, he felt homesick.

He turned at the open door and looked back at the bar where he had spent the evening, propped up on the polished wood surface, his elbows in pools of beer, pushing the flanelette mats awry so that every so often an irascible landlord would pointedly straighten them, cleaning up the beer with his rag. Self-important idiot, thought Skip.

"I thought you was going!" yelled the landlord, a florid man in his fifties.

"I am that."

"Well, get gone, instead of staring back like this was paradise, and close the door before we all catch our death!"

By way of rejoinder, Skip gave a parting belch. Oh, that was a good one, he thought, trying to savour the stomach gases as he did so.

He'd show the buggers tomorrow, he thought with grim satisfaction. He'd show these self-satisfied little southerners what happened when a real fisherman got to work, he told himself as he let the bar door of the *Lobster* swing shut behind him. It would work. And he'd built it himself. Every last little steel bar. And mounted it on his own boat. Two long years and those little men from the Manpower Services Commission sniffing round the workshop trying to find out what he'd done with their forty-quid-a-week grant. Waving copies of *Fishing News* at him, trying to show him how good the price of sole was now, and why wasn't he out there doing something about it? Well, now they would see why.

He turned left out of the *Lobster* – and started doing the Lobster Quadrille. This always happened after a half-decent night in there nowadays. His legs wouldn't stay under him, and he had to keep chasing them to get on top of them. First one, then the other. Then after that they would behave themselves, and bear him home.

At the end of the street he turned left again, and now he was walking along the main dock. To his right, the ships were lined against the quay. Not the big cross-channel ferries – they were on the other side, where they disgorged their load of trucks and holiday-makers – but the merchant ships, coasters and small bulk carriers, towering above him in the night. Their sides and the cranes were reflected in the pools of water that had collected from the day's rain, beaded films of multicoloured diesel spreading over the surface, the damp concrete reflecting the glow of the arc-lights; at the end of the dock the asphalt of the access road glistened in the orange light of the street-lamps. The deck of a freighter, lit for work, seemed like a bubble floating, tens of feet up, in the darkness. From it came the babble of English and Polish voices.

Skip made his way, veering to right and left. He felt slightly sick. He lit a cigarette, taking one of his last two or three Rothmans from its rather crushed packet; it had bent slightly, corrugating the paper near the filter. But it lit, and he took a long drag.

This was a mistake. Saliva poured into the back of his mouth, and then he threw up. But if anyone saw him, they didn't care. Actually it made him feel a bit better, releasing those great gobs of thick brown liquid that gurgled up from deep within him like love or nostalgia is wont to do and then splashed his shoes as they hit the tarmac. He sweated slightly, and felt as if his eyes were made of rubber.

Home was not far away. Skip crossed the main street that ran across the head of the docks, deserted except for a police car which stood by the kerb. Its occupants sat inside.

"Old bugger's pissed again."

"Leave him to it."

"Reckon 'e's alright then?"

"Yeah, no problem."

"Heard something about his taking his boat out tomorrow with that new gear."

"Coastguard know?"

"Told him today."

"'Spect he'll be alright."

"Oh yes. Bugger's always sober in the morning."

They watched Skip make his way towards a side-street past the tobacconist's. Every now and then a little drizzle fell across the windscreen.

"Typical April," said one of the officers, stretching and sighing.

The street that Skip lived in was an ordinary one of semi-detached seaside houses, 1930s brickwork with rose-bushes in the front gardens. He found his key. The house he went to had been divided up into bedsits, and there was a common front door. He opened it after scratching around the socket with his key for a minute or two, and then closed it as quietly as he could so as not to wake the other residents, who were mostly elderly.

It seemed a long way up to his room that night. But by the time he made it he felt a little more sober. Perhaps throwing up on the quayside had helped.

The room had a cleanliness and order that reflected pride in a greater past. The walls were white, the carpet a complicated pattern of bright colours, faded a little with age; so were the curtains, which he now pulled closed, blocking out the orange streetlamps that refracted in the raindrops on the glass and cast a thousand small patterns of their own on the wall behind. He put the kettle on the gas ring and settled back in his easy-chair. He wasn't worried about getting up the next morning, beer notwithstanding. He'd been getting up early for forty years.

He made himself some coffee and smoked another cigarette, his eyes half-closed. In his mind he looked out through another spray-spattered window, great sheets of water running off the perspex, sliding this way and that as the big trawler rolled. He looked at the deck before him; it dipped down below the waves and, when it rose, sent cascades of grey water streaming back across the sides. He saw the sidewinder deck gear, so encrusted with ice that each rope was twice its normal diameter.

He smiled. Then he frowned.

"Tore her heart out," he muttered. "Tore her bloody heart out, that's what they did."

***   ***   ***

KEVIN did have trouble getting up in the morning.

Dawn had broken over the town. It was clearer now, but mid-grey clouds still swamped the sun, leaving a faint orange line along the horizon. Now and then the sun fought back, seeking a crack in the clouds through which it sent a weak ray over the wet countryside. It still wasn't very cold, but there was a brisk wind.

Kevin, at 17, was still growing. Day by day quite unreasonable amounts of food vanished into him. Steaming plates of spaghetti chased casserole dishes of beef stew to join the mighty roast of the day before, to fuel the building of a new human machine. The machine didn't look that impressive, being a shade under five foot ten and rather thin; but his face was open and cheerful, albeit so covered in spots that you'd be hard put to find unblemished skin in between.

Kevin's morning alarm was a radio-cassette machine linked to a central heating timer. It clicked and the radio released a wave of music that distorted the tinny speaker. Kevin stirred.

His eyes closed again, then opened.

Big day today.

He hauled himself upright and first one leg, then the other broke out from under the covers.

"Turn that bloody racket off," shouted his father from the bathroom.

He turned the music down a bit, and as his father left the bathroom he slouched into it. He stood for a moment in front of the mirror, squeezing the spots that had come up during the night.

"Good crop today," he murmured.

He liked it when a nice neat white spot had formed at the end of a lump and gentle pressure could force out a small jet of bloody pus, which would hit the surface of the mirror leaving a satisfying splat. Trouble was you had to clean it off with water because if you didn't it would smear, and even then the water left a little trail of droplets across the surface. Then you had to clean it up with your fingers. However, most of the spots this morning were too small to give much satisfaction, and those that weren't had simply congealed into red weals.

He washed his face, not bothering with the one day's growth of stubble, which was still thin. In his room he dressed; long johns first, then good thick jeans. Double socks; wellies would go over the top. Two vests, then his shirt and a big shaggy Norwegian polo-neck. He would pick up his anorak from the hall later.

In the kitchen, Mr. and Mrs. Tilley were already eating breakfast. Plenty of bacon and egg, preceded by porridge with a load of sugar on top and rivulets of milk slopping around the edges. He ate greedily.

"Big day today," he mumbled between mouthfuls.

"So you keep telling us," said his father, a thinning, greying fiftyish. He slurped his coffee noisily.

"You be careful on that bloody boat," said his wife.

"Been all right before, hasn't it?" said Kevin. "Got a good run of sole week before last. You ate some of it."

"Well, yes," admitted his father. "But it'll be different now with all these wretched hooks and things."

"He's obsessed," said Kevin's mother. "All those dreams of the sea and a picture of a bloody boat on the office wall."

"That's no boat, that's the *Duke of Marlborough*," said Kevin, trying to talk while shovelling another mouthful of bacon and egg, rind and all, into the gaping chasm of his mouth. "It's the best boat that ever fished the Arctic."

"So your damn Skip keeps telling you," grumbled his father. "All this talk of silver sole and whatnot."

"Silver cod," his wife corrected him, her coffee-cup pausing on its way to her mouth.

"Didn't ought to give them grants for these things, all this damn mucking about," went on Mr. Tilley, frowning down at the front page of the *Gazette*.

"It's exciting," said Kevin.

"You want to get a proper job, you do."

"I'd rather be cold and wet than get a job as a forklift driver in a bleeding bogroll factory," said Kevin, now with a slightly surly note.

"It's bloody steady," his father snapped. "And don't go talking like that, show some respect. Bloody bogroll factory. What would you do without toilet paper? Eh? Who do you think you are?"

Without looking up, Kevin shifted his position in his chair slightly so that one buttock was in the air and broke wind with aplomb.

"Now that's enough," barked his father, making as if to rise.

"You ought to apologise to your dad," said Mrs. Tilley, but gently. "It's been all right for us. There's been food and a home and a decent Christmas every year." She turned to her husband. "You let him have his dreams, Ron. He'll grow out of it. And if he doesn't, who's to know? Maybe he's right."

"Oh, sod it," sighed Ron Tilley and settled back into his chair.

"Anyone'd think you were on both sides," he grumbled to his wife after the door had slammed and Kevin had gone. "It's that skipper, that's what it is. Saw him in the Lobster last night, pissed as a fart again he was. He's been filling that lad's head with dreams and stories."

"He'll be all right," said his wife gently. "Drink your coffee, lovey."

Her husband grunted a little less harshly.

Kevin flew through the early-morning air on his bicycle, waving at the milkman as he went, braking at the last minute before the main Brighton road and swerving into it, making one of the big green double-decker buses jerk to avoid him. It sounded its horn, and drew up at the bus-stop as he veered to the right of it, flying through the thin cloud of diesel smoke and on towards the harbour. His anorak stayed where, in his hurry, he had left it, forgotten, draped over the hall stand across his father's umbrella.

*** *** ***

SKIP stood on the stern of the boat, which rocked rhythmically in the slight swell. His eyes were, again, half-closed; he could see the silverware, the flawless white tablecloth, the long, long table where they all sat; David was on his left, someone was making a speech. The waiters slipped past in their penguin suits, high, starched white collars and jet-black cloth, trays of food balanced on their finger-tips, noses in the air.

He opened his eyes and saw the crews worked to ready their boats for sea. A thin morning sunshine had broken through and the sky was blue, but patches of very dark grey cloud hung on above the town, in which the first cars were beginning to move.

There were thirty or forty small boats tied up around the quay. The smallest were the little charter-boats, mostly fibreglass with forward, moulded wheelhouses and tiny cuddies in the bow crammed with ropes and rods. Little happened on them as yet. It was not the best season, although Easter was not far ahead; the first of their customers would come then, hobby fishermen mostly, from South London and Reigate and Tonbridge. One or two of the charter-boat owners were walking around, discussing prospects, with maybe a thought to slip out for a nice bit of bass for the market. Skip wished that they would leave it to the professionals.

Also in the harbour were rather different vessels, wooden craft of maybe twenty or thirty feet, old, clinker-built. Some were lamentably tatty. Others were not. There was *Norma*, thirty years old, built in the town, proud in her scarlet paint and white wheelhouse, which was set well to the rear, which was where Skip reckoned a wheelhouse ought to be. On her deck were piles of pots, ready for lobster. *Norma* would go a long way out to those pots, slow as she was. And her skipper, a steady man, would do well.

Here and there was a forty-foot steelship. Most were actually just under forty feet, to squeeze in under the ten-metre rule, so that they could work inshore. Some were rigged for beam-trawling, so that for'd of their aft superstructures stood tall masts with subsidiary spars on either side, slanting to a common base like a V with a central post. These spars would lower towards the water and haul the beam-trawl. Locally-built, these steelships were the pride of their crews, quite unlike any other type of boat; the engines, big Caterpillars or Kelvins, had plenty of grunt, belting out 300HP and more to keep the boats ahead of the fish. They were sited deep down in the keel to give room for big fishrooms, and their contents could pay. Sole and plaice brought big money on the South Coast. London's hotels, and its new supermarkets with the fishmongers' counters in the corners. Bitty, little things, those fish, thought Skip dreamily. His mind wandered back a quarter of a century again, and he saw the stiff-necked waiters, the trophy gleaming dully on its plinth; John beside him, not yet forty then and still fit, and David, ten years younger, broad shoulders awkward in dinner-jacket, a cigar held strangely in his fingers where a roll-up should be.

The sight of a bicycle swooping down the quay jerked him back to the present. He half-turned and called over his shoulder:

"Lad's here, Dave!"

"Bang on time for once."

"He's not a bad little bugger."

"No, I don't reckon he is." David, six foot and stocky, walked along the quay towards him, burdened with two big pails. "Where'd you want these then?"

"Leave 'em in the stern, next bait cutter."

"Right. What's left to do then?"

"Done it last night, mostly," said Skip. He handed David a cigarette, which the other took without comment. He leaned towards Skip's petrol lighter and, as he did so, caught something on the older man's breath. Then he told himself he must be wrong. Despite all the beer of the night before, Skip looked good this morning. At sixty, he was still a powerful man; his head was large and square, his hair grey but still thick; his mouth was large but ringed with powerful muscles that clenched when he was angry or tense, and then his high, wrinkled forehead would come down to shade his piercing pale-blue eyes with shaggy eyebrows.

"Sorry I'm late," said Kevin breathlessly, screeching to a halt on the quay.

"You ain't, for once," said David.

"Yes he is," said Skip. "Thirty seconds." He bent down and took a piece of bait between his fingers, and flicked it at the boy. It missed. "Good lad. Go and get us a brew, then."

"Yep!" Kevin grinned and made for the shed. He threw his bike against the wall, but it didn't stay there; it wheeled itself forward, the front wheel veered away from the brickwork, and the machine slid down against the wall, landing with a clatter, its rear wheel spinning round and round. As it did so the chain detached itself from the front sprocket and dragged in the dust.

"Shite," said Kevin.

"Language!"

In the shed, John hauled himself off his chair; he was tall, thin, old, bent forward a little, eyes quizzical and humorous. "He'd have you gut every cod on the ship for that, back on the Duke."

"Ain't on the *Duke*, are we?" replied Kevin, bouncing towards the kettle. "Be great if we were. Hey, is that woman here yet?"

"Nope," said John.

***   ***   ***

AT THE kerb in the still-quiet high street at the end of the harbour stood a little light-blue Fiesta car. Inside, Katherine from the *Gazette* prepared for the first assignment of the morning. On the seat beside her were a notebook and a small tape-recorder, and a newish Canon F1 with a zoom lens.

Katherine was a tall, slim woman of twenty-two, recently out of the University of Sussex. Her hair was short and thick, darkish blonde, with a boyish cut. Her face was good-natured, with brown eyes and a snub nose; she had a broad gash of a mouth and, like Skip's, it had strong muscles around the edges, although instead of tightening into a hard purse, more often they dimpled or spread her mouth into a smile that showed her white, even teeth. She was pretty, and knew it, and told herself not to use it.

She had a slight knot in her stomach, as she still always did before starting a job with strangers. She could never quite settle her stomach in the morning, and every now and then she tightened it in response to a slight, sharp protest, wishing that she hadn't bolted her breakfast and left home in such a hurry.

The radio was on and she tapped her fingers gently against the wheel, a track by Terence Trent D'Arby:

Sign *your name* across *my heart, I* want *you to be my* lady*!*

It faded. The time signals went. "It's seven, and time for the latest news on BBC Radio Kent," began the presenter.

She clicked off the radio and glanced at the small digital clock above the mirror. Then she tossed a cigarette-end out of the window, the taste of the smoke blending thickly with breakfast.

She drove the car the hundred yards or so round the corner and onto the quay. It wasn't hard to find the workshop. The temperature seemed to have dropped a little, and a fresh breeze was starting to stir the dirty waters of the harbour.

Katherine parked the car, locked it and went into the workshop. What she saw there was typical of marine workshops everywhere. Wires and ropes were jumbled on the shelves at the side, old calendars with cheesecake pictures covered the walls, mugs with the dregs of yesterday's coffee littered the tables. The room had a single bare, dusty bulb. But the floor had recently been swept clean and a broom was leaning against the wall where it would fall quickly to hand.

She was facing an eager youth, about her height, who grinned at her. He was pockmarked, with a face that looked like the wrong side of the moon, but despite that he wasn't bad looking. Immediately she smiled back, and his own grin got a little broader.

Behind him a thin man in late middle age raised himself awkwardly out of his chair and stretched out a hand to greet her. He held himself awkwardly and she sensed he might be in pain. "I'm John. I do the office stuff. This is Kevin, our gopher. Tea?"

"That'd be nice."

David and Skip were already on their way back across the quay, having seen this vision in black nylon bomber-jacket and tight jeans disappear into the workshop.

"Must be an omen," said David.

Skip nodded. "Reckon it's Christmas."

"Show her your hooks and snoods will you?"

"She might get lucky," replied Skip dourly. He bent slightly as he entered the workshop, a reflex from years of crawling around boats. "Miss Hailey?"

"That's me." She smiled, and shook hands. "We've spoken on the 'phone."

"Yes, well, we'll be off soon," said Skip. "You want to come on board and see the gear?"

"If I may."

"You may."

He motioned to her to follow him and together all of them, except

John, walked across the quay and on to the wooden slats of the jetty. There were many boats tied up. But the jetty wasn't long; their boat lay at the end.

She was of thirty-three feet, fibreglass, with a forward wheelhouse, giving her the look of a cabin cruiser. The whole of the area behind the short wheelhouse was an open working deck, and on this was a strange contraption. On the port side a long steel bar, raised above waist-height off the deck, ran the length of the deck from the wheelhouse to the stern – about two-thirds of the vessel's length; on this bar hung the snoods, dozens and dozens of nylon strands a couple of inches long. At the end of each was a gleaming stainless-steel hook. At the end of the bar, on the stern, was a sort of steel gate and above that a funnel. Meanwhile, at the wheelhouse end, on the other – starboard – side, was a post, again at about waist height, with two little steel bars on top, about an inch apart.

"It looks like a sewing machine," said Katherine, bewildered.

"And it'll change the fabric of fishing in this port!" said Skip with a rare grin. "Now come aboard, you, and I'll show you what it all does."

He leaped down onto the deck, and held out his hand for her to climb over. After a moment's hesitation she took it. "Mind the side, it's a bit slippy, that. From our Kevin throwing up on it every day."

"I never," protested Kevin, open-mouthed.

"What is it?" asked Katherine, raising her camera automatically to her eyes.

"It's a longliner."

"A what?"

"A longliner." Skip thought for a minute, and then continued: "Reckon you think of most of us as putting nets out and dragging them, don't you? Or maybe setting down pots."

"Right."

"Well, some boats don't do that. They put hundreds of hooks on a line, which they then bait, buoy and leave. When you've slipped the one, you nip off and put down another and when you've done that, you come back and collect the first. Simple."

"I see. But I've never seen that done before."

"You won't, not round here. You'll see it in North Wales, where they're lining on the dogs..."

"Dogs?" Katherine had a sudden vision of Basset hounds being hauled, yelping, from the water.

"Spurdogs," said David helpfully.

"I see," said Katherine, who didn't.

"And the Norwegians," Skip went on. "They're the past masters at this game. But there are problems. You see, it costs money to bait hooks by hand. I read of one fella in the *Fishing News*, he'd spent £18,000 in a year on men on the dole as labour, no questions asked, cash in hand. God knows how he wrote it off the books."

Katherine smiled.

"But why fish this way?" she asked. "Why not trawl?"

"Trawling's got its drawbacks," put in David. "You get good fishing inshore. But that's where people snag their nets. No-one wants to come fast, it's dangerous. But it's not just that. Nets are expensive."

"How much?" asked Katherine. She had switched on the pocket tape-recorder but was scribbling in her notebook at the same time.

"Maybe two or three hundred quid for a set on a boat like this. But there's more to it than that," said Skip. "And here" – he gave a slight smile – "is a local angle for your paper."

"Oh good," said Katherine.

"The fish we catch down here have a very high catch-value. Codling, bass. We'll get them fresh to the London restaurants because we're not too far away. But they've got to be in good condition. A trawl damages them. They get squashed. And if we use a gill-net, they damage themselves struggling to get free. This way we'll get nice fresh fish for your tea."

"I understand. So what does this machine do that makes line-fishing easier?"

"A lot." David again. "The hooks will be shot out over the stern from this steel bar. On their way, they'll go through the random baiter. Here, come and have a look."

She looked down the funnel above the line of hooks and saw two savage steel discs. On the funnel was a very graphic little graphic showing a finger being cut off.

Skip grinned.

"It's the lad. He'd be the one to get his fingers chopped off. He's a bit like that."

"And this is the bait?" Katherine looked down into the pail, in which she could see a damp, purplish, half-frozen mush.

"Squid," said Skip. "Frozen squid from France. Here, want a bit?" He dug his fingers in and held up a fragment for her inspection.

"No thanks," she said, nose wrinkling a little. "I've had it in Greek restaurants, though."

"Oh, yes. Nothing's too good for our cod," said Skip

"Cod? I thought bass was the most profitable species."

"Oh yes. But it's the cod *I* want." Skip seemed to lose concentration for a moment. "Always was, always is."

"And here's where the line will be hauled back in," said David quickly, steering her to the post on the starboard side behind the wheelhouse. "There'll be a man standing here to take the fish off as they come in. If he missed any, they'll be taken off by those two steel bars between which the line runs. Then the snoods and hooks will be lined up on the bar along the port side, automatically, ready to shoot again."

"Where does the power come from?" asked Katherine. "Is the line moved electrically?"

"No, no, hydraulically," said Skip, flicking the start-stop lever in and out of position. "See?"

"I think it's ingenious," said Katherine honestly. "Did you dream it up yourself?"

"Oh, no," replied Skip. "The Norwegians have been building autoliners for years, sometimes with precision baiters that attach the bait to each hook with a hammer. Some big Norwegian boats work 10,000 hooks. We'll not shoot more than a thousand from this. In fact, they sold a couple of big systems into Aberdeen some years ago, but the Scots weren't really interested and they didn't make them work."

"So why haven't you bought-in a system?"

"Money," said Skip crisply. "We'd be paying upwards of £25,000 for a rig like this. It took me two years to design and build this, but I reckon I spent less than a third of that. Get it back in 18 months' hard fishing and then the sky's the limit. I'll licence more systems and we'll build one for one of 'em ten-metre steelships, and we'll work inshore with 3,000 hooks and more. Oh, I'll be the King of Cod again yet, you'll see."

"Again?" Katherine smiled and lifted her chin slightly.

Skip seemed to be about to say something.

"Come and see the rest of the boat," said David.

They showed her. "It's not a *real* boat," said Skip. "Just fibreglass. Plastic pig." But she admired the decking and the woodwork in the wheelhouse, shiny iroko, beautifully-kept; and saw the arsenal of instruments in the wheelhouse, radio, radar, a small echosounder, even a colour video plotter that gave you an electronic chart on which you could follow your course, and flick a switch to give you an overlay showing wrecks and buoys or fishing limits, or pipelines, or the whole lot; and zoom in and out to see larger or smaller areas of the chart.

"Japanese?" she asked.

"British," replied Skip with satisfaction. "And the engine – a Kelvin from Glasgow. And the boat's a Lochin 33 from Southampton." He grunted. "I'll tell you, this country'll do it yet."

From the starboard side came the sound of an engine. They turned; through the wheelhouse door they saw one of the ten-metre steelships bound for the open sea. She chugged past against a background of masts and derricks, under the great green flanks of a Baltic freighter that had arrived overnight. The steelship's beam-trawl gear was up and someone had hung a bucket from it. Men in wellingtons and jerseys busied themselves around the deck. The small steelship was painted a bright, warm scarlet and this and her brilliant white superstructure were reflected in the still-calm water with crystal clarity. Behind her spread a silvery-white wake, clusters of seabirds wheeling and calling above its boiling surface.

Skip grinned.

"Reckon it's about time we buggered off and all," he said. He held out his hand to Katherine. "Thankyou for coming, Miss Hailey. Nip down around six and I hope I'll show you some damn fine cod."

"I'll buy some off you for my supper," said Katherine, shaking the hand firmly.

"It'll be on me," said Skip. "'Bye, lass."

As she scrambled over the side and up on to the jetty, she flashed a smile at Kevin, who was bent over the line of hooks, separating snoods that seemed too close together. He returned it.

"'Bye, Miss," he called. "Don't work too hard,"

"Shan't," she said, and gave him a big wink. He was delighted, and his smile broadened.

Ropes were untied and the vessel moved forward from her position in her berth, the Kelvin burbling briskly into life to join the mixed band of Sabres, Mermaids, Listers and Ivecos that were pushing their vessels out to sea. As the stern swung away, Katherine caught sight of the name on it and realised that she had forgotten to write it down. She did so now.

She waved a last time, turned and walked back to the workshop. In it, John was sitting at a table, jotting down figures, having left the vessel shortly before her.

He hauled himself out of his chair again.

"Please don't get up," said Katherine quickly. "I just called to say cheerio."

"Thanks for coming," he replied. His voice lacked the cheery, open quality of Skip's and David's.

"Are you not going to sea?" she asked him.

"No."

"Do you always stay on shore?"

"Mostly, now. Bit of trouble with my joints."

"Arthritis?"

"Not quite. Got blown up minesweeping," he said. He smiled slightly. "Long time ago, now, that. I did get better, and the joints never bothered me much, not really. It's just the last ten years they've ached a bit."

"You were *minesweeping*? How old were you?"

He laughed. "Fifteen. It was right at the end of the war. I'm fifty-seven now. Matter of fact, we weren't minesweeping ourselves just then. We were putting to sea. One of them Wellingtons had just flown over, with those huge magnetic rings round it, to set off the mines, and we thought we were in a swept channel. More fool us."

He smiled.

"What did you think of our longliner, then?"

"I'm fascinated," she said. She was. Something about Skip had caught her imagination."Can you answer a question for me?"

"Surely."

"The boat's name. *Silver Cod*?"

John nodded. "That was a big prize they used to dole out every year for the best-fishing boat and skipper. Won that, we did, years back, on the *Duke of Marlborough*. When was that now? 1964, I guess. Maybe '65."

"You were sailing with Skip then?"

"Yep."

"How come you all came down here?"

"Same reason there's good men in Hull now, hanging round with nowt to do," said John. He wore a slight smile. "You know what happened to the East Coast fleet?"

"A little. Not a lot," she replied. "I know it was something to do with Iceland. But it was a long time ago, wasn't it? I was only nine or ten at the time."

"Do you want to hear the story?" He seemed a little cautious now. "I'd not want to bore you."

"You won't bore me," said Katherine. "I'm not doing much more this morning, anyway. Just popping down to the General to see how many fresh corpses they've had in overnight."

At this he laughed, and it was a rich, full laugh, totally lacking in malice. "You never did have that cup of tea. Set yourself down, young lady."

She did as she was bid, looking around the workshop with its friendly, busy clutter. Bits of pumps and gear littered the benches along with notebooks and invoices; a garish calendar, overlaid with dust, hung on the wall at shoulder-height, depicting last December's lady-for-you from some manufacturer of refrigeration equipment. An old black telephone sat on a workbench, half-covered with flimsy invoices, its handpiece covered with oily fingermarks. It was quiet in the room, save for the sound of the gas-ring hissing as John made tea, but outside as if from another dimension came the sounds of men carrying equipment to boats, shouting and calling to each other in morning greeting. It reminded Katherine of being ill as a child, maybe with late-winter 'flu, lying in the quiet while the sound of traffic filtered in from the street outside.

It did not take John long to make two big, strong mugs of tea. Like everything else in the room, the mugs had the marks of an gear manufacturer on them, left over from Christmas. John's bore the logo of a net importer at Romney; Katherine's, that of a winch-builder in Yorkshire.

John settled himself back into his chair.

"Well, I'm no storyteller really," he said. "But I was born on the East Coast and when I was young, there was one hell of a fleet there. All the big companies had fleets of maybe ten or twenty ships each, big boats of up to two hundred foot, sidewinders mostly."

"Sidewinders?"

"They'll bring the catch in over the side, so the superstructure's aft to give space. Later we had a lot of stern trawlers, with for'd superstructure and gantries over the stern. But I was on sidewinders right to the bitter end."

"Where did they fish?" asked Katherine. "There isn't much for a fleet that size to catch close inshore, is there?"

"No, not so much. But they were designed to go a long, long way out," said John. He nodded. "A hundred and fifty years ago, Yorkshire men found the Silver Pits. That's right out in the North Sea. We built our fleet from there northwards until we were off Iceland, and right round into the White Sea, and around Spitzbergen, and some of the lads used to go to Grand Banks – right over there off Newfoundland." He paused. "You know where that is?"

"Canada," said Katherine. "Near where the St. Lawrence comes out into the North Atlantic."

"That's it."

"Did you fish off Newfoundland?"

"Not a lot. North Cape of Iceland, mostly, and Skip used to like the White Sea, North Norway, that way."

"When was that? In summer?"

"Dear me, no!" John chuckled. "All the days God sent, year in, year out, and the wind would cut you like a sword."

"But what about the icebergs?"

A grin. "What about the buggers?"

"Didn't you hit any?"

"Naah... No need. Plenty ice enough in the hold already." Still grinning, he shrugged. "It depends how good you are, doesn't it? Never so much as hit an ice cube with Skip. Never did hold back, though. Never was joking, that man."

"How many crew would you have?"

"Oh, could be twenty or so."

"How did you live? Weren't you at sea for a while?"

"Oh yes, three weeks at a stretch, maybe. The quarters were pretty cramped. At least you had heads by the time I was twenty-five, thirty."

"You mean the toilets."

"Save you a freezing arse in the winter, I can tell you."

"You mean you didn't always have them?" Katherine's eyes rolled.

"Ah, no. Lost the odd good man that way, did Hull and Grimsby. You could follow your arse over the side if you weren't careful. Some of the owners...Well, that's another story." He sighed. "But with Skip you always had a decent bunk and somewhere to dry your clothes, and you didn't notice much more. You'd be working maybe thirty-six hours at a stretch. After a good haul, you'd be at it that long gutting the fish and getting 'em below. And if it weren't a good haul, you'd not go back to bed. It were shoot and haul, shoot and haul till you were fair fit to drop.

"Skip was hard for that. If he thought he could shoot he'd put the gear our and it didn't matter if your arms were dropping off, and I've seen a man complain when the order came to shoot, 'Get off my bridge or I'll kill you,' he says back, an' I reckon he would have struck him if I hadn't stepped forward and told the man to get gone. I was mate then."

"You make him sound cruel," said Katherine sadly. "He does look hard, but he doesn't look a vicious man."

"He never was, and I was glad to be with him," said John. He shook his head. "You see, a skipper was as good as his last haul. One good grossing and he was king for a day. Get a bad trip and he'd have to fight before the Company would give him another boat. If he didn't push the men hard enough, or argued about the state of the boat, he wouldn't get another trip either. Skip did answer back and he mostly got away with it because they knew he was good. Once he went too far and they put him on a coal-fired heap of gribble-worm. He didn't get the message, though; he came back with the only good grossing that week. Had to give him the *Duke* back then. You should have seen him that week, reading the grossings in the *Fishing News*. Laughed like drains, all of us..."

Another quiet smile, but it slipped away.

"And that's why I was glad of him. He'd only push it so far. He was hard, but there were skippers'd have you over the side and not give a damn. But Skip, well, if he caught a man going to bed with wet clothes on and without a hot meal he'd pull him, and me, up sharp. 'John,' he said to me one night, 'I've got to make them do this and if I don't they'll get someone worse. But I shan't kill them. You see they're warm and dry.'"

He looked across at Katherine.

"Drink your tea, it'll get cold."

Katherine smiled. "I forgot it. You said you weren't a good storyteller."

She turned around so that she was facing John, her elbows on the table. Her hands were cupped round the warm mug. "Anyway, go on. Some of the skippers pushed too hard, did they?"

"Oh yes. But I reckon they never did get the really big grossings. Because if a man pushes things too hard, he'll come unstuck in the end. Skip knew that. Mind you, when *Lorella* and *Roderigo* were lost, everyone got a shock then. This was in the mid-fifties. It was winter and they'd gone north of Iceland. The rest of the fleet weren't far away. Their gear iced up. The crews knew what was happening, mind, but they couldn't steam south because they couldn't turn broadside to the storm. They sank and they'd known they would for at least a day. *Roderigo* sent messages right until she went over, as they knew they were going to. Twenty-odd men on each boat. Lost with all hands."

"Why didn't the other ships come alongside and take them off?"

"Not in those seas. All they could do was listen. After that there was a Royal Commission. But it takes years for boats to change. But then one winter in the late 'sixties we lost three Hull ships to icing off Iceland inside a fortnight. Just one survivor, there was, a bloke from a ship called the *Ross Cleveland*. Everyone else from the three ships was lost, nearly sixty in all. We got regular reports from the weather ship after that, and when they said stop, go home, my God we did. Good thing too, because *everyone* did. No-one dared stay and sneak another haul to keep in with the Company, and put his men in danger.

"One day we were working off the North Cape of Iceland and the weather ship came on. 'Everyone stop fishing,' they said. Now, they almost never said that. Only if the seas were running so high, the ice so bad, that we wouldn't have a chance. Skip was on the bridge. He was just about to shoot and he turns round to me and says, "Get the gear in, we're going home." We'd only shot twice. And this Scots voice comes over the VHF. Peterhead man, he was, skippering an English ship. By Christ he was a head case. 'I'm going to shoot once more, lads," he says. I hear another voice, one of our own skippers. 'Well you're a murdering bastard'.' John took out a small tobacco-tin and slowly untwisted the lid. "And do you know, he didn't shoot. He turned for home. No-one was lost that trip."

They sat in silence for a moment. Katherine watched him take a thin cigarette-paper and roll up, quickly and deftly; although his hands were well-worn and calloused, his fingers were slender and agile. He placed some tobacco in the paper and teased it out so that it ran the length of the cigarette; then he thickened it up with more, rolled it, sealed it after passing his tongue along the seam, and handed it to the girl. She nodded and took it, and lit it with his big petrol lighter that lay on the table.

He started to roll another for himself.

"Why did you do it?" asked Katherine. "Why did you go fishing? Wasn't there something else to do, in those years, just after the war, and in the 'fifties, when people were doing so well?"

John thought for a moment. He sat back in his chair, moving his mug slowly around. It was nearly empty; just a little tea floated in the bottom, a slight grey skin forming across the surface. His back was to the door, and his face in shadow. Finally he said:

"I'll tell you of a trip I made, must have been the first one after the war. We'd been minesweeping up to then – we went on for some months after VE day. It were a filthy job. And then suddenly it was over. I'd never really fished properly, see, because of all that. I suppose I was about sixteen, seventeen, by then. And we did our first real trip, long before the *Duke* this was, she wasn't built for another ten, twelve years. Well, we fished North Norway. It was a good trip. It was December – just before Christmas, and very cold, but flat calm. That's the best fishing weather, cold and dead calm. We did well.

"Anyway, we turned for home, knowing we'd got a good grossing. It was rationing, remember, and fish is good food. We stopped to coal in Norway, and then steamed past Trondheim, knowing we'd be home for Christmas – I reckon it was about the 21st. I took a turn on deck that night and it was still calm, but it had clouded over. Then just before midnight as we worked our way past the fjords, the moon slipped from behind the clouds and lit their edges and there were a few stars, and then this moonbeam floods across the water, like someone's dumped gold in the sea."

He took a drag on his cigarette. Katherine said nothing for a moment. Then:

"And did you get home for Christmas?"

His face cracked into a grin.

"Yep. But it wasn't that we did, it was the way we knew we would, just then, and then the moon..." Suddenly he looked concerned, and turned towards her. "You do get me, don't you, lass? Some things always make a man feel like that."

"Do they?" said Katherine. "Yes, I suppose they do. But you haven't answered my question."

He smiled quizzically. "I have."

"No you haven't. Men don't freeze and die for a scoop of gold on a cold sea."

"Don't they?"

"No."

"I did."

"You're still here."

"Yep." He sighed. "*Duke* ain't, though."

"No, she isn't," said Katherine. "So that's what you're going to tell me about now."

"Do you really want to listen to all this?" he asked, half-seriously.

She checked her watch. "I'm interested." *I could write this,* she thought. *A feature. I could write a feature. Double-page spread, maybe.* "I do need to go up to the General before the last of the night shift knock off in Casualty. But it'll keep for a few minutes yet. Now, tell me about the *Duke*."

"All right, I will that. Well, *Duke* was side-launched at Cochrane's of Selby before you were born." He stopped, and looked at her. "When were you born?"

"January 1967," she said.

"All right. Ten years before you were born. A sidewinder, a hundred and eighty foot overall, with a Mirrlees Blackstone main engine, and twin Lister auxiliaries to give us heat and light and work the winches. Decks of iroko. The wheelhouse in teak. Aft superstructure. She was the most modern boat sailing out of the East Coast then. The Company built three like her at Cochrane's. None of the others did so well. We all three of us came out of Hull in a line one summer's morning, all in a row, *Duke of York*, *Duke of Gloucester* and *Duke of Marlborough*. That was us. Last out and first home, to catch the markets. Best grossing of course. Skip took her for the first time in 1960. Not bad going. He wasn't much over 30."

"How long were you on her?"

"A long time but I didn't sail on her till the year we won the Silver Cod, so that's in the mid-'sixties. I was with the boat on and off until 1974."

"And that's when it was all over?"

"For us it was. Some of the newer boats lingered on a bit longer. It was the Icelanders. Fishing limits. It had been rumbling on for some years. Well, since the 1890s, really. Then the Labour Government said they'd back us to the hilt and then signed an agreement with the Icelanders. Two hundred miles. Well, that finished us. By that time the Norwegians didn't love us too much either."

"Didn't you feel bitter? Why did the Government run out on you?"

"We didn't know then," said John. He furrowed his brow. "We think we do now. The Yanks have a big base at Keflavik in Iceland. We think the Icelanders leaned on them and they leaned on us."

"So you must feel a bit bitter then."

"Yes and no. I don't really understand politics. I understand fish, and I know the Icelanders wanted to conserve stocks. Well, that's all right. Thing is, they offered us a quota that might have kept a few boats at work. But the government mismanaged the talks and threw that away." He shrugged. "What can you say? Mind you, you see the Icelanders shipping great container-loads of cod into Hull today and you do feel a bit bitter then.

"But I've been angry anyway. One morning in Spring Skip and I meets up on the dock, 'Where are you going?' he asks me. 'Down to sign on for a trip,' I says. 'I've just seen Bert' – Hallsey, he was the company manager. 'Sitting behind a desk like a brothel-keeper,' Skip tells me. 'We've done with you, Skip, you're not going anywhere, or the *Duke*, come to that, he tells me. We're decommissioning.' And so they were, sod 'em. Thirty years but I was a casual – though that may have been wrong, they tell me now. And they got huge decommissioning grants for bringing the boats out of fishing. Some got sold outside the Common Market or out of the industry, as well, so they won both ways. They did that with *York* – she became an oil-rig support vessel and may still be afloat now, for all I know. But *Gloucester* and *Marlborough* went to the torch."

Katherine nodded. "So what then?"

"Well, Skip and I tried to make a go of things with an inshore boat, and David came too. We quite enjoyed the work, but we couldn't make it pay, and we lost most of what we had. There was just enough to buy this Lochin we've got now. We came down here because the fish prices are high, high-value species too; and you can fish close inshore and make money."

"Are you making any?"

John grinned.

"Sometimes. But that mad bastard" – he jerked his thumb out to sea – "he wants to make more. He's going to take us back into the North Sea with a 65ft. sidewinder. It's not the same, but we'd go out as far as the median line with Norway, go out of Hull or maybe

Scarborough. I reckon he could do it. But only if he does it this time. We won't last much longer together. David's still quite young. But Skip and I, well, we're getting old. And bitterness does hard things to you."

"Do you think Skip is bitter?"

"Skip? Oh, yes. He's bitter. But he's a fighter, that man."

Katherine nodded slowly. "Will this machine work?"

"The autoliner? Yes."

"You sound pretty certain."

"I am that. But it's not whether it'll work. It's whether it's in time for the three of us."

"Four," corrected Katherine. "Don't forget young whatshisname."

"Kevin? No, it's not the same. He's a good lad but if we stop, he'll do something else. Old Skip's been filling his head with dreams. Well, they may come true. But if they don't he'll go and fish with one of the ten-metre crews. If that works out and he's still yearning for adventure, well, he'll get a berth on a Scottish boat fishing Rockall, perhaps."

"And what'll you do?"

"Me?" He shrugged. "Beer and a cig, that's all I need now. I'll go on the social."

"You don't sound too convinced."

"I might not have the choice."

***   ***   ***

KEVIN stayed by the stern. It was the most sheltered place. It was calm now, but he knew that when they passed the breakwater things would be different.

They followed some way behind the red-and-white ten-metre steelship. She was still reflected in the water, but the wind was freshening and every now and then her image broke into a thousand pieces; after a while you could barely see it.

Skip held *Silver Cod* back a little, as her pace was harder than the steelship's; the glassfibre boat could make a comfortable 15 knots as a matter of course. He sat at the wheel in his big black Bostrom skipper's chair, scanning the skies ahead.

Kevin did that, too. He was starting to feel cold now. The sky was still blue, but with low black clouds covering patches of it, instead of the more usual pattern of white cumulus towering up behind.

The breakwater approached, lighthouse on the end. A car was silhouetted against the bright sky. One or two figures moved slowly along the mole in the distance. As they moved closer Kevin could make out the outline of some steps leading down to the water, then he could see two boys, maybe a year or two younger than him, lounging on the lower steps, unconcerned by the slippery green slime where the tide had been. They were smoking, tipping their ash into the water in an awkward, affected way.

David came out of the wheelhouse and stood on the deck for a few moments, hands in pockets. He was trying to remember the gale warnings from that morning. The usual litany flowed through his mind. *Rockall, Force 5. Freshening. Biscay. Force 5. Freshening. German Bight. Force 4. Malin. Hebrides.* For twenty or thirty years that voice, always identical, had been as much a part of his life in the morning as pulling his socks on. So much so, in fact, that it flowed into his mind like electronic information poured from one computer into another by landline, never displayed, simply stored to be there when you needed it. Now he keyed retrieval. What flashed up on his mental screen did not concern him unduly.

It didn't when they passed the breakwater, either, although it wasn't a smooth transition. It never was with Skip. The steelship was out of his way. He brought the boat up to 15 knots, and then they were out; and the personality of the sea changed completely.

It didn't normally catch Kevin unawares. It did today. Dreaming, his mind slowed a little by the chill, he staggered backwards, his back hitting the longliner rack, and the hooks stuck into his sweater. The boat rocked and pitched, the sea coming up nearly to the freeboard, although it would never actually come over except in rough seas. These weren't.

Kevin steadied himself, laying his bare hand carefully on the top of the steel rack, and carefully disentangled two or three hooks from the fabric.

"Silly bugger," said David, hands still in his pockets. "All right, then?"

"Yeah, I'm okay," came the reply.

"Mind youself, lad," called Skip from the wheelhouse. David thought his voice had a rather rough edge to it. "It'll get worse."

"No problem," said Kevin cheerfully. He did not feel cheerful. He wished he had his anorak with him.

He looked down at the water; it never bored him. David turned and sauntered back into the wheelhouse.

"What d'you reckon?" he asked, jerking his head at the horizon.

"All right."

"Think so. Seen a lot worse in April."

"Seen a lot worse in June," grunted Skip. "'Specially where we come from."

Once again, David smelled a faint hint of something he did not want to smell.

"All right, Skip?" he asked brightly.

"Sure, why shouldn't I be, Dave?"

"I'll go and check the grub and things," said David. "I stowed it all in a bit of a hurry last night."

"You wanted to get to the boozer," said Skip.

"Will tonight and all."

Skip grunted again, wordlessly this time.

David ducked down into the doorway in the front of the wheelhouse, below the line of the windscreen, and went into the cabin in the bow. This was a small but comfortable place with two bunks arranged in a vee, so that their ends touched each other in the bow. He felt only mildly irritated.

Below them were the teak doors to the lockers. It was these he opened now. Crouching on his haunches, steadying himself against the rolling of the boat, he opened the locker.

He wasn't looking for the oilskins. Noticing that he had forgotten to stow them, he was, again, only mildly irritated. He didn't always bother anyway. Skip hated them and David only used them when working on deck in very heavy seas. He sometimes liked Kevin to do so, but bothered less and less. The lifejackets were there all right, though. Again, it wouldn't have bothered Skip if they weren't, and it didn't really worry David. Everything else was in order.

But David wasn't interested in the gear. He found what he was looking for, a large bottle of brandy given them by a French skipper whose pots they had recovered and returned after someone had carelessly trawled them away. They kept it for medicinal purposes and had used less than a third.

Until the previous evening. It was still over half-full, but David could see that it had been got at. He frowned, and looked at it for a minute or two.

"Are you staying in there all day, man? Get up here and let's have a look at the plotter," came the gruff bark from the wheelhouse above.

Without speaking he put the bottle back exactly where it had been. He fastened the locker door securely and returned to the wheelhouse.

Skip continued to look straight ahead.

David started to manipulate the plotter. It had tracked their course out of harbour. The shape of the breakwater was clearly visible and took up much of the screen. He punched two keys and they shrank, broadening the scope of the brightly-coloured display map in front of him. Now there was a lot of clutter on it. Two more buttons and the wrecks and buoys disappeared. And with the sort of fishing they would do that day, they wouldn't need to worry about underwater pipelines and cables either, so he got rid of them as well although they were ready to be recalled at a touch, carefully delineated on-screen in red and yellow so that they could be quickly distinguished from fishing limits and other information if he needed them.

"Bring us out a bit," said Skip. "Round to starboard. Let's have a look at the Seven Sisters."

David did as he was told.

"We'll put the first line down here," said Skip, jabbing the screen with his finger. "That's where we got that good run of codling Monday week."

"Yes. Shall I plot it?"

"Go on."

David worked swiftly. First he pressed another combination of keys and the plotter's software placed on the screen a series of red triangles, markers he had put there after a good haul. No-one outside the crew would ever see these and a duplicate set of disks were locked in the safe at the office.

"I think it was this one here."

"Give me the Decca."

David called up the red and green Decca references after moving a cursor over one of the triangles. He read them out.

"Yep, that's it. Give us a course then."

Once again it took a second or so. David simply merged the map with the previous one on a yet smaller scale, showing their present position, lined up the cursors, and read out the heading the screen then displayed. Smoothly Skip changed course, taking the vessel port side to the onshore wind so that it rolled a little more and pitched a little less.

Before long, thought David, we'll mate up the plotter to an autopilot and we won't even have to do that.

"Still miss the old pencil and compass, then, Skip?" chuckled David, jerking his head towards the locker where the charts and log tables were still stored as a back-up.

Another grunt. Normally quick to defend the role of his pencil and compass, Skip didn't seem to want to say much today. David shrugged.

"Everything all right, Skip?"

"Why shouldn't it be?"

"Just asked."

"Well, don't, all right? Get out there and see if that little bastard's tangled up the snoods yet."

David said nothing. He turned and was halfway out of the door onto the working deck when he heard, or thought he heard, Skip mumbling something. He strained his ears. He hesitated for a moment, and then stepped out onto the deck.

Once on deck, he turned and looked back into the wheelhouse, but the light streaming through the forward screens reduced everything to a silhouette. He could see the radar screen, the cursor rotating slowly to display the land mass to starboard, and then the open sea to port, with one or two blips a mile or two away – he could still see the small steelship on the horizon; and the colour video-plotter showed up clearly too, with its red and yellow lines delineating fishing limits and coastline, and the Decca co-ordinates of Monday week's good run still displayed. A little daylight shone on the wheel and he noticed that Skip was holding it tightly, his knuckles a little pale. Everything else was in shadow.

Kevin was still standing on the stern, legs together, arms crossed tightly on this chest. He was pulling his sweater close to his skin to feel the body-warmth in the wool.

"Why didn't you bring your anorak, you silly little fart?" asked David.

"Forgot it," replied Kevin. "Can I have an oilskin?"

"No you can't. We left them behind. As we often do," said David. "Get in the wheelhouse, out of the spray."

Kevin moved, rather slowly, towards the wheelhouse.

David turned and looked out over the port side towards the open Channel. Years of experience had taught him to judge the weather and he realised that they would have a brisk day, but with no serious trouble. Although patches of blue sky endured to landward, and shafts of sunlight briefly lit up the chalk cliffs, to seaward the grey clouds had started to join together. The boat was in shadow. The lower clouds were not particularly dark, but seemed so against the yellowy-whiteness of the cumulus above that showed through their cracks, so that the sky resembled crazy paving in reverse. Here and there, there were patches of white light on the surface of the sea, where a crack in the clouds' crazy paving had become wide enough to admit the light; but more often David could see thin veils of mist that he knew were rain squalls moving across the horizon. None were near, but the air had started to thicken and sour slightly the way it does before the barometer drops.

David lit a cigarette, match cupped in hand, drawing it in the first flash of phosphorus before it blew out. He tossed the match over the side and watched it disappear as the boat rolled to port, then reappear, tossing madly, as the vessel rolled again, and the sea came up towards the gunnel, sending a fine spray across his body. Thousands of tiny bubbles rose in the water and joined to make a thin, broken skein of white that spread across the grey-green surface.

Kevin came out of the wheelhouse.

"I thought I told you to go inside."

"Skip says to get out, we'll be shooting soon."

"It could be another hour," said David.

"Well, that's what he said."

David glanced at his watch. They had changed course at about nine; it was coming on for half-past.

A chance sunbeam cut across them, making the spray in the air sparkle. Kevin parked himself on top of a locker immediately behind the wheelhouse and found a little shelter; Skip seemed to forget about him. David wondered why Skip hadn't set the autopilot. He knew their course well enough and would have no trouble checking it against the screen if he wanted to. Still, if he was happier at the helm, perhaps that was the best thing today.

David left him to it, and stayed on the working deck, self-sufficient in his thoughts, facing the stern, legs apart to steady himself against the rolling of the vessel.

He was right; it was another hour. Their course took them slightly to seaward, and the coastline fell away from them; they were now several miles out. Once or twice the shape of a big tanker appeared on the horizon, coming through the Dover Strait on the last leg of a long journey from Kharg Island to Rotterdam; or a freighter, its derricks stark against the sky, on its way from Gdansk or Hamburg to Massawa or Bombay. Strange, those long passages in a man's working life that began, not on a dock, but in a minute spark that clattered a telex machine, or a line of type on a photocopied sheet, passed from one suited man to another as they walked the floor of London's Baltic Exchange under vaulted ceilings, taking sheets from under the arm of someone they did not know and scanning the hulls for charter, free in and out, Western options, May, June. Then that smudged line of type would change and grow into a freighter, tied up under a humid tropical sky that tipped monsoon jets through the night onto the glistening concrete where men of other races shouted and hauled and grumbled, and harassed white men stood with sweat-stained bills of lading, and spotty young seamen rode in rickshaws. Or, if they were less lucky, they baked on the deck of a crude carrier in the Gulf, trying to think of the daily danger money instead of the menace that crossed the pitiless pale-blue skies above them. Sometimes, thought David, he could feel his world grow smaller, and knew that Skip did too; felt it crowd around them, saw horizons draw nearer; felt themselves growing old. Once, he remembered reading *The Surgeon's Log* in his bunk as they steamed homeward from a fruitless trip to the White Sea. For a short time, he had wondered; there were tropics, or Latin ports, or the high-paying trips to the Gulf, maybe his for the taking instead of the relentless cold. But then there was a good trip, then a hard one in a boiling sea, then a new ship and then his mate's ticket and there never was much time for reading.

The engine slowed, but the vessel did not stop. She was making about five knots when Skip poked his head out of the door.

"All right, we'll shoot here," he announced.

"Have you marked the plotter?" asked David.

"Don't have to. We know where we are."

David raised his eyebrows slightly, involuntarily. Skip seemed to avoid his eyes. He looked instead at Kevin.

"Get to baiter."

Kevin started to move, slowly.

"Come on, jump to it."

"I'm cold."

"You're not cold. Christ, lad, see you in a northerly."

"I am so." His voice sounded unsteady and slightly slurred, as if he had been drinking.

"Effing jump to it." Skip's voice was full of menace.

Kevin did move then, but not quickly. However, he was soon at the stern. David glanced at him briefly, but now he would have his hands full; they both would.

David took the orange buoy at the end of the line and threw it in the water. The line started to feed out and he stood by the rack separating the snoods, ensuring that each hook was six inches or so away from the next. Kevin seemed to wake up a little. He took the pail of mushy squid and started to feed it into the top of the funnel on the stern.

David stood back a little and watched the hooks coming out over the gunnel, anxious lest they be badly baited. But the baiter was working perfectly, and Kevin seemed to know instinctively at what speed he had to feed it.

"Baiter's doing all right," David called out to Skip, who had fixed the vessel's helm onto autopilot. He had automatically headed them slightly to seaward, although the coast was a good few miles away now and showed only as a narrow line on the horizon.

"Yes, it seems fine. I'm glad now we didn't muck about with precision baiters and hammers," said Skip. He seemed more cheerful now, but there was a slight aggressive tone in his voice which David did not like. He knew this man well, but there was something that wasn't quite right. "Watch those snoods, Dave ...Easy, easy. Speed about right?"

David nodded. It was hard work, but he could keep up and thought Kevin could. "'Bout five knots, yeah?"

"Thereabouts."

It did not take them long. They shot five hundred hooks and dropped the second buoy. It bobbed lazily away in the wake of the ship, their hopes and dreams strung out behind it. Standing on the stern of the ship, David watched thoughtfully as it fell farther away behind.

Out of the corner of his eye he could see Skip standing, arms akimbo, at the wheelhouse door, looking in the same direction. Still on autopilot, *Silver Cod* forged her was forward at a steady six or seven knots.

He's forgotten, thought David, I bet he has.

The orange buoy diminished until it was hard to pick out by eye. David stood, frozen, for a few minutes, and then pushed past Skip into the wheelhouse.

"What's up with you?"

"Mark our bloody position. Or we'll never find the fucking lines agan!"

Skip said nothing and David realised that he *had* forgotten. He worked quickly, fixing a red triangle at their point of travel. Then he pushed the cursor back along the line that the plotter had marked as they travelled it, until it was just separated from the triangle by a quarter of a mile or so, and took a bearing. He sighed with relief. The autopilot had been running the vessel, so the course should be accurate. Even if Skip was pissed out of his mind by the time they came back, he could simply set a course for the triangle and then head back on that until they found the buoy.

If Skip had got his sums right about the tide.

Arms still crossed, Skip turned and moved slowly into the wheelhouse. David wondered if his balance against the rolling of the boat was usual.

"Done your Boy Scout bit, have you?"

"I have that. No thanks to you," said David quietly.

"Button up."

David grunted.

"Let's have a look at the area round *Scot*, then," said Skip.
"You gonna shoot out there?"
"Why not?"
"Bit of a way."
"So what?"

David jerked his head in the direction of Kevin, who was standing on the stern. Once again he had crossed his arms over his chest, each hand on opposite upper arm, hugging himself. He was shivering. He was looking down at the deck, not happily. David would have called it quiet desperation.

"Him? Nowt wrong wi' lad. Shoulda' brought his jacket this morning."

"'Course he should," said David. "Bloody stupid. But I don't reckon he's all right."

"There's fuck all wrong with him. What he needs is a bloody good clout round the lughole," said Skip. He was staring straight out in front of the vessel and his voice was maybe half an octave above normal. "An' I'll tell you summat else. Reckon you could do with one as well yoursel' sometimes."

"Cut that out," said David sharply. "We can shoot inshore, can't we?"

"Well I've chosen not to," said Skip quickly. "Good run of gurnard we got out on *Scot*, first neap tide."

"Not after gurnard. After codling," said David mulishly.

"Shut up," said Skip, looking straight ahead.

David looked at him for a moment, and then moved out onto the working deck.

He tapped Kevin on the shoulder.

"All right, lad?"

"No," said Kevin, slowly and quietly, so that his voice could barely be heard above the wind and the rising revs of the engine. "No, Dave, don't reckon I am."

They had turned out to sea. The boat rolled and pitched, doing perhaps a couple of knots more than she needed to. David turned towards the wheelhouse. Skip's burly silhouette, in shadow, couldn't be seen against the grey-white of the sky, just the outline of the VHF and below it the unblinking colour screen of the plotter, and the radar screen, image sweeping round and round in synchronization with the neat little Furuno radar scanner on the wheelhouse, right behind the white cylinder of the liferaft which lay across the roof.

David lowered his gaze a little. He saw Skip's back in the entrance to the bow cabin.

A few spots of rain joined the spray on the white fibreglass roof. On the horizon, the patches of silver were gone and there were dark grey smudges instead, where water fell upon water from small, angry black clouds that stole across the curtain of white that covered the sky above them.

*** *** ***

AFTER she took her leave of John, Katherine left the seafront, pausing only to buy a *Guardian* and a pack of Marlboro Lights. The little Fiesta churned over a couple of times and then clicked into life. She drove down the seafront.

She had written nothing down while she was sitting with John; somehow she had not wanted to, but she could see a good feature developing around the longliner, and its relation to the past. She needed to talk to Skip along the same lines.

A few early holidaymakers strolled along the seafront now. Pulling past the dock, Katherine drove along the promenade proper, above the long, smooth beach that made the town a resort as well as a port. Newly-painted green wrought-iron benches were placed up and down the promenade, between electric lampstands that were made to look like the gaslights they had once been. Wires curved between them to hold the bunting in the summer.

She turned the car away from the promenade and drove through the narrow, busy streets of the town's shopping centre, crawling through the tail end of the morning commuter traffic. The pavements were already busy with shoppers, many with children in tow. Besides the big Woolworth's and Sainsbury stores there were many small chemists and tobacconists with their cardboard-cutout Kodak advertisements and little clusters of buckets and spades hanging outside the doors.

Katherine stretched in the driver's seat, yawned, and lit a cigarette.

She was, as she had told John, on her way to the General Hospital to see what last night's corpse-count had been like. Probably not high, but it was the day you didn't go when there was something worth reporting. One day when she hadn't bothered, there had been a young girl knocked down outside a pub; the driver had been a local councillor and he'd been drunk.

The General was on the inland edge of town, with a modern housing estate on one side, and on the other the Downs, sweeping down to the perimeter of the hospital, their brow high in the distance, the grass a moist light thin green; white clouds rose above the ridge, and then blue sky above them. Katherine felt quite cheerful. It had been a lousy winter. Spring was proving late and blustery, but bright.

She parked the car between an aged Allegro with dulled paintwork and a newish Jaguar, perhaps that of a visiting consultant; and walked towards the cuboid white building with large windows and rows of white tiles. There was an antiseptic feel to the building itself, and one sensed the statistics of the patients admitted, discharged, died, gallstones removed, ingrowing toenails, cirrhosis and catarrh, hæmorrhoid and hæmorrhage, slipping neatly into a clean white computer and blinking on a green-white screen. Once, when she was young and didn't know she couldn't take the sight of blood, Katherine had wanted to be a doctor. She had thought one took the long watches of the night in a tiny room off a dark but cosy ward in some sootstained Victorian pile, no strip lights but a soft pool from an anglepoise over the night-nurse's desk; a damp fog outside and the thick smell of an autumn night, mugs of tea and crises, death amid distemper. But she had never imagined a place like this.

The aluminium doors hissed and slid back smoothly as she approached. She sprang slowly across the thick rubber floor of the lobby. One or two people waved cheerily as she approached.

She passed the reception desk.

"Morning, Hannah," she said to the middle-aged lady behind it.

"Morning, Kath," came the reply. They both smiled.

"There goes the vulture again," she heard as she rounded the corner towards Casualty.

Katherine hesitated for a moment in the corridor, but then walked on.

The spring mood had evaporated.

Sighing, she went on towards Casualty. It was near-empty; a nurse was dressing a young boy's hand and chatting cheerfully to him as she did so. She looked up and smiled briefly as Katherine came into the room.

Dr. Bryce was leaning against a cabinet, enjoying a moment of peace, the dregs of a cup of tea in the mug beside him.

"Ah-ha. Friend or enema?" he said with plummy cheerfulness.

"I've heard that one before," said Katherine.

"Never mind. I have some jokes about suppositories, but I expect you'd take them as innuendo," said the doctor. Katherine groaned inwardly.

Bryce was thirtyish, plump, not very tall, with short, smooth black hair, round glasses on a round face and a bow tie. Katherine did not dislike him, but found he could irritate. "What news here then?" she asked him, leaning her bottom against the cabinet opposite his.

"Nothing to write home about," replied the doctor. "Or rather, nothing to write in the *Gazette* about, haw-haw. Body count as such is only one this morning, I'm afraid."

Katherine whipped out her notebook. "Any details?"

"Old lady, bronchial pneumonia, had been ill with what was thought to be just a fever for several weeks, admitted last night, died early this morning."

"Age?"

"Seventy-eight."

Katherine jotted this down, not expecting to use it. "What else?"

"Lad came in with a fractured skull, came off his motorbike where the High Street meets the Newhaven road."

"Any other circumstances?"

"Car pulled out in front of him."

"I see. Do you know if he stopped?"

"Oh yes, I think he rang the ambulance."

"But you reckon he'll be all right?"

"The boy on the bike? Oh, I should think so, but he's not my problem now. And that, my dear Katherine," said Bryce, stretching and yawning, "is your lot, today. Have a cup of tea."

"I might," said Katherine, letting a small smile escape, "if you talk to me about something off the record."

"Now what could I have to talk about on or off the record?" asked Bryce.

"Fishermen," said Katherine. She took a seat at Bryce's small Formica table while he busied himself with the kettle on the sideboard.

"What about them? See plenty of them in here," said Bryce, not turning.

"That's just the point," said Katherine. She leaned her elbow on the table and rested her chin on her hand. "I'm interested in doing a feature to accompany an article I covered this morning."

"Oh yes," said Bryce, searching for the sugar.

"It's an article I'm writing about these blokes who've invented a new longlining system."

"A what?"

"Never mind. Anyway, they went off to test it this morning and I'll check with them this evening. I just got talking to one of their workmates on the quay, and he was telling me all about the old days and the deep-sea fleets and whatnot. And they were saying that there are some profitable species of fish on this stretch of the coast. There certainly seem to be plenty of fishing boats."

"Plenty of fishermen getting themselves hurt, too," said Bryce. He nodded. "Yes, I can tell you about a few cases."

"Industrial accidents or drownings?" asked Katherine.

"Both. Plenty of industrial accidents. You'd think it was drownings that did most of the damage, but it's bloody well not, you know. And as for drownings, it's hypothermia you should be asking me about. Most of them don't go over the side before they die of cold."

Katherine nodded. She started writing vigorously in her notebook, having left the tape-recorder in the car. "Well," she said, smiling sweetly, tilting her head, chin still resting on hand, "shall we open Dr. Findlay's casebook, then?"

"Och aye, we will that," said Bryce, smiling back. He sat down opposite her. "A common one is chaps losing their footing and falling into things, be it the sharp edge of a gunnel or tripping over an engine box. Had one like that off an Eastbourne boat, one of those little inshore craft, who had his leg snapped in two at the knee. The shin was bent forward at an angle to it. Made one hell of a mess of the knee and by the time they got him here, his joint was swelled to the size of a football. I must have removed a pint of arterial blood and pus before we could get him into the operating theatre. Real workaday stuff, but the man won't walk easily again for the rest of his life. Just a moment's carelessness."

"Is that what it was?"

He frowned.

"Do you know, it was and wasn't. One of his chums brought him in and I remember asking him how the hell it happened. He told me it was a heavy sea and I asked him why they were fishing in it."

"And?" It annoyed her when people she was interviewing paused for effect. Bryce sometimes did that.

"They said they had to go because there were cod coming inshore as the weather turned colder, and that was later than usual; and they hadn't had the chance to take their cod quota that year. They had to take it all, because it was barely enough and by the time the fish turned up, they were all in hock to the bank anyway."

"But there are other species, aren't there? What about bass?"

Bryce shrugged. "You'd better ask the fishermen that. Maybe they're subject to quota as well."

Katherine nodded and made a couple of notes in her notebook. Then she looked up.

"Okay, Findlay. Another leaf in the casebook, please."

"Roll credits." Bryce gave an oily smile. "Why do we all remember that programme, when it's long dead?"

"I don't know," said Katherine.

"And *Emergency Ward 10*," said Bryce, a slightly faraway look in his eyes. "Ah well. So that's a typical accident for you, but there are other ones. When they gut fish at sea, they often do so in a bit of a hurry so that they can deliver gutted fish to the markets before everybody else and get the best prices. At least, that's what one of them told me after he'd brought in his mate who'd sliced his own thumb off. Idiot."

"I doubt if he needed telling that," said Katherine.

"I didn't bother," said Bryce. "He was unconscious for loss of blood." The kettle boiled and he got up to pour the tea, carefully drying out each mug with a cloth before sprinkling the tea in the strainer. "I'm trying Earl Grey. I find it very refreshing towards the end of a long turn."

"What did you do with this guy? Try to sew his thumb back on?"

"Mr Cryer had a go. They'd got plenty of ice on board, being a fishing boat, you know. But there wasn't time. The man was in deep shock. It had taken seven hours to get him here."

"Seven *hours*?"

"Well, these chappies sometimes don't have VHF on board, and when they do, the weather may be so foul that you can't medevac. Mind you these RAF chopper chaps always try. Most of the serious casualties we have here from ships, not just fishing-boats, come in that way. It's striking just how many people they do save. Often in dreadful conditions. You should talk to them, Katherine. Perhaps they'd take you up."

She didn't mention that they'd done so six months earlier. "Tell me about a serious casualty."

"Right. How about the chap on the Newhaven boat who tried to fix the engine one day when it was overheating? He unbolted the pipe from the engine cooler – the coolant runs through the keel, rather like the a car's runs through a radiator. Anyway, he was showered with boiling water and got ninety percent burns."

"Didn't it occur to him that the pipe would be full of boiling water?"

"Apparently not," said Bryce. "And I couldn't ask him. He died of shock ten or fifteen minutes after we admitted him."

"I remember that helicopter winchman who won the George Medal," said Katherine.

"Yes. About a year or eighteen months ago, wasn't it?"

"That's right, but I can't remember exactly what it was for."

"It was a Frog boat. They brought the man in here, and he survived," said Bryce. "I wasn't on duty that night, but Cryer told me about it later. Now *that* was an interesting case – a piece of machinery going wild and damn near killing someone."

Katherine brushed her lips lightly with the end of her pen. "Go on."

"It was a trawler from Boulogne. They shot their gear – I think that's what they say – and then they hauled the nets back in while a heavy sea was running. Now, apparently the net is sometimes hauled in by a winch that gets its power from the main engine. In a rough sea, the propeller came out of the water for a crucial second or so and the engine-revs shot up – and the speed of the winch with it. There's a clutch thingy to stop that happening, but it failed. The man was leaning over the side manoeuvring the net over the gunnel, and it caught him and damn near took his arm off." He made a little gesture with his hands and smiled, as if he was an engineer who had solved a complex mystery.

Katherine winced. "And then the RAF took him off in a heavy sea."

"That's right. And brought him here."

Katherine leaned back. "That's horrible. You mentioned hypothermia as well, but I confess I don't even know much about what it is."

"Neither do fishermen," replied Bryce. "That's why they keep dying of it. They don't know how easy it is to get, and they don't know how to recognise and treat it."

"But what is it, exactly?"

"You get cold." He sounded sometimes as if he was talking to a schoolgirl, thought Katherine.

"I know that. But how do you define it?"

"Your body temperature drops by more than a degree centigrade under normal," said Bryce. "When the core temperature of the body sinks, a number of things happen. The first symptoms are lassitude as the body burns up more and more of its reserves, and then what may well appear like drunkenness manifests itself. Eventually the victim will lose all co-ordination and sink into a coma."

"How soon does death follow?"

"It's awfully difficult to say because it depends on the strength of the individual. Willpower plays a part. There was a fisherman who went over the side in Iceland and survived many hours. But the average survival time in north European waters in winter is as little as thirty seconds. In English waters, even in summer, the risk is considerable. In the Bristol Channel you may only have two hours."

"You've looked into this," said Katherine, smiling slightly.

"God knows I've seen enough of it."

"So. If someone falls into the water in winter he drowns in two minutes, does he?"

"Well, it isn't necessarily actually drowning." Bryce frowned. "You want me to go into this?"

"Why not? Perhaps I could write something and cut down the death-rate a bit."

"Yes, maybe you could," he said thoughtfully. He nodded. "Okay. When someone gets cold, the supply of blood to the limbs is curtailed by a constriction of the blood vessels. Now, what happens if you force a given volume of liquid through a smaller pipe then it was travelling though before?"

"It raises the pressure."

"So now you know how these men die."

"I see. So instead of dying of drowning, or what we actually think of as dying from the shock of the cold, they have a massive heart attack." Katherine nodded slowly.

"If you don't get to them in time, yes. The trick is to apply the heat gently to the area of the chest. Gently. Apply too much heat and the opposite happens; the blood flows back to the limbs suddenly and puts the same strain on the heart for different reasons. The other mistake is to give the poor bugger brandy. It does makes you feel warm, but it actually depresses body temperature. The worst thing is when they put the man into a blazing hot engine room and slosh brandy into him. He dies. It's as simple as that. What's needed is gentle heat, to get the patient into a survival bag as quickly as possible. Which, like liferafts, lifejackets, flares, spanners, etcetera, tend to be a bit sporadic on fishing boats!"

"Perhaps they can't afford them."

"Survival bags are only a couple of quid." He sighed. "They don't carry them because they don't *know*. And the other gear they often don't carry because it's unmanly, or tempting fate, or some other such codswallop."

"Is that why fishermen are so prone to hypothermia? Wilful neglect?"

"Actually, that would not be fair," said Bryce slowly. "Ever heard of chill factor?"

"Oh, yes," said Katherine. "I can remember being lectured about that by a very handsome, hunky Norwegian ski-instructor."

Bryce frowned.

"Yes, I know the type. You mean he knew what it was?"

Katherine laughed. "Men. Yes, handsome men do have brains sometimes, just like pretty women."

"I would never have thought it," said Bryce. "But I wouldn't know. Not being handsome, or hunky, you understand." He paused for a strategic split second.

"You have my sympathies," said Katherine. He coloured slightly. "You were talking about chill factor."

"The wind can lower the effective temperature on the body's surface by an amazing amount," said Bryce, his face a little red. "Yet the thermometer may well read the same. Now, fishermen rarely bother to consult the thermometer to see whether it's safe to go out. Barometer yes, thermometer no. Get them out there on deck and the spray soaks their clothing and then a breeze, even a mild one, will do it. Even in July. One of the crew says he feels cold. And the captain says, it's not cold, it's July, the sun's shining, get back to work you soft bugger. By the time someone twigs what's really going on, it may be far too late. Even if they give him the correct treatment. And they won't."

"Because they've never been told," said Katherine.

"They've never asked," said Bryce. "They're ignorant bastards."

* * *   * * *   * * *

SEVERAL hours after Bryce had spoken, when morning had turned to afternoon, David stood in the wheelhouse of *Silver Cod*. It had been a complicated half-hour, but he was used to it.

First they had made their bearing, some way off the coast now, and, when the track on the plotter screen coincided with the bearing, he told Skip in taciturn tones. The boat stopped and David switched screens, looking now at the colour video sounder that would show them the marks of the fish below, telling them what they had and where to find it.

He enjoyed this. Years ago he had started by using the so-called paper sounders, echosounders that did the same job but spewed out hard copy in the shape of a graph on a page, a little like those used by meteorologists to keep a track of barometric pressure and temperature. Now those days were gone. Swiftly and skilfully David interpreted the colour graphics.

"Want to know what we've got?"

"Not particularly." Skip didn't bother to look at him, or the sounder screen.

"There's a bit about. Quite a bit. Let's get cracking, shall we?" said David. He felt a little cheerful for the first time in hours.

"I'll tell you when," said Skip dully, continuing to stare forward through the windscreen.

David looked at Skip for a moment. Then he left him, and went out on to the working deck, where Kevin was sitting motionless on the engine cover.

"Get ready to shoot," he said.

"Are we going home then?" asked Kevin without turning. "I'm damn cold."

"You can't be *that* cold, Kev," said David. "Not in late April. For God's sake, no wonder Skip's in a foul mood." He felt the thick spray scatter against his cheek.

"I'm cold," repeated Kevin, softly and slowly.

David looked at the sky. There was a fair amount of blue showing now; the odd island of dark-grey cloud, the odd patch of clear blue and, stacked up between them, mountains of brilliant white. The sea remained choppy but he had seen it much worse, and he didn't feel cold.

"Will we go home after we shoot?" asked Kevin in a dull monotone. He kept his eyes fixed to the deck, and his speech seemed unsteady.

"No, I expect we'll come back to haul this line when we've hauled the other one," replied David. "Are those snoods ready?" But a brief glance told that they were not.

He let out an oath and started to separate the tangled snoods and hooks on the rack. Kevin did move now, and stood on the stern beside the bait-cutter, hair twitching in the breeze.

David watched the boy carefully as he worked the hooks out.

Kevin was feeding the squid into the funnel. He moved slowly, but as far as David could see, all the hooks, dragged out behind the buoy he had just dropped, were properly baited.

When they had finished, Kevin sat down on the engine-cover again.

"Go on inside the wheelhouse, lad," said David, a note of concern beginning to show in his voice.

Kevin stood up slowly and made his way unsteadily to the wheelhouse.

He emerged a minute later.

"What are you doing out here again? I told you to go inside."

"He ain't having it."

"Screw this," muttered David, and strode into the wheelhouse.

"What's the problem with Kevin coming inside for a while?" he asked tightly.

"Who're you to ask," said Skip. He continued to stare in front of him, although he was making a course correction. David's eyes fell automatically to the video-plotter.

"You're twenty degrees out," he said, without really thinking.

"Fuck off," said Skip.

"You haven't answered my question."

"What question?"

David took a deep breath. Then he said:

"The lad's cold."

"Should've brought his bloody jacket. Keep the little bugger out there and make him put up with it."

"What's the point?"

"What's the point to anything?" asked Skip.

"Why did we build this liner, then?"

Skip didn't answer. But he did look down at the plotter and start to measure the bearing of the first line they had shot from their present position, and feed the course into the autopilot. David let out a sigh of relief and turned back on deck.

It took them an hour or so to get back to the first set of buoys. The afternoon was wearing on now. Skip had the vessel on autopilot and, apart from the occasional sortie to the front cabin, he did nothing, staring though the screen as the land came slowly back into view, first as a smudge on the horizon, then as a green-and-white line; above it, the sky showed patches of blue and white more often than the grey and white that persisted out to sea. In the wheelhouse it was not cold; on the aft deck, thought David, it felt only a little cooler; then the spray stuck to his clothes and caught the wind, and he did feel a little cold then.

Skip's trips to the front cabin became more common and he no longer waited until David's back was turned before making them. The smell of brandy started to permeate the wheelhouse.

Halfway between the waypoints that marked the positions of the two lines, he realised that Kevin was completely motionless on the engine-cover. Quickly he went into the cabin himself and half-filled a hip-flask full of brandy. He checked the little gas-stove as well, and made sure that the steel hot-water bottle was ready to be heated up; they kept it there in case of unscheduled nights aboard. He decided not to use it yet, and went out to Kevin with the flask.

"Drink this," he said. "It'll warm you up. And for God's sake remember your anorak next time."

Kevin took the flask. His hands seemed imprecise and, although he used both to hold the flask, he seemed unable to drink without spilling quantities down the front of his jumper. But he managed to swallow a fair amount, coughing as the liquid scorched the soft flesh at the back of his throat.

"Have a bit more," said David.

He did. David took to feeding him nips now and then and the lad seemed to sit a bit straighter, although he didn't say much. But his silence didn't worry David too much. No-one says a lot when they're tired and freezing.

The buoys came in sight. By now it was well on in the afternoon, and the light was already mellowing

Silver Cod throttled back and came alongside the buoy.

Skip emerged.

"Stand by the posts and be ready to retrieve the line," he said roughly to Kevin. "And for Christ's sake stop looking at me as if you were a codling that'd just been gutted."

Kevin didn't move.

"Oh, for fuck's sake get out of my way," Skip roared. He picked the boy up under the arms and fairly threw him into the wheelhouse, where he managed to collect just enough strength to catch his balance and sink into the skipper's chair. His eyes closed.

Skip either didn't notice or didn't care; David did, but now he was busy. He stationed himself beside the two vertical posts on the port side through which the line would run as it was hauled, ready to take the fish as they came over the side; the posts would remove any he missed. Skip hauled the buoy in, detached the line and linked it to the mechanism that would reel it in and onto the rack on the starboard side, ready to be shot again. Now, they would find out whether it worked at sea as well as it did in harbour, where there were no fish on the hooks.

"Ready then?" asked Skip. It sounded like a threat.

"Take her away."

Skip pulled back the hydraulic lever. Its stainless-steel shaft clicked into place and, with gurgles and vibrations, the line started to come back in.

The first, empty, hooks began to appear, bait still sticking to the barbs. They snagged and pinged but came through the gate, David quickly separating the snoods before they went back on the rack. Once, one of them snagged too hard. There was an elastic and metallic sound and it detached itself, flying through the air to hit David's cheek. It scored his cold skin painfully, leaving a small red scratch.

"Christ Almighty," he said, putting his hand to his cheek.

"Get your eye, did it?"

"Nah."

Quickly he began working again, making a mental note to check where the hooks were snagging and deal with it.

It took them ten minutes to haul the line. They had caught three codling.

David would have liked more, but he was not disappointed. How well the fish took the bait was, he knew, a function of the bait itself and of the time and the tide. But the machine worked. Of that there was no doubt.

So there was a smile on his face as he looked up to speak to Skip. When their eyes met, he felt as if he had turned towards the sky on a bright summer's afternoon to see a front of jet-black clouds edging towards the sun.

"What's the matter?"

"Three frigging fish, that's what's the matter."

"But the liner works."

"It don't if there's no fish."

"So we got our sums wrong about where the fish were," said David. "Sod that. The liner works. All we've got to do now is – "

"Shut up, man. We're going for the other line now."

David straightened his back from the stooping position he had adopted over the rack. "Lad all right is he?"

"'Course he is."

David followed him into the wheelhouse.

"Then why is he unconscious in your chair?"

"He's not unconscious," said Skip. "Lousy bugger's shamming."

"Is he hell!"

Kevin was sprawled in the chair, his head heavily over to one side, his legs splayed out at a strange angle. His hand hung over the padded armpiece of the skipper's chair and he was clearly unconscious, making no effort to steady himself against the movement of the boat although the pitching kept bumping his head, quite hard, against the aluminium window-frames. His face was off-white with pale greyish shadows in the hollows of his cheekbones. Strands of dark hair, still lank with spray, were plastered to his forehead.

David forgot about Skip for the moment. Grasping Kevin under the armpits, he hauled him out of the skipper's chair and dragged him towards the entrance to the cabin. It was not easy; the boat was pitching and Kevin was completely inanimate, his hand catching under the chair-frame and instrument consoles.

Somehow he managed to get the youth onto a bunk in the forward cabin, straighten him out and toss a blanket over him.

Next he lit the gas stove, which to his relief remained steady on its long metal legs; then he managed to force a little more brandy between the boy's lips. When the kettle boiled he filled the hot water-bottle and placed it on Kevin's chest, hoping that it would not scorch the skin too badly and wishing that the boat was big enough to have a proper engine-room. Never mind, he thought, this will do nearly as well. He tied the scorching bottle to the boy with the arms of his own sweater.

Just as he completed his task he felt the engine rev and the bow come about.

David shot out of the cabin as quickly as he could. Skip was sitting forward on the edge of the chair, still staring straight ahead. The video plotter was switched on, still displaying, in enlarged section the spot where the first line had been dropped. Nothing else. Skip did not have any idea of his position or bearing.

"Turn for home," said David softly.

"Mind your own business."

"It is my business."

There was no answer.

David looked at the figure hunched over the wheel. There was little in Skip's eyes except a sort of quiet desperation. He was drunk, but David knew that that was not the real problem. Now it was his turn to see a quarter of a century stripped away before his mind's eye, to slip back across the years to an evening when the silver tableware gleamed softly and genteel men leaned over your shoulder with champagne-bottles, chilled, held in white cloths; and Skip, alone amongst them, was assured in his surroundings, because if he wasn't, he simply would have dismissed them as meaningless.

David could hear the voice of the slim young man who stood before them to present the trophy, speaking in glowing terms of enterprise and skill and courage and the forging of the country's industry, every industry, in the white heat of technology. Skip sitting there, lapping it all up.

He heard Skip's voice reaching back at him from the present day.

"They tore her heart out, David," he said slowly. "They tore her sodding heart out."

David reached forward, grasping the other man under the armpits to lift him out of his chair the way he had Kevin. But he had misjudged the mood of the moment. You do not lift a skipper out of his own wheelhouse chair.

"Take your bloody hands off me," roared Skip.

He pushed his hands onto David's chest, wild-eyed. It took David a few milliseconds to understand that he had misread the situation. He had never been responsible for Skip before. It had always been the other way round.

He raised his knee into Skip's stomach. It wasn't a hard blow, to wind the older man; rather, he used it as a pivot to swing him round so that he half-laid, rather than threw, him on the floor. Skip sat up, after lying immobile for a moment. But now his mind was where David had thought it to be a few minutes earlier. He watched, apathetic, as David called up their Decca reference on the plotter with one hand and reached for the VHF with the other. He switched the VHF to the emergency frequency in seconds, simply keying-in the correct LED reading. A second or so later, Skip heard him say:

"Mayday, mayday. Mayday, Mayday. This is *Silver Cod* at" – he read off the Decca co-ordinates – "requesting emergency medical assistance, crew member suffering from exposure."

The voice of Newhaven coastguard filled the wheelhouse as if he had been there.

* * *   * * *   * * *

KATHERINE'S day had gone much the way it usually did. After the hospital, she called at the magistrate' court, where two youths were arraigned for smashing a butcher's window. She stayed awake long enough to see them fined £50 each and then drove to the pub next door to the *Gazette*'s rather soulless offices above Woolworth's. Here she squeezed the Fiesta into a motorcycle-sized space and repaired to the bar.

She found the news editor and the production artist enjoying a liquid lunch and she joined in. Two pints later she returned to the office, not drunk but with that slightly ratty feeling one has when one has drunk more than intended, but without making a proper job of it. In this mood that she gazed without enthusiasm at the screen in front of her, wondering whether she, word-processors and beer would ever really mix. It was just before five and she was trying to write an item for tomorrow on the opening of a public right of way from the council estate to Sainsbury's supermarket. It went through a middle-class street and was bound to cause trouble. She had got as far as loading the disk and proceeding to the copyright warning on the software. She had been staring at this with a fascination born of boredom for about five minutes when the telephone rang.

"Hallo?"

"Is that the *Gazette*?"

A piercing female voice, middle-aged, reeking of sherry and white Rover cars.

"*Gazette* newsdesk," she replied.

"I'm ringing about the footpath," said the voice.

There was a delay of several seconds.

"Are you still there?" asked the sherry fume.

"Yes. Yes, I'm sorry, my mind was elsewhere," said Katherine. "I was expecting a call about the strategic arms talks. Gorbachev promised to let me know first."

"I beg your pardon?" Genuine bewilderment.

"Nothing. Yes, I presume you mean the footpath to Sainsbury's from the Peterloo Estate. We are covering it."

"Yes. Well, I think the planning committee have made a disastrous mistake." Another pause.

Katherine managed to keep her sigh inaudible. "Why, madam?" she asked eventually.

"Well, can't you see what it'll mean? Imagine all those people from the estate trooping past our back garden to *Sainsbury's*."

"Shocking," said Katherine. "Can I have your name and address?"

She gave it. Katherine gleaned a few more quotes from her and put the phone down as soon as she decently could.

She looked at the screen.

"Press space bar to continue," it replied.

She complied. A series of options flashed up on the screen. Idly she pressed a couple of keys and found herself looking at this morning's story about the butcher' shop window.

"Bugger," she said.

The phone rang again.

"Hello?" she said impatiently.

"What's wrong with you? Had a bad pint this afternoon, have you?" said a friendly middle-aged voice at the other end.

"Something like that," she said, relaxing and smiling a little. The voice belonged to the duty controller at the coastguard station on the cliffs outside. "Sorry, Jim. I've just had some snotty old cow on about the Sainsbury's footpath again."

A chuckle at the end of the line.

"'Fraid one of those council strays might devalue her prize pekinese, is she?"

"That sort of thing. People who put coal in baths," said Katherine. "Okay, Jim. What's new?"

"Just a routine medevac."

"Go on then."

"I'll read out the SitRep. Half a mo." She heard him shuffling papers at the other end. "16.30 hours. Westland Sea King helicopter answered call to Newhaven coastguard requesting evacuation for youth aged 17 from fishing vessel *Silver Cod* off Haven Point.

Aircraft now proceeding to vessel. Victim believed suffering from hypothermia. Medical advice being given by radio."

"Oh shit," said Katherine.

***   ***   ***

It was a routine call for the helicopter crew, who were on standby. As it was daytime they were ready to fly at a quarter of an hour's notice.

Neither did they expect any real problems. Their yellow Westland Sea King helicopter, like one or two of the many dotted around the coast, was equipped with the latest rescue avionics. An artificial horizon had been built that would enable them to hover, in the dark, ten feet above unstable seas, and hardly move an inch. Infrared sensors on board could help them spot the body of a man at the foot of a cliff in darkness. But none of this would be needed today. There was a brisk onshore wind that would keep the water moving, but not badly; perhaps force 4 or 5. They had worked in worse. It was daylight. And hypothermia cases could at least be moved.

The crew flew the aircraft out across the downs. It had been raining inland earlier in the afternoon, and the sky, now partly clear, had a fresh, limpid appearance; a deep film of water covered the tarmac and as the Sea King's rotors sped up, the water was lifted skyward in a veil of spray that caught the rays of the sun and split them into the colours of the spectrum.

The winchman sat still with the same slight tightness he always had in his bowels before an operation, knowing that those that seemed easiest could easily turn out to be the worst. But he didn't dwell on it. Instead he looked down as the aircraft crossed the perimeter fence, climbing all the time so that the trees and hedgerows, cars and cows declined in size until you could hold them between your thumb and forefinger. Every now and then they flew into patches of sunlight and the Westland's shadow appeared on the fields below, like a demented hunchback cantering across the countryside, shape twisting and distorting as it leapt a hedge. They shot across the clifftops and the world fell away beneath them, the shadow dropping like a stone. The waves breaking against the base of the cliffs were not too heavy, but the drift of the spray betrayed a stiff breeze that the winchman had already studied in the scarves and hair of the walkers on the clifftop. He brought his mask, with its intercom, close to his face.

"Sea's not too bad, but there's a bit of a blow. Say twenty knots."

"Okay. We'll think it through," replied the captain.

The voice of the co-pilot cut through with a course correction. The captain complied. "Give me ETA."

"17.09."

"Get him on the VHF, will you?"

There was a pause as the co-pilot raised *Silver Cod* on the VHF and told David to fire a flare.

He had not been idle, carefully checking that the blistering hot-water bottle was securely fastened to Kevin's chest; once or twice he had tried to slosh a little more brandy into the boy's mouth, but realised that he was wasting his time. He checked, too, that the working deck was as clear as possible and the entrance to the wheelhouse door was unobstructed. About Skip, it was pointless to do anything. The man was sitting in the skipper's chair, but he was like marble; he must have been steadying himself against the movement of the boat, but there was no evidence that he was moving a muscle. David ignored him.

Medical advice was given, briefly, by a supercilious doctor from the General – not Bryce, who was off duty and would return at six. The doctor told David to keep the patient warm and dry. David simply said that he had already done so. He didn't mention the hot-water bottle lashed to the boy's chest, and the doctor didn't ask. "Should I give him more brandy?" David had asked. "No, that won't help," said the doctor. He did not elaborate.

The ETA was accurate. David heard the engine just as they asked him to loose off a flare. It was some time since he had handled a Very pistol, and he did it cautiously, knowing it had never been fired. It functioned perfectly.

It helped the pilot pick him out quickly. At eleven minutes past five he was hovering over *Silver Cod* and the winchman was on his way down as David dragged Kevin's inert body out of the wheelhouse door.

The winchman landed neatly on the deck; his feet parted briefly again from the iroko planking before settling firmly. He wriggled out of his harness, which was a simple strip of leather called a strop, exactly like those one sees on walls in barber's-shops. His hand felt the bulge in Kevin's chest. In maybe thirty seconds he had the metal hot-water bottle detached, and rolled it off the boy's body. It hurt his fingers as he did so, but he said nothing, glancing instead at the face to see if there was any evidence of life. There was no clue apart from a sallow blueness around the corners of the mouth.

The strop was circling around him; the small boat was pitching quite heavily in the blustery wind.

"All right," he said. "Let's get him up there."

David lifted the boy's shoulders while the winchman manoeuvred the strop into place. A moment later Kevin was rising towards the helicopter, vertical, with the winchman simply hanging on.

David watched them go, face tense. The two bodies on the end of the cable continued to gyrate, black against the light of the sky. The helicopter looked small in comparison, many feet up, its squat shape in silhouette against the blue and white sky, rotors whirling. It looked like an enormous dragonfly.

* * * * * * * * *

"You want to be a *what*?"

"Journalist," said Katherine. She smiled sweetly.

"Good God," said the lecturer.

They had been sitting in her tutor's cubicle-like seminar-room, the walls lined with books that failed utterly to convey the cloistered peace of an Oxford don's retreat. Outside the steel-framed plate-glass windows a late spring wind had been whipping across the short grass of the nearby sports-field.

"But journalists," her tutor said gravely, "chase ambulances."

"You've been watching too much television," she replied.

"That's a fine comment for a member of your generation. What the hell do you want to do that for, anyway?"

"Variety. Human contact."

The tutor glanced down at his notes. "It seems a sad waste of what will certainly be an upper second, Katherine. Maybe a first."

She shook her head crisply, lips pursed. "No. Look. Trainee vacancies on local papers are so hard to get that I might well need that first just to chase ambulances, cover thefts from butcher's shops and live in a bedsit with a gas ring for two years."

"You've thought this out, haven't you?"

"Oh, yes. So will you give me a reference?"

"Well, there was never any question about that," he said, laughing. "No, I'm just wondering what you want with chasing ambulances."

She laughed too.

A year later, that conversation came back to her as she sat behind the wheel of the trim Fiesta, lighting a Marlboro Light, her eyes trained on the tiny, distant ambulance. Her vision was strained by the blur of the mesh wire fence that ran round the perimeter of the airfield.

Behind it the grass glistened with raindrops; about two hundred yards away, reflected in a puddle, the ambulance was parked on a tarmac apron.

She jumped at the sound of a tap on the window. A clean-shaven face peered at her from under a peaked cap.

"Afternoon, Miss."

"Hello."

"Waiting for something?"

She nodded. "A helicopter."

"Relative, is it? 'Cos you'd be better off down the General. Not that I don't understand, but..."

"It's OK," she said. "Actually I'm a journalist off the *Gazette*."

"Give us your ID then," he said.

She brought her press card out from her inside pocket and handed it over. He glanced at it briefly.

"Okay, Miss. Just like to keep a check on people hanging round the perimeter fence, that's all."

She grinned. "Right you are. But I'm not a Peace Woman with wirecutters."

"That, Miss," said the guard, "would be a shocking waste."

"Sez you." She broadened her grin. "Male chauvinist pig."

"Know a way to a man's heart, don't you?" he chuckled. "Don't hang around too long, will you?"

"Why? Bad for your blood pressure?"

Still smiling, he made a dismissive gesture and sauntered back towards the main gate.

Katherine switched the grin off and leaned back in her seat. The radio clattered out the latest chart line-up. She switched it off.

She wondered if she might have been better off parked away from the airfield, facing the sea, where she would see the Sea King as soon as it approached; she would need a head start if she was to beat the ambulance to the General, although it was only a mile or two, for the route cut across a busy shopping street on the edge of town.

She didn't want to wait in Casualty. Not today. They would let her, they knew her, but...

Vulture.

She got out of the car, admiring the view across the town to seaward; the weather was less changeable now. She could feel the sun on her face. She blew her smoke into the damp air and searched the horizon for the small yellow speck that would turn into a helicopter

It appeared low, close to the horizon, as if flying straight at her. It gained height a little to cross the cliffs. As the noise of its engine broke, she tried to see if it was the right one, but she knew it was.

I bet the car doesn't start.

It started.

Twice she nearly had an accident; the first time was when, chopping her way through the end-of-day traffic in a suburban shopping street, watching her mirror for the ambulance's blue lights, she suddenly saw an elderly Cortina reversing out of a parking space; the driver had made a mess of parallel-parking and was trying to tidy it up. She missed him by a bumper's width. Then she had to turn right and then left across a busy stream of traffic. After a minute or two of waiting she started to ease her way out of the traffic, but no-one would stop. Eventually she pushed her way out far enough so that an angry BMW driver was forced to stop. It would have taken him but five seconds to let her through. His face turned puce with fury; a youngish, plump man, about thirty, she guessed. She ignored his blaring horn and made her way, loathing him.

She parked as close as she could to the front entrance of the hospital and half-walked, half-trotted across the springy rubberized plastic of the floor, dodging the odd white-coated staff member who glanced at her as she weaved her way between the changing shifts; most of the office staff had left now, but a few hung around, talking on corridor corners, hands in pockets.

Up ahead were the double swing doors into Casualty. As she approached, one was flung open, and a fire-extinguisher appeared, base-first, to wedge it. The fire extinguisher wobbled once or twice and settled on its base, and a hand appeared and let the door rest against it. The head of a wheeled bed appeared, a drip on a pole above it, and behind it followed three or four anxious nurses to propel it through the door.

Katherine just managed to flatten herself against the wall in time to let it past.

"Get out of the way, you stupid bitch," hissed one of the nurses. Katherine recognised her as one who sometimes did duty with Bryce. Katherine had not been in the way at all.

In Casualty, there was a small waiting-room and she entered it. It was a plain room, devoid of the usual magazines, save for a few tattered copies of *Punch*; this was not a place where people felt like reading. She sat down in one of the low chairs, closed her eyes for a moment, hands on the chair-arms, and then opened them to look around her.

There was a middle-aged couple in the room, and she guessed at once who they were. They were talking in low voices.

"Don't you worry, pet, he'll be fine," Mr. Tilley told his wife. "Silly little sod just got himself a bit cold, that's all. Tell you, all he needs is a hot shower and a good dollop of that stew you've got on for tonight and then into bed with a good book and a hot-water bottle."

"I dunno, Les," said his wife weakly. "All this business with helicopters and that. They wouldn't bother if they didn't reckon he was sick, would they? What did that copper say? Suspected hypothermia? Isn't that what old ladies die of in winter?"

"Ah, well, that's different, you see," said her husband, his own voice betraying forced confidence. "They don't know what's happening to them, do they? Takes weeks, doesn't it? Well, you know, Kev's been got off quick, hasn't he?"

"I dunno, Les," repeated Mrs. Tilley. "All this charging about on boats with that old soak of a skipper. Reckon you ought to get him into the factory after this lot, Les."

Her husband forbore from repeating what she'd said to him that morning over breakfast.

"I'll get him fixed up, don't you worry," he said. "Maybe we could get him in to study a trade. He's good with his hands and he's got plenty of common sense with machinery. Mind you, if I caught that boozy old Yorkshireman, I shouldn't leave much of him."

Katherine doubted that, seeing the thin, slightly stooped frame of Mr. Tilley against the rollicking shoulders and barrel chest of Skip. But neither said any more, because from that moment one could pick up the sound of a siren in the distance. Then it ceased, and the ambulance arrived seconds later.

Kevin was manhandled into the building with maximum speed

and minimum fuss. A nurse kept the couple back in the doorway with a gentle arm.

"There's a cardiac arrest team who'll want to have a look at him as soon as he comes in, just to make sure," she said kindly. "Don't you worry, now, Mrs. Tilley, it won't be long before we know whether everything's all right."

Katherine couldn't see much from behind these three, but she saw the stretcher wheeled past and caught a glimpse of a blue-grey face on the pillow, spots showing a bit darker, a sort of silver-foil survival bag wrapped tightly around him up to the chin. She watched the nurse, who she recognised as the same small woman who had bitten her head off a few minutes earlier.

Somewhere inside, the cardiac team, summoned from all over the hospital by bleeper the moment Kevin left the deck of *Silver Cod*, was at work, quickly, quietly, in near-silence. Everything they knew would be tried, chests could be thumped and stimulants injected as they searched the green screen for the blip of life. If they failed, they would know that everything had been done, that the organization had been immaculate, right from the moment that David had shoved Skip out of the way and into the skipper's chair and taken the microphone, and the message had been passed by the coastguard in seconds and the helicopter, on fifteen minutes' standby, had lifted off in barely five, playing cards scattered around the messroom as space-age figures ran across the wet, gleaming black tarmac. And then the ambulance with its engine running as the helicopter turned to land, and the team standing by at the General, impassive.

There was no "if only"; it had simply been too late.

Katherine saw the nearby set of double doors open slightly and then close with a smooth rush of air. No-one came through them. Mrs. Tilley emitted what sounded like an animal cry, half-sob, half-howl, a primeval throwback to cubs lost in the snow. Katherine noticed an old blue anorak hanging over the woman's arm.

* * *   * * *   * * *

THE early-evening sunlight streamed through the window of the pub next to the newspaper office, the bar almost empty still, for it was just a quarter to six; those who went straight home had gone, the more sociable were waiting for their colleagues in the office. It was a handsome room, refurbished a year or so earlier but with traditional materials; the high bar stools were covered with comfortable blue cloth, not plastic, and the bar itself was a good solid mahogany. The floor was bare, sanded, polished wood. The foot-rails under the bar glinted in the sunlight that also caught the rows of upturned pint glasses waiting in neat rows.

The barman pulled back the pump-handle and a pint of bitter frothed into a straight glass, giving off a faint aroma as it did so. Katherine always enjoyed the first pint of the evening, work done. The three of them, herself, the layout artist, and the news editor, sat in a triangle on stools just beside the bar. The layout artist nibbled at cheese-and-onion crisps.

"So he snuffed it, then," said the news editor.

"Yep," said Katherine, crossing her long legs.

"Could be the lead tomorrow," said the news editor. "See what turns up. Give us a crisp, John."

"Weren't you charging about getting background material on that boat today?" asked the designer.

She nodded. "Yes. Got stacks. Don't know what I'll do with it all now."

"Good human interest story," said the news editor. "Maybe you could do it as a feature. Did you get a pic of the crew?"

"Yes, just looking over the equipment before they left."

"Well, there you go then. Got the film in?"

"Rod took it round to the lab. I saw him on my way back from the General."

"Good girl. We can splash those in the morning. Even get Bill doing one of his tub-thumping editorials. You know, the price of cod and all that, Neglected Industry in Holiday Town."

"Yes, I'll take care of it all," she said wearily. "Thanks, Mike." She took the pint the designer handed her and drank it a third of the way down. "Shit, I needed that."

"Did you get a word with the parents at the General?" asked the news editor.

"Are you joking?"

"No."

She didn't comment.

"Well, all they could have done was tell you to piss off," said Mike practically.

"I didn't exactly feel like being told to piss off by them at the time," said Katherine.

"That's no excuse," said the news-editor, half-serious.

"Well, I'll get Rod to knock up some pictures of the lad from the roll I shot in the morning and I'll nip round and see them tomorrow," said Katherine, eyes on her beer.

"Yeah, that'd be good. Mind you, you got to be hard, Kath, strike while the iron is hot, you know?"

"Oh, God, piss off, Mike," she said.

"Sorry, kid." He grinned. "Must have been a funny sort of day."

"Was a bit. Look, I'll sort it all out in the morning. You're right. It *will* be good, but I think I'll go and watch telly now," she said.

"Fair enough. See you in the morning."

She drained her pint quickly and, hiccoughing a little, went out into the street. She was about to get into her car, but something drew her towards the harbour.

* * * * * * * * *

KATHERINE saw David before he saw her. He was walking slowly along the main prom, on the seaward side, his jacket and canvas bag slung over his shoulder. Tall, well-built, but without the barrel-like pugnacity of Skip, he was walking with his head down and his face in shadow. He walked slowly but steadily.

"David?"

He looked up. There was something rather broken in his face.

"Oh, Miss Hailey."

"Hallo. I'm sorry about what happened." A sudden thought struck her. "You do know yourself, don't you?"

"'Bout Kevin? Oh aye. I've only just got in but I heard it on VHF as I came up breakwater."

"Did you think he was dead? When they took him off, I mean?"

"If truth be told I didn't really know," he said dully. "And if that crazy fool had let me get him into the wheelhouse quick, this would never have happened. But, you know who's really to blame, don't you?"

She shrugged. "Tell me."

"I am."

"Why?"

"I could've given lad an oilskin, but I didn't bloody put them in the locker, last night, did I? Too bloody keen to get to the pub, that's me."

"Oh."

They were silent for a moment. Then:

"But you said that Skip wouldn't let you get him in."

"Eh? Oh, in the wheelhouse, yes. Skip just said keep the soft little bastard out on deck."

"Then you're not to blame," said Katherine. "Look, I went to the General today, before they brought him in, I mean. And the doctor there was talking about hypothermia. If you'd been able to keep him out of the spray, you'd have been all right. If you tried..."

"Oh, sod it." David shrugged. "Save it for the inquest, love. Lad's dead and we killed him. That's enough, isn't it?"

He hoisted his jacket higher on his shoulder and turned to go.

"David?"

He turned his head and looked back over his shoulder.

"The machine?"

"The longliner? What about it?"

"Did it work?"

"Work? Oh yes, it worked." He gave a sort of twisted smile and fished in the canvas service-issue bag by his hip. He brought out a headless codling, still moist, of about two pounds. "Have some cod for your tea, love."

"No ta," she replied. "I think I'll eat meat, just this once."

He put the fish back in his bag.

"Keep smiling," he said.

He walked off down the prom. Katherine watched him go, then turned towards the harbour. It was only a few hundred yards, and she was soon passing the serried ranks of fishing-boats, mostly in and tied up now, although some of the harder-fishing 10-metre men would stay out overnight and land to the dawn market. There were few people about; here and there someone was painting on one of the boats, or checking a piece of gear that had played up during the day's work.

The sky was still full of clouds, but they had broken and scattered, and the westering sun came out from behind a ridge of grey and lit its edges orange for a moment or two, shooting beams out across the sea, which caught silver at the wave-crests. It was calm now, with only a gentle breeze, and it promised to be a pleasant sunset. Not too sure what else she would be doing, Katherine walked on towards the breakwater.

The sun, shining from her right, lit a silhouette on the end of the mole. A thickset figure sat on a bollard, smoking.

As she approached, the figure resolved itself, but she already knew who it was.

It took her several minutes to reach him. He did not turn or move a muscle, but she knew he knew she was there. She sat down on another bollard a couple of feet away.

"Hallo," she said quietly.

"Good evening, Miss Hailey," he replied. His voice was leaden, but it lacked the brokenness that she had sensed in David's.

"Are you all right?"

"Yes, yes." Skip stretched himself a bit from his hunched position, and she noticed that he had a nearly-square piece of white card, about ten by eight inches, in his hands. On the back was a stamp which she thought was National Union of Journalists logo. She could just make out the words *Evening Telegraph* underneath.

"I'm sorry," she said.

"What about?"

"Kevin Tilley, of course."

"Yes, of course." His gaze remained fastened on the other end of the mole opposite them. A small steelship chugged past them; on the deck sat a few men, in boots and woollen jerseys, holding knives, gutting codling. The deck had old-fashioned fishboxes on it, half-full of fish. The usual seabirds wheeled and called in the wake. On the stern a crewman emptied a bright-yellow bucket full of offal into the water.

"David says it's his fault," said Katherine. She wondered why she was speaking.

"I wouldn't say so."

"The oilskins, he means."

"Oh, we never bothered anyway." Skip sighed. Katherine caught a faint whiff of brandy on his breath, but he did not seem drunk. "Sometimes I even used to tell him not to stow 'em, if we were in a hurry." He flicked his cigarette-end over the edge. "No, there's only one man in the dock, Miss Hailey. I thought I could spot a man in trouble, real trouble I mean, on the working deck. Well, sod it, I've been doing it for thirty-five years. But you know what?"

"What?"

He had turned his eyes towards her. They were a little red. He looked tired; not grief-stricken, not broken, not desperate; just very, very, very tired.

"I was drunk," he said with a clean, open cadence, as if he were a lab technician giving figures. "I was so worried, so obsessed with my last real chance. I'm sixty-one, Miss Hailey. So I drank. Because I didn't know if it would work. Forty-five years at sea, and forty years a drinker too, but I've never touched a drop between breakwaters before. Thirty-five years on the bridge, first with my mate's ticket, then as a skipper, and I've never lost a man, 'cept twice. There was a lad went over the side in the White Sea once, must have been in sixty-two or three. And a man got a grappling hook hit his stomach and bled inside. They flew him to Gilbert Bain's in Lerwick but he didn't make it. But those were accidents. Just... accidents."

"Hypothermia," said Katherine. "They said it down at the General. He told me you can't spot it if you don't know how, and people get chilled on deck with the spray, even when it's – "

"Oh, Jesus Christ, don't give me that." He raised his voice in a sort of snarl, but it was directed inwards. Katherine sat silent for a moment.

"Anyone'd think cold had only just been invented," he said finally. "All this stuff about new ways to freeze to death, well, I don't know. But I'll tell you summat, I've never crawled to any man, Miss Hailey, and I've suffered for that. But I've stood on my own two feet for sixty years. I killed that boy. I'm going to say so, there, in that inquest. I've never crawled to anyone. Not a bloody soul. And I'm not going to crawl to myself."

Katherine nodded slowly.

She took out her cigarettes and gave one to Skip, who took it with a grunt of thanks. They were silent for a moment.

"Tore her heart out," he said softly. "They tore her bloody heart out."

Katherine stood up. She looked over his shoulder and saw that the white card was a black-and-white photograph, eight by ten inches with a black and white border, immaculately printed. It was the front three-quarters or so of a ship, tied up by a quay, seen from landward; a slightly old-fashioned vessel with a rear superstructure, and tall derricks instead of the smaller beam-trawls she had seen that day. A large vessel, she had a black hull and a white gunnel and superstructure, but both were streaked with rust. The name on her prow was *Duke of Marlborough*. On the quay in front of her, scattered around in scrapyard fashion, were pieces of machinery. They were quite clear; they included a vast main engine, and on either side of it, two smaller ones, the auxiliaries, like lungs.

Katherine laid a hand on his shoulder.

Behind them, two or three youths on racing bikes wheeled and circled like gulls, each with a cigarette between their lips, awkwardly, as if they were unused to them. A mile or so away, on the main prom, cars and buses passed silently back and forth. In front of the workshop door, opposite *Silver Cod*, another racing bike lay on the ground, front wheel pointed skyward; the chain dragged on the concrete and the back wheel moved slowly a few inches one way, then the other, in the soft breeze.

II Summer

From where he stood, Terry could see the whole of the atrium and the surrounding balcony, as well as most of the floorspace below. He stood leaning on the polished hardwood railing of the walkway that ran around the building's central space, basking in a pool of yellow sunshine that spread patterns across the carpeted floor. Above him was the building's glass-and-steel, high-tech roof. He tipped the ash off his cigarette into the potted plant beside him.

There were numerous potted plants. They lined the balcony and popped up in all the empty offices, often the only object in those rooms, which had a smell of fresh paint and varnish and clean new carpets. Some symmetrical soul had placed all the plants in the same positions, in the corner and next to the powerpoint or telephone socket. In the entrance hall, on either side of the inner doors which led into the light-well below the atrium, two tall ashtrays had been placed; they stood guard, their polished metal cylinders reflecting any visitor as he walked towards them from the smoked glass of the outside doors.

Terry heard the murmur of voices from the light-well below and peered over the balcony. After a moment two figures emerged from beneath the balcony across the well and started to walk slowly, talking, across the open floor. From above he could see the Chairman's mop of silver hair and broad shoulders, the careful cut of his charcoal suit; and the balding head of the chief accountant, not quite as tall and clad in a lighter shade of grey.

Something had struck Terry as missing when the two had followed him into the building. Now he knew what it was. Neither carried briefcases, giving them what he thought was a casual, unprofessional air. As they disappeared below the balcony on which he stood, he raised his own brown leather-covered case with its gleaming combination locks and placed it in front of him on the railing. He opened it, and then listened for footsteps on the stairs behind him.

He heard the hiss of the door opening and the sound of a voice, unmistakeably the chairman's, deep and rich, and, for some reason, a little diffident.

"You meet quite a few of them nowadays," he said quietly. There was a grunt of assent from his companion.

Terry waited a second or two while the door closed and, choosing his moment carefully, snapped the lid of the case down into the locks, securing them with two sharp clicks. Then, and only then, he turned and smiled.

"A beautifully-planned building, wouldn't you say, Alistair?" He was addressing the Chairman.

"It certainly has a remarkable, er, *regularity*," said the chairman. "Do I mean that? What word do I want, Mr. Davis?"

"*Symmetry*, perhaps, Chairman," said the accountant. His own voice had a slight burr that might have come from the West Country. "Even the ashtrays. Did you notice?"

"The ashtrays? Ah, yes, those two in the hall."

"The atrium is good, isn't it?" Terry waved his hand vaguely at the ceiling over the light-well. "It gives a feeling of light and space."

"Surely there must be energy losses through that ceiling," said Davis. "And doesn't it become rather warm in that light-well?"

"I should have thought it was, er, infernal on a fine spring day," said the Chairman.

"Oh, but one wouldn't have people working in that space," said Terry hurriedly. "It's meant as a sort of promenade space."

"It's still square footage we have to pay for," said Davis.

"And the price per square foot does seem rather high," commented the Chairman, again with that slight diffidence that Terry found odd in one so powerful.

"That reflects its close proximity to London," said Terry. "And good communications."

"I had hoped to save a considerable sum of money on rental," said Davis. "Otherwise it isn't worth uprooting our staff."

"At least here they wouldn't be too isolated from amenities," said the Chairman. "But do we really need a promenade area? In Covent Garden they appear to find the pub quite adequate for that, especially with the new licensing hours."

Davis chuckled. "Quite so."

"Ah, but we have excellent pubs here in the countryside," said Terry quickly. "In fact, let's go and have a spot of lunch. It's – " He looked at his watch. "It's nearly two."

The Chairman hesitated. "What do you think, Mr. Davis? I'd like to hit the Chiswick Flyover before the Friday afternoon holocaust." He smiled slightly.

"So would I, but it should only take an hour or so, surely," said Davis. "It's only seventy or eighty miles. Are you anxious to get back?"

"No, not especially." The Chairman made a move for the door.

This threw Terry out of kilter. *I'm supposed to take the lead*, he thought, *act positive. I shouldn't have let them wander round the building on their own anyway, bad psychology.*

"In fact," the Chairman was saying, "I should love an excuse to be late for dinner. My wife has invited some dreadful bore from the Arts Council. I expect he will spend the entire evening spewing fearful drivel about the shape of sculpture in the wake of socialist realism or something. Is this the way down, Mr. Malcolm?"

"Eh? Oh, yes, er, straight down the stairs and across the lobby." With fancy footwork Terry managed to take the lead again in the hall, having been frustrated on the stairs, which were too narrow. He led them towards the doors, which had brown-painted steel frames. Through the polarised glass the sky looked blue and white; as they emerged, blinking, into the strong sunlight, it reverted to a white summer haze.

"Would you like a lift?" asked the Chairman courteously. "Or did you bring your car?"

"Is he taking the piss?" Terry asked himself, but there was no hint of it on the Chairman's face. Out loud he replied: "It's the BMW over there," and pointed to a white BMW of the smaller kind that was drawn up by the kerb a few yards away. "I'll lead you to the pub. It's only a couple of miles."

"Perhaps you would give us directions, in case we lose you," suggested Davis. He had already guessed that the young estate agent's sales psychology included a leaden right foot.

"Oh, it's quite easy," said Terry, surprised that anyone would admit to not being able to keep up. "Turn right, then right again along the Basingstoke road. Follow that for a mile or so, then a turn to the left brings you to the village. The pub's in the middle of it."

"Very good," said the Chairman. "What sort of pub are we looking for?"

"Oh, a nice pub," said Terry, construing the question as social, rather than geographical. "It's been done up very nicely. I'll see you shortly, then."

The Chairman nodded. He climbed behind the wheel of the dark-green Jaguar and switched on. Above the gentle whirr of the twelve-cylinder engine he caught the revving of the BMW and a slight whiff of exhaust intruded over the wood and leather of his own car. He sighed softly, and followed the BMW out of the car-park.

"What do you think of the building?" asked the accountant from the passenger seat.

"I think it's a bit soulless for a publishing company," replied the Chairman. "We've been happily in organised chaos in Floral Street ever since my grandfather ran the firm. Really, John, I'll be looking for quite substantial savings if we're to move. I'm not sure that we'll find them here."

"I don't think so either, now I've talked to this chap," said Davis. "He admits that the lessees would be looking for a premium. Moreover I rang Home Counties this morning and I gather that the head lease has been sold to an investment company. Apparently it was in *Chartered Surveyor* last week."

The Chairman smiled. "I see. So they'll cream a little off the top. From us."

"More than a little," said Davis. "According to *Chartered Sur-*

veyor Weekly, they've been trying to find occupants for more than six months."

"Have they?" The Chairman glanced across at his companion. "That's interesting. I thought this area was supposed to be incredibly sought-after."

"It is, but I feel the increase in rents has slowed just enough to worry some of the property companies. It's become so competitive that they've all hacked their profit margins to the bone and they can't afford to drop their rents by even a penny per square foot." He thought for a moment. "It's not obvious yet, Chairman, but with these rising interest rates the bubble's beginning to wobble. Maybe all over the south-east. But not burst. Not yet."

"Hmm," said the Chairman. He looked at the rear of the white BMW, fast disappearing in the distance. "Bad news for chaps like that. I suppose they'll go back to wherever they came from. I wonder where that was?"

"Some obscure polytechnic in suburbia, I expect."

"I hope not," said the Chairman. "My daughter's at one of those."

Meanwhile Terry had reached the country road, as he had described it; actually a long strip of tarmac that ran straight and level between market gardens, with the odd light-industrial site. He was humming, tunelessly but cheerfully. If he could shift this one, the investment company that had bought the head lease would be confirmed clients. Personal clients. He liked the thought, and was looking forward to a good lunch. And a drink. He fingered the lapels of his Hugo Boss suit. He reached the pub several minutes ahead of the Jaguar, which had made no attempt to keep up. He waited in the porch and the three men went in together.

Terry led them through to the dining-room, an airy new extension built onto the back, where the tables were crowded with diners, almost all male and suited.

"They do an excellent steak here," he said, beginning to steer them towards a corner table. Then he realised that neither Davis nor the Chairman had followed him.

"Do you mind if we just settle for a beer and a sandwich?" said the Chairman apologetically. "Really, I mustn't be too late."

"Are you sure?" asked Terry anxiously. "The meals here are really excellent."

"Thank you, but my wife gets quite infuriated if I can't manage her massive spreads in the evening," the Chairman replied firmly. "How about you, Mr. Davis?"

"Oh, a pie or something will do," said Davis. "Look, there's an empty table over there in the corner. I'll grab it while you order."

Terry was allowed to buy the drinks.

"A pint and a half of bitter and a spritzer," he told the barmaid.

"What's a spritzer?" asked the Chairman curiously.

"Have you never had one, Alastair?" said Terry.

"I confess I haven't had the pleasure."

"A white wine and soda."

"Ah."

The barmaid returned from the pump.

"Let's see, now," she said, "that's a pint and a half of bitter...and a white wine and soda."

Terry pushed three pound coins across the counter.

They sat down beneath an array of horse-brasses, the table patterned by diamonds from the extension's windows behind them, which were leaded. The two clients began on their steak-and-kidney pie and chips and beans.

"Good filling stuff," said Davis approvingly. He nodded towards Terry's plate. "You watching your waistline, Mr. Malcolm?"

"I like to keep fit," replied Terry defensively. On the plate in front of him was a plate of salad with a slice of quiche.

"Oh?" The Chairman managed to keep his eyes off the packet of Rothmans that was on the table beside Terry, going slightly soggy in the beer-slops. "I suppose you're one of these chaps that go jogging, are you?"

"Not jogging," said Terry, between crunches of green salad. "I play squash a lot."

"I confess I've never played," said the Chairman. "I used to enjoy fives at school."

Terry wondered vaguely what fives were, but his mind moved on in an instant.

"I love squash," he said. "It's competitive. Like me."

"Indeed," said the Chairman. Terry might have, but did not, see a slight smile on the Chairman's lips, but it was soon gone. "Do you bring the same approach to your work?"

"Of course. I really enjoy bringing off a deal. I'm always watching to see if I can" – he was about to say "get one over", but changed his mind. "I like to make the most of anything going for me in a business transaction. It's natural, isn't it?"

"Then perhaps we'd best be a little careful," intoned Davis in his slight West Country burr.

"Oh, no," said Terry quickly, a little horrified. He had missed the gentle humour in the accountant's voice. "I mean you try to reach some agreement that profits both sides."

"Indeed," said Davis. "I was only joking. So what will the weekend hold for you? A good thrash on the squash courts?"

"Oh, yes," said Terry enthusiastically. "After that a couple of beers. Then tomorrow I'll go gliding." He let the word hang, waiting for the others to respond.

Out of courtesy, they did.

"That sounds enterprising of you," said the Chairman. "Where do you do that?"

"Oh, it's an airfield north of here, on the edge of the Midlands," said Terry. "It's great. It's a gliding club. About ten of us joined as trainees all at the same time and we had a race to see who was going solo first, then for the silver, then for the bronze, I don't suppose you know what those are?"

"Yes, I do," said the Chairman.

"Well, for the silver you've got to glide upwards into cloud, so you've got to have radio training," explained Terry, "And for the bronze you've got to do a cross-country flight. I'm really looking forward to doing my silver. I guess you haven't been in a small aircraft that often."

"I flew Seafires in Korea," murmured the Chairman.

"Well, it's quite something being in that little bubble in the sky. You ought to try it sometime. The view you get, it's just fantastic. Especially when you've had some practice flying and you can break off and look at the scenery sometimes."

"Have you reached that stage?" asked Davis, again with a subtle smile in his vocal chords.

"Oh, I think so," said Terry. He gave a guilty start. The *deal*. "So what did you think of the building?"

"A very handsome structure," commented the Chairman.

"We can contact your solicitors about letting arrangements," said Terry, setting down his knife and fork. "Would you like me to set that in hand, Alastair? Do it this afternoon if you like."

The Chairman had been sitting back in his seat, his hand near his chin, smiling quizzically, as Terry talked about gliding. Now he sat up, straightened his back and pursed his lips before saying:

"That won't be necessary. We have a number of options to consider, but I think that with the premium, the building is probably out of our range. There are other factors, but I think it unlikely that we'll be taking it on."

"Come on, it's an *excellent* building!" said Terry, a cold feeling spreading in the pit of his stomach – though this was also due to a tomato that had not been properly thawed before being removed from the freezer. "It's the ideal place to move staff who've been forced out by rising prices. Look at the rail and road links."

"It was those that brought us to look at it," said the Chairman, "but I am concerned about running costs, about the vast atrium that consumes so much of what I assumed would be useful floorspace, and by the, er, slightly antiseptic nature of the site and its surroundings."

"Eh?" said Terry, puzzled.

"In light of this," finished the Chairman, "I don't think the savings justify us moving out of London, particularly as we're not being forced out; our lease has ten years to run."

The meal finished quietly. Terry saw them off philosophically enough. He watched as Davis went to the passenger side. The Chairman followed him and unlocked the door, holding it open.

"Thankyou, Sir Alastair," said Davis as he got in.

"Shit," said Terry under his breath. He smiled and waved.

* * *   * * *   * * *

THE Jaguar breasted the rise onto the Chiswick Flyover.

"Well, we both voted Conservative," said Davis.

"I don't think I voted for the likes of him."

"Perhaps, Sir Alastair," said Davis, "you should send your daughter to finishing school."

The chairman chuckled. "Don't be impertinent. By the way, are you still free for golf tomorrow?"

* * *   * * *   * * *

SOME years earlier, Harold Grieves and Partners had itself moved, as the first stirrings of the office boom had compelled it to search for better premises than its Berkshire high street shop-front in a quiet town. The town itself had grown and today Grieves occupied a modern suite of offices on the edge of it. This had upset some of the older staff, who resented having to get the car out to collect sandwiches at lunchtime. It would also have upset Harold Grieves had it not been for the fact that one Rotary dinner too many had hardened his arteries to the steel-like consistency displayed, to his distress, in some of his son's business dealings. The son opted to have Harold cremated, against the latter's wishes, but cleaner, less messy, and cheaper too. He then traded-in his father's Rover in favour of a BMW, which was, he felt, somehow more suitable for the prevailing climate, and abandoned residential for office agency. He also abandoned his studies for the Royal Institution of Chartered Surveyors, which were, he felt, about as relevant as a City and Guilds in motor engineering were to a car salesman.

This afternoon, John Grieves was leaning back in the green cloth swivel chair behind his desk. Terry was pacing up and down in front of him, his jacket off; over his white shirt he wore a waistcoat with a shiny back. The waistcoat was buttoned tightly over a developing paunch (in truth, Davis's remark about watching waistlines had rankled a bit). In his early thirties, Terry remained chunky and nuggety and muscular, however, and the paunch was still far from obvious. He wasn't tall, but he was very solid. His hair was cut fairly short, although a little less so since he had noticed it thinning on top. In fact, this was Terry's imagination; his thick brown hair was very healthy.

"Well, did you close the deal with Sir Alastair Kellet?"

"*Sir* Alastair," snorted Terry. "Who the hell bothers with titles nowadays anyway?"

"Is that the answer to my question, Terry?"

"You haven't answered mine yet. What about the decision on my partnership?"

"Give a bit of breathing space, Terry, old son. Daily business first, eh?"

"All right, all right." Terry was not exactly pacing, more doing a sort of high-speed fidget standing up. "I think so. He'll be in touch."

"Triangle Investments would love to know." John sat forward and shuffled the papers on his desk. "They really want to shift that bloody lease. It *matters* to them, Terry."

"Well, partnership matters to me," said Terry.

"All right. There are one or two things to be sorted out and then we'll make a decision."

"What sort of things?"

"Oh, just formalities about suitability."

"Christ, John, I haven't got two heads. I do the same sorts of things as everybody else, wear the same sort of clothes, is that the sort of thing that's important?"

"Not quite, but related. Like I say, Terry. Formalities. Let you know this time next week."

"Okay, okay," said Terry. He decided that it was time to beat a strategic retreat before John pressed him too hard about Kellet. "See you Monday."

He went out, jacket over his shoulder, and pulled the door behind him as an afterthought. It didn't quite close, but drifted open a few inches. John left it.

It was half-past four. Terry had assumed that the Kellet appointment would take up the rest of the day. It hadn't, so he was at something of a loose end.

He decided to go home.

He walked down through the offices where the secretaries sat with their word-processors, each one sitting on an individual desk, three on each side of the room in a neat little row. The room was lit by strip-lighting and had light-brown walls and a dark-brown carpet. There was nothing else in the room.

"Hallo, ladies!" called out Terry.

One of them glanced up; she had been reading a bodice-ripper under her desk.

"Sold St. Paul's, have you?"

"St. Paul's?" he asked, puzzled. "That isn't one of mine."

"St. Paul's Cathedral," she replied, looking back at her bodice-ripper.

"Oh." He managed a laugh. "But I'm onto a real good thing with this Newbury property. I've sold the lease to a publisher, a real-live knight."

"A what?"

"Sir Alastair Kellet," said Terry in mock-posh tones. "I've just had lunch with him. I think he'll take the lease."

"Congratulations," she said, turning the page of her novel.

"Have a good weekend," he called cheerily.

Somebody grunted.

He strode out into the street and got into the BMW parked outside. Tossing the suit jacket onto the passenger seat, he started the engine and pulled away, cutting through the traffic towards the other side of town.

Terry lived in another, similar town about fifteen miles away. He travelled a mile or two away from the outskirts on a main road, and covered a brief stretch of dual carriageway onto a smaller A-road. The afternoon sunshine had changed in quality as the heat of midday faded; no longer did the strong light of the August dog days turn the sky white. Instead a hint of gold had appeared, and the countryside had mellowed, with the fields turning a darker, livelier shade of green, and the sky had faded gently to blue.

Terry did not notice this.

He accelerated up the slope from a roundabout, and followed a slight curve in the road, staying just inside the white lines. As he did so a police Rover came towards him, and he backed off with a guilty start, just as the BMW hit the apex of the bend. As he did so the car's tail twitched slightly. His heart jumped, but the car stabilised itself of its own accord and he plunged on down the road, congratulating himself on his skill.

The road narrowed, the hedges closing in, the white lines gone, tall trees lining the verges. A long straight, a bend, then the steepening hill over the apex of the Berkshire downs. Terry loved breasting this rise so that, at its apex, the car lifted and he could sail over the crest. He watched the speedometer – forty, fifty, fifty-five, sixty, sixty-five.

The BMW didn't leave the ground, but the body lifted gratifyingly on its suspension. Terry braked gently, wondering if he dared hang the tail out round the bend at the bottom of the hill. Instead, he slowed and slowed into the bend, automatically feeding in more throttle as he came out of the other side.

Busy doing this, he did not notice a long line of horses travelling in the same direction, but occupying the opposite lane, so as to be against the traffic. The road was just wide enough for him to get by, so when he did see them, he decided not to slow.

The six or seven horses were being led by an instructress from a local riding school. Behind her were strung out both advanced learners and raw beginners, carefully spaced out so that no two complete novices were together. She heard the sound of the engine strengthening behind her. Too smooth to be an old banger driven by a hooligan, too fast to be a local, too noisy to be a gentleman.

The car shot by at about fifty-five, with perhaps a foot or two to spare, and then it was gone.

"BASTARD!" screamed the instructress.

The horse immediately behind her was the only one to panic. A skittish two-year-old, it reared up on its hind legs. Thirteen-year-old Cecilia grasped the reins tightly. Then she tried to hang on to the saddle. But it was too late, and she slid onto the rump, rolled over onto her left, and fell, her foot catching in the stirrup. She landed on her head, and her body skidded along the ground. The foot in the stirrup twisted awkwardly, and her leg stuck out from her body at a crazy angle. Her foot finally came free from the stirrup after what had seemed to everyone watching to be an eternity.

Two older pupils calmed the panicked horse. Cecilia lay on the ground where she had fallen. The instructress ran over to her, having first made sure that someone was holding the reins of her own mount so that it did not wander across the road.

Cecilia rolled in agony.

"Your head! Are you all right?"

"My head hurts," said the girl. She smiled weakly. "But my hat stayed on. I think I'm okay...Oh, Christ! My LEG!"

She sat bolt-upright, trying to hold the twisted knee, and nearly screamed in agony.

"Helen, go and find a 'phone and call an ambulance. And the police. Quickly."

"Don't worry, Sissy," said one of the older girls, kneeling down beside Cecilia as another went to comply with the instructress's orders. "I got the pig's number."

*** *** ***

THE PIG steered his car into the outskirts of the town where he lived, blissfully unaware of the pain he had left behind him.

It was an ancient town and was probably the one chosen by George Orwell for his between-the-wars elegy for England, *Coming Up for Air*. Terry did not know that, and if he had, would not have been interested, though he would have told everyone anyway. He drove impatiently around the square with its one-way system and narrow streets, past the statue of a bygone and probably mythical monarch, and between the two shops where Grieves owned the head lease and was trying to shift the long-term tenants so that he could propose a trouble-free road-widening scheme to the local council, which would then purchase the properties. He passed the garage and came out into the short stretch of open road that led to the estate where he lived.

This had been built five years previously on an abandoned airfield. The developers had offered the neat new detached houses onto the market at an attractive price, but they had rapidly become dearer so that this was now quite a desirable place to live. The mortgage had damn near broken Terry three years earlier but he now felt that the investment had been a good one.

He left his car outside, planning to go out later. There was a short driveway, no side-passage, and just a small patch of garden at the back that Eileen, his wife, used occasionally but he did not. Wondering if she was back yet from her work at a local hairdresser's, he let himself in with his Yale key, having to jerk open the light wood door, which had warped with the winter rain.

Eileen was in the kitchen, chopping turnips for dinner.

"I'm back."

"I heard you." A high voice, with that slight note of complaint in it which Terry had noticed lately, and resented.

He went into the kitchen. His wife was a slightly-built woman, but of average height, standing about equal to Terry, who wore mildly built-up shoes to compensate. Her long, straight, mousey hair hung across her shoulders. Her face was rather thin, her mouth small, and she had neat grey eyes.

"That kid who sees Mrs. Hutchins was round there today," she said, without looking up.

"Oh yeah. Getting her oats is she?" Terry wrenched the cupboard open, looking for the Nescafe. The wrench was necessary because the door had warped during the wet winter.

"I dunno, Terry, I think he's just her nephew or something."

"Hope so. Talk about mutton dressed up as lamb," said Terry, shoving the cupboard door shut and putting a big dollop of coffee into one mug. He hadn't shut the door quite hard enough and it swung open. "Shit, I forgot to pay the instalments on the video."

"I've done it," she said, not looking up from her work. "I don't like that lad coming round here, Terry. It's that rusty old car. Specially in the evening."

"Bit of an embarrassment," said Terry. "I wish she'd get her front door painted, too. " He turned for the kettle and his forehead collided with the sharp edge of the cupboard door, which was hanging open. "Jesus Christ, can't you close that door?"

"You opened it."

"Well, you were standing right next to it," said Terry, aggrieved. He strode through the narrow hallway to the toilet. He shut the door behind him but it swung open, having warped a little in the damp air back in the winter. It swung back against his buttocks. Eileen could hear the heavy stream of urine clattering into the toilet bowl.

"When are we eating?" he called out above the waterfall.

"'Bout seven."

"I want to go out about seven-thirtyish."

"You said. Aren't you going to stay in some night?"

"Might tomorrow. Got to go gliding earlier," called out Terry. "Fix me some sandwiches or something"

"I got you some scotch eggs from the Superstore."

"And what else?"

"Those individually-wrapped pork pies you like."

"That'll do."

"You're always bloody out."

"I'm making contacts." He pulled the plug, not bothering to put the lid down. "And stick some coffee in a thermos for me, will you? Thanks."

He went through into the living room and dropped himself onto the slippery surface of the maroon leather three-piece suite that he and Eileen had bought a couple of years previously. Only another year, and we've paid that off, he thought with satisfaction. Then maybe we can get that car for Eileen and she'll quit bloody moaning.

He picked up the *TV Times* to check if there was anything he should get her to video for him while he was out. The list of films did not please him.

West Side Story. Yeugh. *Brief Encounter*. He looked at the dates against them. 1957? 1944? Not encouraging. Ah, a TV-length pilot for a new American detective series. He was about to call out the times to his wife when the doorbell rang.

Walking to the door, he noticed a white police Rover standing outside and wondered what they were doing there. He noticed Mrs. Hutchins's curtains twitching.

He opened the door with a bit of a heave. Two tall policemen stood on the doorstep.

"Mr. Terence Malcolm?" enquired one of them lugubriously. He was well-built, about fifty, with a rather craggy face and bushy eyebrows. His companion was much younger, with dark hair and eyes and a pale face.

"Good afternoon, officer," said Terry, taken aback. "May I help you?"

"I believe you may," said the older of the two.

"Ask away."

"Perhaps not on the doorstep, sir."

"Oh, yes, sorry. Please come in." Terry led them into the living room, wishing that the toilet cistern wasn't still gurgling from his recent pee. "Please take a seat. May my wife fix you coffee? Tea?"

"That won't be necessary, thank you, Mr. Malcolm." Neither sat down. The older man took out a notebook and a pen, and jotted something down. "Are you the registered keeper of a white BMW 318, registration E836 CWL, registered owner Grieves and Sons Ltd.?"

"Yes, I am," said Terry, who had been about to sit down but quickly straightened up again when he realised that neither of the policemen were going to. "It's my company car."

"Were you driving it today, Sir?"

"Yes, I was."

"Very good. Mr. Malcolm, we have had a complaint from a member of the public in relation to an alleged moving traffic offence. I should warn you that you may be subject to prosecution and that anything you say may be taken down and used in evidence against you." He coughed. "You are not, of course, obliged to say anything at this juncture."

"Oh," said Terry. He went a little pale and started searching his memory.

"Were you driving on the A338 at about five o' clock this afternoon, Mr. Malcolm?"

"Was I...? Oh, er, yes, I believe so. I was on my way back from work a little early."

The policeman looked at his watch. Not quite six. All right. He nodded at the younger officer, who went to the police car and removed a small black box.

Terry watched with growing alarm.

"Were you aware of a group of horse riders proceeding in a northerly direction between Hungerford and Wantage, Mr. Malcolm?"

Terry frowned. "Yes, I believe I was."

"Can you estimate your speed as you passed them?"

His frown deepened. "No, I can't, officer. It wouldn't have been very fast. Why?"

The policeman didn't answer. The younger had re-entered the house carrying the black box.

"Have you been drinking today, Mr. Malcolm?"

"Just one drink at lunchtime."

The officer nodded perfunctorily. "Would you be prepared to take a breath-test, sir?"

"Of course," said Terry, with a confidence he didn't feel.

The test was done quickly on an Alcocheck machine. Terry had been through this before. As on previous occasions, it registered negative.

"Thankyou, Mr. Malcolm. I must warn you that you may be subject to prosecution under the Road Traffic Acts for dangerous driving," said the older of the two officers, snapping his notebook shut.

"May I ask what this is all about?" asked Terry.

"One of the horses shied, apparently due to the manner in which the vehicle passed the group," came the reply. "A thirteen-year-old fell and has since been taken to hospital."

Terry felt as if the frozen tomato at lunchtime hadn't quite thawed out yet. "Is she seriously hurt?"

"They'll X-ray her head, but they think it's all right. But there's a possibility of serious damage to one knee." He nodded. "Thank you, Mr. Malcolm. We will be in contact with you in due course to let you know whether the we'll be taking any action. That will be all."

They let themselves out.

Eileen came hesitantly from the kitchen, where she had stayed for the duration of the interview.

"What was all that about then?"

"You heard. And where were you when I needed you?"

"Do you reckon that girl's badly hurt?" she asked anxiously.

"God, my licence!" moaned Terry. "My job!"

"They can't take your licence away for that, can they?"

"Don't you see? I'll be totted-up, under the points system," he groaned. His licence already had a number of points.

He went to the toilet, just managing to get his pants down in time without crapping himself. The door swung open as usual, and he didn't bother to push it shut, although it jolted his knees.

Eileen went on chopping turnips in the kitchen.

* * *   * * *   * * *

"It's a good thing they've never done me when I've been really ratarsed!" chortled Terry. He waved his cigarette about then leaned across at Steve over his bottle of Pils. "Here, do you remember that time after the Grout party when we couldn't find the doorlock?"

"Yeah!" Steve grinned. "And there was you driving down that one-way in the square, bit quicker that way you said – and they stopped you and – well – good thing it was daylight, eh?"

"Bloody right!" They both roared with laughter.

"Mind you," said Terry, "did my heart good the way we got pissed-up with all those ancient chartered surveyors standing round, looking like they couldn't swallow their plums in their mouths!"

His expression grew a little more serious.

"Hey Steve, you want to swap favours?"

"Anytime," said Steve. "What sort of favours?"

"Information," said Terry.

"OK. Let's trade," said Steve.

He was a tall, slim man with slicked-back short blond hair. He worked for Triangle Investments, and was a couple of years younger than Terry. The latter found him a little weak, but liked to use him to keep an eye on what Triangle was up to; and anyway, they both enjoyed a game of squash. Which they'd just had. Terry had, as usual, won by a small margin, which had improved his mood. Steve had made him work for it. Together they had charged around the court, grunting, sweating, their faces a little red as the ball smashed into the wall, each imagining that they were swatting a reluctant client.

Now, showered and changed, they were upstairs. The club had been converted by the Council from an old gaol, and had been neatly done. The drinkers in the bar were all smartly-dressed, like Terry and Steve; formally turned out in new Levi jeans with razor-sharp creases, sports shirts or carefully-chosen sweatshirts, sneakers so bright white, orange or red that they dazzled your eyes, and often neat zippered collarless jackets, though never with the sweatshirts. Bottles of lager or Guinness could be seen on every table, along with the odd white-wine-and-soda. Both lager and Guinness were available on draught, but no-one was drinking it that way.

"You first," said Steve.

"What do I get in return?"

"Let's see if it's worthwhile."

"Okay." Terry leaned a little closer. "Those shops around the street that comes off the market square, back in my neck of the woods. You know how everyone hates to squeeze between the pavements? Well, it's a main road, isn't it?"

"Yeah, that's really old-fashioned, that," said Steve. "We've got the freehold on the two on the east side of the street. You've got the two opposite, haven't you?"

"Yes. And there's road-widening in the air."

Terry nodded. "Right on."

"Come on. Council'll never wear it. Old Colonel Bollocks has vetoed it more times than I can remember," said Steve.

"No problem." Terry shrugged. "Old Grieves reckon's he's nobbled him."

"You're joking."

"No. Straight up. Pinkerton's were after taking those leases off you, weren't they?"

"And we may sell," said Steve. "But not if you're right. So Grievesy has nobbled the Colonel, has he?"

"Yep. Dunno how he did it."

"That's all right. I think I know." Steve sat back, smiling. "I think I know, old son. Why tell me this? If Grievesy heard you tell me what you've just told me he'd fucking kill you."

"He won't hear," said Terry. "Will he, Steve?"

"Not from me."

"OK. Now I want something back."

Steve's mind was racing with possibilities. He could easily block the sale of leases to Pinkerton's. Anything he made on those properties, he'd take a commission. Now Triangle and Grieves would talk each other up on prices. The compulsory purchase orders would not be necessary if both companies reached agreement. The consulting engineers likely to be on the scheme would want to avoid delay. They were an associate of Pinkertons. So the latter would go for the properties at a much higher premium than they were offering now. Both he and Terry would make good commissions on the deal.

"You've made the grade," he said. "Shoot."

"I want to know why I'm being blocked for partnership with Grieves," said Terry carefully. "I think you can tell me. I think Triangle's bringing pressure. It's that blasted office space, isn't it? That deal I nearly shifted today?"

Steve looked at him for a moment.

"No, the deal's irrelevant," he said. "Or nearly. It's a social question, Terry."

"What the hell are you talking about?" Terry nearly spat out his Pilsner.

"They like you to be compatible," Steve said, and shrugged. "It's our MD."

"Your MD? Christ, I get along with him all right, and the rest," said Terry, puzzled. "I've played squash with him. Jesus, Steve, I've even screwed his wife."

"Does he know?"

"Nah. So what's the problem?"

"Your trouble, me old mate," said Steve, "is that you ain't on the square yet."

"Ahhhh…" Suddenly Terry understood.

"You ever been invited, Terry?"

"Yep. Couple of years ago, one of the guys in Pinkertons. Said I'd think it over. Wasn't too keen. All the funny handshakes and that."

"Oh, Christ, don't worry about Masonic ritual," said Steve. "It's all treated as a joke here. You don't imagine a bunch of estate agents and computer programmers take all that, seriously, do you? It's only the old guys like Colonel Bollocks who like everything done properly. I knew you'd been sounded out, Terry."

"So I damaged myself by turning it down?"

"Easily put right." Steve lit a long brown cigarette and tossed the empty book of matches from an Oxford restaurant into the ashtray. "All I've got to do is pass the word that you'd come in. I can do that tomorrow. And then you're hunky dory. In fact I gather Grievesy wants you in partnership. He's sick of taking all the risks. Tell the truth, I think his bottle's going."

Just then the MD of Triangle walked past them. He gave them a cheery nod. He was in his late thirties and looked younger. His wife, tall and dark and thin, was with him. They seemed to be about to join Steve and Terry, but the woman, with a sidelong glance at Terry, steered her husband on.

"You've shafted her, have you?" Steve grinned. "Doesn't seem to want to know you tonight, does she?"

"Silly bitch," said Terry.

"How'd'you do it, anyway?"

"She had too much one lunchtime, and I drove her home," said Terry. "I moved in there quick. She made like she didn't want it."

"And you reckoned she was panting, did you?"

"Well, she'd been friendly enough at lunchtime," Terry shrugged. "Just a quiet one. Did it there on the sofa. Took her out for a drink afterwards and she seemed all right. Bit quiet, mind you."

Steve stretched.

"Ho well. Want to be driven home, do you?"

"You mind? Don't fancy being watched out for tonight. After that silly business earlier on."

"No problem." Steve made to pick up his Adidas grip with the smart white racket-handle sticking out of it.

"Hang on, let's have another Pilsner first," said Terry.

"Don't want to get a blowjob from the police myself, you know, or I'll be out of a job. I've had two or three."

"Oh, you'll be all right," said Terry confidently. "Anyway, we've got to, haven't we? Shake on the trade. Keep shtum. And two or three's nothing."

"Okay." Steve wanted to make sure that Terry never played a double game over those shops. He stuck out his hand.

Terry grasped it warmly.

"No, not like that," said Steve. "You put the thumbs like this, here, you see, and then..."

* * *   * * *   * * *

STEVE drove Terry home. He had a BMW 318i. This rankled with Terry, who had an ordinary 318. When I'm a partner, he thought, I'll get even with all these bastards.

After dropping him, Steve drove on up the A338 towards his own home on the outskirts of the city. He always enjoyed the sensual feel of the wheel between his hands. It was a long, straight road but at one point it did kink right and left through a narrow dip beside a pub. He eased off the throttle slightly as his headlamps picked up the black-and-white chevrons of the warning sign.

He eased the wheel to the left, deciding not to bother dropping a gear. He took a careful line across the apex of the bend, his rear wheels thumping gently across the white line. As they did so the car's rear slewed a little to the left. The wheels chirruped. He jerked the wheel a little farther left. The car stabilised, and he just managed to hold it through the bend, swinging out far enough for the summer grass on the verge to brush the offside of the car.

A long white police Rover eased out of the pub car park.

Steve didn't fight it. He stopped at once, pulling his nearside wheels over onto the verge. He stabbed the hazard warning-light switch and got out of the car.

A burly policeman approached him, tall, with a craggy face and bushy eyebrows. His companion stayed in the car, speaking on the radio.

"Good evening, sir," said the policeman politely, with a touch of the local burr in his voice. "No need for those." He indicated the hazard lights. Steve had not realised that only the offside ones were visible from behind, giving the impression that the car would shortly pull out. "Have you been drinking?"

"Not much, officer," said the victim, politely. He felt slightly sick. "I've just been to drop a friend off from playing squash. I wouldn't be on this road otherwise. I don't know it well."

"No indeed," said the officer. "Would you have any objection to taking a breath test?"

"No, of course not," said Steve, letting a little aggression creep into his voice.

"Very good, sir." The box was produced. Steve followed the officer's instructions. He watched with rising horror as the lights on the box changed. Oh, Jesus, he thought. He had just taken out a massive mortgage on one of the new Barratt's starter homes near the city. No licence, no car, no job.

"I'm afraid, sir, that we must ask you to accompany us to the police station," said the officer politely. "Sergeant Wallace will drive your car for you, sir."

*** *** ***

IT DIDN'T take the two policemen long to regain their position by the road. This time Bob had chosen a bay on the motorway junction, where it intersected with the bypass. It was now nearly midnight on Friday, nearly time to end their shift; all the locals were back from the pub now, and they were after the long-distance boys, tanked-up after the office and then onto the road for their weekend homes.

"Bob?"

He turned. Tom Wallace handed him a large sandwich, made with crusty loaf. "Can't eat all of these. Bloody good, though."

"Ta." Bob bit into the sandwich. "Mmm. You're right. Looks after you all right, doesn't she?" After his beginning on the beat, Tom had been transferred into Traffic; Bob had been in it for years. Tom had been married for a year.

"She certainly does." Tom smiled. "Your lady out of hospital yet, Bob?"

"Tomorrow." The older man yawned and stretched. "No problems. Day early in fact. Just one of those things when they get to a certain age. Nothing to worry about."

They munched peacefully for a minute or two.

"Bob?"

"Yep?"

"You on the square, are you?"

Bob laughed. "Don't really go now. Was into that, oh, ten, twelve years ago. Jacked it in."

"Why?"

"Oh, it's all changed," said Bob, chewing thoughtfully. "Never did care for all that funny handshake business, but you knew where you were with anyone you met there. Friendly too. Get all the brass together for dinner and they'd have a whale of a time, everyone happy together. Get back on duty the next morning, it's yes, Sarge, right away, Superintendent, but you knew they liked you well enough. Now, well, it's all these thrusting bloody kids, isn't it?"

"You reckon?" Tom looked at him. "You don't think I ought to join, then?"

Bob looked back. "Might help you."

"So you think I should?"

"Up to you."

He was silent for a moment. Then:

"Better off just being a good copper really."

He thought he saw a smile of relief cross the younger man's face in the dim light from the sodium lamps that lit the dual carriageway's surface, giving it an eerie, yellowish appearance.

Just then a car shot through the summer night in the fast lane below them.

"What do you reckon? Shoving on a bit, wasn't he?" said Tom, straightening up.

"Maybe," replied Bob. He was tired, and the miscreant, though speeding, had been running straight and true. "See what kind of car it was?" Doubtfully, he started the engine. As the Rover SD1's eight alloy cylinders burbled into life, Tom said:

"Three-series BMW, looked like to me."

"Was it now," said Bob. "Wanker's motor, eh."

The big Rover shot down the slip road like a hound of hell emerging from the Stygian gloom.

* * *   * * *   * * *

TERRY shoved open the ill-fitting door and snapped on the lights in the hall. The living-room was dark; his wife had gone to bed.

He made himself some coffee, his mind wandering on to that MD's wife. Nice and tight, she'd been. Bit dark, though, and that big nose. Wonder if she was Jewish? Had he been screwing a Jew? Screw a Jew, the rhyme ran through his slightly befuddled brain. Screw Jews. Ah. *That* was the sugar. He poured the salt out of the mug and into the sink. Think she gave me a dose, as well, the cow, he thought. Good thing Eileen didn't get it or I'd have had no peace.

He drank the coffee. A little slopped out of the mug and a brown mark spread across the Formica.

Must go to the bog.

He made for the one downstairs, not attempting to close the door but simply letting it swing across his buttocks.

Upstairs, Eileen could hear him thumping around. Eventually he came up and undressed. He lay down heavily in the bed, which was a double but rather narrow, and a little too soft. The sheets kept coming detached from under the mattress because they weren't quite wide enough.

"You might at least have turned the hall-lights out," said Eileen. That slight and whiny voice. "Why can't you come home a bit earlier? You said you'd be home by ten tonight!"

"So what? Me and Steve had to talk business," he replied, and belched. He was not particularly drunk, but had that rather let-down feeling when the beer began to wear off.

"It's just that I'm alone at nights. It isn't as if we had a baby I was looking after."

"If I've told you once, I've told you a thousand times," said Terry. "We can't afford a baby. We've still got payments on the three-piece suite, and you want a car as well. Baby'll have to take its place in the queue, won't it?"

He tried to make love to her.

"Not tonight, I'm not feeling well."

"You're never feeling well when I want it. Silly cow."

He went to sleep. Eileen did not. She lay awake for a while listening to his soft snoring, and then when, once again, the pain in her bladder got a little too bad, she stepped softly downstairs in her nightdress. She closed the door of the toilet behind her and crouched down on the bowl, trying to pee. Not much came out. It was very dark. And very painful.

"Cystitis," the doctor had told her. He gave her a prescription for some antibiotics. He answered the unspoken question. "Yes, you could have caught it off your husband. But quite often it's all completely innocent. Do you wear tight jeans?"

"Yes," she had replied miserably.

"How often do you change your underpants? Every day?"

"Three times a week." She felt desperately humiliated.

"That's not enough if you wear clothes that are tight-fitting round the groin, however clean you are."

"My customers in the salon like tight-fitting jeans," she said sullenly, not looking at him. "My husband likes tight-fitting jeans."

"Well, try and wear slightly baggier ones," the doctor told her crisply. "And if I were you I'd change my briefs twice a day, while you've got this."

She had slunk out of the surgery wishing that the ground would eat her up.

The door of the toilet swung open again. From her position on the bowl Eileen tried to push it shut, but she couldn't quite reach. She looked apprehensively through the hall at the front door, hoping that the light in the toilet wouldn't illuminate her so that she could be seen through the window.

* * *   * * *   * * *

A FEW hours later, about forty miles to the north, the first rays of morning sunlight felt their way through the tall fronds of the hedge behind the little kitchen-garden. They paused for a minute to caress the ripening tomatoes, Roy's pride and joy; and then entered the kitchen where he stood cooking an early breakfast.

He had poured a little vegetable oil into the frying pan and was adding just a little every now and then, just a little, just enough. He didn't prick the big sausages that sizzled in the pan, preferring to watch the skins split slowly to reveal the succulent meat inside. They were excellent sausages. In a few minutes four tomato halves would be grilled slowly at eye level, their surfaces powdered with basil.

Four big sausages. Roy licked his lips. Two nice big free-range eggs. He would have liked three, but Katy would have said he was greedy, though she would have laughed as she said it. Now for the tomatoes. He was almost giggling as he tiptoed out into the kitchen-garden and bent down to pick his breakfast.

"God, you're such a pig!"

He looked up. Katy stood in the back doorway of the cottage, wearing a simple, light-blue shift over a white blouse. She was barefoot, one foot arched down so that her toes rested on the bare earth below the step. Little of the baby was visible under the shift just yet, but the bloom of pregnancy lit up her pale, freckled face. The sunlight caught her rust-red, curly hair. Tiny lines were forming around her eyes now that she had passed thirty led like arrows to the eyes themselves, which were dark-blue and glittered when she smiled.

"Roy, where do you put it all in that beanstalk frame of yours?" Her voice, well-bred, jerked him out of tomato-worship.

"I know why you're up so early to see me off," he grumbled. "You didn't get up to wish me a good day's gliding. You want me to cook breakfast." He straightened his tall, thin body and pushed his glasses back on his nose. They had slipped to its tip as he concentrated on the tomatoes, and this, with his slight premature balding, had given him a scholastic air as he studied the tomato.

He manoeuvred his way past her. Four fresh sausages settled in the pan. Now he concentrated on the scrambled eggs, adding three more and slicing a loaf thinly so that it would make good fried bread. When the tomatoes were safely under the grill, he reached for a tin of baked beans on the shelf.

Katy busied herself with coffee and before long a rich, roasted smell rose from the percolator. "And of course I've made your sandwiches," she said. "They're in the box. And spaghetti Bolognese for tonight."

"Spaghetti Bolognese?"

"Uh-huh."

"That's nice."

"Watch that fried bread."

They ate at a large table next to the back window in the small, cramped living-room of the cottage. There was an old, deep, plush sofa. The television stood before it, an ancient Dynatron black-and-white set, in a beautifully-fashioned rosewood cabinet, with an old-style speaker-grille underneath. Geoffrey used it as a drinks cabinet, having taken the innards out when he couldn't get new parts for it anymore. On the sofa sprawled mounds of exercise books, last night's marking, probably tomorrow's as well. They were both teachers.

"Listen to this essay," said Katy, picking up one of the books while jabbing a huge sausage with her fork. "It's by Alan Gosset. He's eleven. 'The sun sank below the horizon like a huge tomato'." She laughed.

"I expect it went 'plop'," said Roy. "I ran into Donald in the snug last night."

"Oh yes. How's he?"

"Not bad. He's just broken up an old Mini with rotten subframe mountings, and he's got a nice pair of part-worn half-shafts."

"Oh, excellent," she said, looking up from her meal. "With that and the carburettor you got off the scrapheap last week, we'll have it running soon won't we?"

"Oh, yes."

"How much does he want for these bits?"

"I'm taking him round a crate of home-brew."

"Can we really afford to run a car, Roy?" She frowned. "Even a Mini? I mean, we've always managed without, haven't we?"

"I know," said Roy, thinking with regret of the Volvo 121 he'd had at college. "But I think we'd better have one now. I don't really like to think of you carrying a child on the back of a bicycle. And you'll need to get to work while you're quite heavily pregnant, if you're not finishing till March."

"Mrs. Smith needs me until then. She can manage with a supply teacher for the summer," said Katy. "Still, it'll be nice, won't it? Our own little car."

Roy nodded. He was worried about the cost. But he liked the little car. It was a quarter of a century old, with the original pale primrose paintwork and light, bright blue seats, a button for the starter on the floor and long plastic strings to open the doors, set inside massive door-bins that could carry three bottles of milk.

"I think the gliding will have to go soon, as well, darling," he said reflectively.

"Oh, no." Katy put down her knife and fork. "I suppose I shouldn't while I'm pregnant, but really, Roy, there's no need for you to. You're getting most of your flights through instructing, now, so it's not costing us much."

"I know. But I don't really enjoy instructing," said Roy. "I mean, I have people like that prat – what's his name? Terry Malcolm, the bloke who was at university with us. It's not just that he's hamfisted, there are ways round that, but he's just not prepared to work at it.

He just wants to say he can do it." He did not say that there was an outside chance that someone like that could kill him.

"You could remain a member of the club. And Alan Ryan gives you goes on his Slingsby now, doesn't he?"

Roy sighed. "Well, we'll see." Alan Ryan was a wealthy local farmer with a beautiful single-seater. Roy helped him to maintain it and, thanks Alan's kindness, there was no need for him to be earthbound.

They drank their coffee in silent contentment. The matter of whether or not Roy would go on gliding was allowed to rest. He spent a quiet half-hour with *The Independent* before going to the side-passage, where he kept his elderly racing-bike.

The five-mile run to the airfield from the village was one that he always enjoyed. The village itself was on a B road, and this twisted and turned through combes and hollows before plunging through a wood, where he turned left onto a narrow country road that took him over steeper hills, so that he marvelled at the way when, driving through this county on the main road, he used to think it flat and dull.

It took him twenty minutes or so to reach the airfield, which had been abandoned after the war; once used by Bomber Command, it was now part industrial estate, part grown wild and part of it, what had been the main runway, still serviceable. This last was still maintained, for the benefit of gliders, light aircraft and microlights.

The club had its headquarters in the old control tower, next to the hangars. Roy propped his bike up against the wall and went up to the top floor. It wasn't yet half-past seven, but several members were there.

"I think we've got all four instructors," said someone. "May as well kick off."

Roy was offered a thermos of tea but shook his head.

"Alan Ryan's cried off," said his neighbour. "I think he may be over later."

"Is he instructing?"

"Not today."

Roy made a mental check of how many pupil-members he'd have to take up, and there were plenty. They'd only get two circuits each, and his own private flight would be much later in the day. His particular pupils weren't encouraging. A professional woman, quite young, who was quick and competent, but who he disliked; another girl, very young, a secretary, who was making slow progress, but would go solo if she could gather a bit of confidence; and Terry Malcolm, who had far too much.

Or did he? wondered Roy.

"I see you get to fly Plummet Airlines again today," said the senior instructor, grinning. "Sorry, Roy. Dick was going to take him today but he might not turn up, so I'm shoving the bloke off on you."

"Don't worry." Roy shrugged. "The other two are OK."

They went out to ready the aircraft; the pupil members should have helped, but only a few were there to do so. It was not a rich club. Each member paid forty pounds a year, plus two pounds per launch. If they chose to use one of the club's three ancient K7s, there was no extra charge but there might be an awfully long queue.

The fuselages were wheeled out of the hangars and the wings checked for even the slightest pinhole in the fabric that might have spelled danger. Panels were opened up so that the control lines could be checked, rechecked and checked again. Then someone sat in the cockpit and went through the check procedure. Today Roy did this, swinging the rudder and ailerons while someone stood at each wingtip to make sure that they did as they were told. Next he tapped the surfaces of all the instrument dials to be sure that there were no cracked glasses, and inspected the operation of the canopy and its catches; and checked the ribbon taped to the screen, which the pupil would balance on the horizon to maintain the aircraft's attitude.

There was a shout of annoyance from one of the other aircraft.

The chief instructor, Sanders, was crouching beside the cockpit of the oldest aircraft, where he had been inspecting the skid.

"Roy, nip over here and give me a second opinion, will you?"

Roy went over. All the aircraft had a single nosewheel half in, half out of the fuselage, underneath the cockpit, the axle flush with the bottom of the airframe. Ahead of this was a skid which helped support the aircraft on the ground, and would protect it if the wheel wasn't the first thing to hit the ground.

Two bolts were missing from the row that held the metal facing on to the skid. Two bolts were not really serious, but more could go during a day's flying, so they'd have to be replaced before the aircraft went anywhere.

"I think we'll have to scrub this one, eh, Roy?"

"Not for the whole day. Harry'll be round at ten and he can fix it. I'll mark the log and grab him when he turns up."

Sanders nodded. "Someone just suggested that we get it in the air and bring it in when he turns up." He raised his eyebrows. "What do you think?"

Roy knew that Sanders had no intention of letting it go.

"No," said Roy. "We'll need everything that flies today but no."

Sanders nodded, satisfied. Next week he could sleep in and Roy would do the inspection. He had wanted to know what Roy would do, that was all.

There was a roar of a powerful engine. They had started one of the two tow cars, a 12-cylinder Jaguar too decrepit to go on the road. Pity there wasn't much in the way of a silencer, reflected Roy as the whiff of exhaust fumes spiced the clear morning air. It had automatic transmission, useful when towing.

"Ready, Brian," called someone after hitching a line to one of the gliders. The car trickled gently away, keeping to walking pace, two members supporting the wingtips and a third staying by the tail. It would take them a quarter of an hour to reach the main runway. The main towline had been in the Jaguar's boot and Roy decided he might as well go and inspect it on the runway. He walked out at the wingtip of the second plane, towed just as gently by Sanders in Brian's rotting Austin.

Some members found this lengthy procedure trying. Roy only did when the wind was especially raw. Today, the walk was no hardship. He enjoyed looking at the airfield, at the old, broken, overgrown runways and landing bays. It was peaceful now, the hedges at the edge of the field shimmering in the morning light, the day not yet hazy, the sky blue, the world slightly tinged with gold. The member holding the other wingtip was enjoying a post-breakfast cigarette and they walked in companionable silence.

Ghosts do not seem to walk in daylight. Roy had been on the airfield as the sun went down and felt surrounded by them. This had been an Operational Training Unit. Crews nearing the end of their training flew from here on their first missions. He imagined the terrified nineteen-year-olds, a year or two out of school, strapped into a back turret, watching the ground slowly begin to move below the muzzles of their guns, the aircraft behind slowly turning onto the tarmac, a great bowlegged bird, a malignant mastodon pregnant with death. What was it like to sit there knowing that if you were hit by flak, it would probably get your balls first, then go for your guts, fear sealed around you by a hideous skin of cold, vibration and noise?

"Okay," said the other member.

They turned the glider into one of the bays beside the runway. On the tarmac itself, Sanders was strapped in, ready to take the first flight. The K7 in which he sat had landed heavily the previous week as well. It had been Terry, thought Roy ruefully. Alan Ryan had been instructing. He had climbed out white-faced and scrubbed Terry for the day. The aircraft had undergone a detailed inspection during the week and today, again, Sanders took no chances.

The towline had already been stretched out on the ground and inspected. Brian found a fray. Quickly and expertly he took out a large knife and spliced it. He asked Roy to inspect the splice. Both gave low grunts of satisfaction. If the line broke during take-off, the glider could land on the car. Worse, the tail-down attitude of the aircraft under tow could result in a stall, with neither enough airspeed nor altitude to correct. There was a slight depression in the runway where two members had gone in, tail-first, some twenty years previously. One had died of a broken neck. The other was in a wheelchair.

Such incidents were mercifully rare. That had been the only major accident in the history of this club, and safety standards right across the country were high, despite the age of many of the aircraft.

I'm going to have to give it up, thought Geoffrey sadly. It's not fair on Katy and the child to take even the slightest risk. That's why Katy's given it up. And we can't afford it now.

"Can you do the business, Roy?"

He turned, and saw Sanders waving what looked like a pair of ping-pong bats from the cockpit. He smiled, and cantered over. Taking them from Sanders, he went and stood by the wingtip, some feet away.

Sanders had been through the cockpit checks.

"All clear above and behind?"

Both men were looking.

"All clear above and behind," confirmed Roy. His ears, as well as his eyes, were straining.

Earlier, the man now holding the wingtip had secured the hook on the end of a cable to an eye directly below the pilot. Then Sanders had checked it to ensure that it slid smoothly to the ground when he pulled the cable release. If it snagged, the cable could back-release on takeoff. That could easily panic a nervous or inexperienced learner.

Roy saw the pilot's fingers lift in a prearranged gesture in the cockpit. Still checking the sky above and behind them, as well as in front, he started signalling the tow car. The slack in the rope was taken up, and the aircraft started moving forward; slowly at first, then with gathering speed. The tail and wings came up and then it soared into the air at a punishing angle, nose up, tail down. As the tow-rope came close to vertical, the watchers on the ground saw the glider's nose dip; and, at about 1,000 feet, Sanders released the rope. It looked like a reverse version of the Indian rope trick as it coiled itself back into the ground.

Sanders did not waste time. He made a brief circuit and then wheeled over them, heading for the far end of the runway. The large glider passed slowly overhead, its bright red body and white wings and tailplane catching the morning sunlight. Slowly, slowly, and then that low, familiar hum of wind in rigging and fabric, a graceful Aeolian harp.

The aircraft turned and began its landing approach. Sanders judged it nicely, knowing exactly where the eye end of the tow-rope would have been placed for maximum convenience. The aircraft touched the ground square on its nosewheel, the skid not touching down until it had slowed down considerably. Then when it did, there was the familiar graunching sound. A wingtip dropped and the aircraft came to a halt right beside them.

Everyone grinned with pleasure.

Sanders was unstrapped now, getting out of the cockpit, making a note in his logbook and in the aircraft's.

"All well?" called out Brian.

"All well." Sanders chuckled. "Mind you, I can't tell with these K7s sometimes. It's like flying a truck." He liked to fly by his fingertips. In silence. Just the rushing of the wind. He was an ex-airline pilot. Someone once asked him why, after thousands of hours on intercontinental jets, he now flew simple gliders as a hobby. "If you'd ever spent eight hours flying on instruments and a ninth hour stacked up over JFK, you wouldn't ask that," he'd replied.

An hour later, Roy sat strapped in the cockpit of the K7. In front of him was the young woman, a management consultant from Reading, who was his first pupil of the day. They were going through the pre-flight checks.

"Weight?" asked Roy.

"Nine stone two," she said with a flash of irritation

He smiled slightly to himself. He checked the chart against his own weight; she was lighter than the previous passenger. They were within the tolerance of the ballast already on board, but he would need to check the trim carefully in the air. He made a mental note to check that Connie had the stick far enough forward on takeoff. He watched as she conscientiously pulled her webbing-straps tight, having removed her pen and her cigarettes from her breast pocket. The canopy came down.

"All clear above and behind?"

"All clear above and behind."

Sanders was waving him out. The graunching sound started as they moved down the runway.

Roy kept his hands and feet on the controls, but the woman knew what she was doing now. She was *feeling* the aircraft, rather than trying to remember how far she'd needed to push the stick the previous week. They felt themselves pushed back into their seats as the aircraft left the ground at its usual steep angle. Head back, feet in the air, sitting together in a tiny perspex blister. The altimeter turned; 500, 750.

1,000 feet.

Get on with it, thought Roy. I told you to do it yourself this time. Five more seconds and there's going to be a back-release that will shatter your confidence for the rest of the day.

Just in time she pulled the lever and the cable fell away. She had split her concentration beautifully and already had the K7's nose dipping at exactly the right angle.

"Right-hand circuit," Roy told her. "Keep scanning the sky."

He could see a little microlight below and slightly to the left. What a horrible little thing, he thought absently, like a cross between a kid's tricycle and a late-Victorian flying machine.

"I have control."

He sensed her surprise.

"There's a microlight down there. Wait and see what he's going to do." But Roy had known it was there before he gave the order to turn. Connie knew this. Once again he felt her irritation.

"Make your observations. Turn when ready."

She turned slowly, with soft, fluid movements. The nose came up slightly. Connie noticed that the marker on the screen was well above the horizon. She pushed the nose down.

"Nicely judged turn," said Roy through the intercom. "Very fine stick movements. Don't let the nose come up too far in the turn." When she had, he had watched the airspeed fall to 100 knots. That was when he had started concentrating. Really concentrating.

"Okay, straight and level."

He allowed himself to drink in the view. They were passing over a vast country mansion. He could see the stables, see the rich burgundy roof of a car in the drive and smell the rich burgundy in the cellars. There were few clouds today, just summer haze. The ground looked flat and dull. Some days the light and shade were cast upon the ground by grey and white clouds that split the sunbeams as they passed through the moist air to the earth, and then this was the most beautiful place one could imagine.

Even at less than 1,000 feet with a pupil on board.

The aircraft gave a slight jerk. Instantly his grip tightened.

"Thermal. Let's go for it. I have control."

"Your aircraft."

He kicked the rudder over and found the stream of warm air that was rising from the earth. Round and round they went, tightly, ever-tightening circles.

Roy straightened out. "Damn, lost it," he said. "Made fifty feet though. Okay, Connie. Your aircraft."

"I have control."

He debated whether to look for thermals with Connie today. No. Stick to basics for now.

"Position us for landing approach," he said through the speaking-tube.

"Okay. Where do you want me to aim for?"

"No, you choose your course. I'll put you right if you go wrong."

The aircraft described a broad, sweeping circle. He found himself willing her to pick the right course. Port, starboard, starboard a bit...

Just a fraction too high and too fast.

Her hand was going to the airbrake. The nose came up gently. They drifted downwards breast-first and the fields and hedges slipped past with what felt like increasing speed, although actually they were slowing. The aircraft's shadow chased it across the fields.

Ahead on the runway they could see another glider being readied for takeoff. It was a long way ahead. But it was on the runway.

He'd lose more height, touch down early and risk having to push the aircraft.

"My aircraft."

"You have control."

He pulled the stick back a bit more and hit the runway with a gentle thwack, thinking, God, I wish I could kiss the runway gently the way bloody Sanders does. One day, one day.

They skittered to a halt some twenty yards short of the other aircraft.

"Walkies," said Roy, grinning.

They joined the other members pushing the aircraft forward. The other one hadn't been hooked up yet. Roy craned his neck and could see why. There was a microlight manoeuvring on the tarmac some yards ahead.

Sanders was standing at the wingtip of the front aircraft.

"He's been farting about up there for about five minutes."

"I'm sick of microlights. "

"I got a cure for microlights."

"Go on."

"An 88mm."

Roy chortled. The microlight lifted off into the sky.

"Okay, Connie," said Roy crisply. "We've got about five minutes before we hook up again. You're doing nicely today, good fine touch on the controls. You got the right line on the landing approach. If it hadn't been for this crowd farting about you could have taken her in. Just one thing. You're leaving things just a little late sometimes. I would have had that hook out earlier on the way up. You were OK but you could have been too late."

Roy couldn't fault the attention with which she was listening to him, but he felt at every moment that she resented being told she wasn't perfect. It was during this conversation that Roy's heart sank as he saw a white BMW 318 rounding the end of the runway and bouncing like an eager dog towards the bay, going far too fast.

He put Terry Malcolm out of his mind for now.

Once again he put Connie through it. This time she let the cable out, if anything, a little too early. They had a successful flight and thermalled twice. Gaining good height, they stayed aloft for twenty minutes. A good gliding day, thought Roy. A clunky old K7 could stay aloft indefinitely, but only in ideal conditions, expertly flown. A more modern single-seater could do it much more easily.

"Bring her round."

He left the entire landing approach to her, pleased with the way she delayed her turn into the finals twice to see what a light aircraft was doing.

Then they were going in.

She waited for him to say "My aircraft". He didn't.

Come on, girl, he found himself urging her in his head. Bit more airbrakes. Ohhhh-kay! The hedges started to speed up again. He said nothing. Just don't lose your nerve, girl. Don't push the stick forward. You've got a mile of runway. Settle her nose-up, like a bird laying an egg.

She levelled-up a little early and they hit the ground hard, but not dangerously so. He prayed that she would keep calm as the aircraft bounced, keep it straight, so that he didn't have to take control at the eleventh hour and shatter her confidence.

The aircraft rolled to a halt, but several tens of yards beyond the bay. From the latter came the sound of ragged cheers.

"I seem to have given us a rather long walk," she commented bloodlessly.

"It'll be shorter next time," he said. "And we'll have to inspect the skid, because we were just a little heavy. But you did all right."

He parted company with her, signing her logbook and noting, "First landing. Rough but safe. Very good stick and rudder control."

"When can I go solo?" she asked tentatively.

"Three to four weeks," he said crisply. "Maybe five. I want several perfect landings, but you're much closer to solo today than you were last week."

She managed a management consultant's smile for him.

He wouldn't wait five weeks; he would turn her loose in three. But she wouldn't have any warning. None of Roy's ever did. Better that way. He glanced down at her logbook. Should go solo in about thirty flights. Average, then, maybe good.

An hour or so later he was strapped into the rear cockpit again, reading another logbook. Terry was strapping himself in the front. The logbook was speckled with comments. He hadn't gone solo yet. Alan had written: "Stick and rudder control coarse. Needs better observation. Needs to think more in the air." When Terry read that he'd gone out and got pissed. He'd told Steve he was hoping to go solo that week.

"You've landed, then?"

"Yes. No problems," said Terry. It occurred to Roy that the pupil was nervous. Fear of failure. You could always tell it, see it in the collarless zip-up jerkins, Levis, immaculate sneakers; fear of failure. They couldn't keep calm in the air.

"We'll have you land today."

"Yes, of course," said Terry. There was an air of surprise in his voice which sounded simulated. "I've done it before."

Roy kept his temper.

"Backlaunch with Alan last week."

Terry didn't reply.

"Release the cable when you're ready. Don't hurry. If you're late I'll intervene."

They went through the final checks. These, at least, Terry knew off pat after forty-two flights.

Takeoff.

He kept a gentle forward pressure on the stick. He knew Terry wasn't aware of it.

Terry released the cable far too early.

Roy took over straight away. As he put the stick forward he kept the stick dead straight, feeling Terry trying to peel away from the runway. The airspeed climbed to a hundred knots and he pulled it round at just four hundred feet.

"I have control," he said.

Terry did not respond.

He brought the aircraft in and coldly made a note of the flight time in Terry's logbook. Four minutes.

"We're going straight back into the air," he said. "Follow my instructions this time. Better to release too late." He paused for a minute, and then said: "Don't let your bloody ego feel punctured because I might have to slip the cable before you do." His voice was cold.

Still Terry said nothing.

"And never attempt to turn with the airspeed down. You did right to try and turn away from the runway, but get the nose down and the knots up first. Otherwise you'll sideslip. Got it?"

Right, Roy, said to himself, making a decision that he knew was unprofessional. I'm going to push you this time, brat. You're getting this aircraft up and down yourself this time, and if I have to take control, I'm not flying with you again. Let Alan and Sanders scrub you if they want to.

This time, Terry released a fraction of a second too late, but there was no back release. Roy didn't look for a thermal. He made Terry bring the aircraft straight round. The pupil was concentrating very, very hard. His movements on the controls were stiff and jerky, even by Terry's standards. Fear of failure.

"Right, bring her in."

Terry was thinking hard at last. The route he took on the landing approach was perfect. He brought the stick back.

He brought it back too far. Too late, he went for the airbrakes, instead of slowing them with them first. Geoffrey took over.

"My aircraft," he called calmly.

There was no let-up in Terry's pressure on the stick.

"My God," he told himself. "The little berk's gone mad."

Terry was gripping the stick hard, very hard. Just in time Roy managed to shove it forward enough to prevent a stall, and then pull it back enough so that they would bellyflop down before they ran out of runway. He could see the parked tow-car at the end of the runway approach with frightening speed. The doors flew open at exactly the same time and the occupants dove for the verges in perfect unison. Real Keystone Cops stuff, thought Roy grimly. Be funny if it wasn't so fucking dangerous.

He chose his moment carefully, then yanked the stick back and shoved the airbrakes out full. They dropped the last twenty feet like a stone. The skid hit the ground with an almighty crack and the wings slewed first one way, then the other. They wound up in the rough.

There was silence for a moment. Then Roy released his webbing straps and lifted the canopy. Like Terry, he was white with fear.

"You idiot," he said quietly. "You stark, staring... pratt. Why didn't you release control?"

"I could do it," said Terry urgently. "I knew I could do it. I've done it before. So I hung on."

"If I believed you," said Roy, taking a step towards him, "if I really thought you were *that* stupid, that you disobeyed a command in the air and put us in danger just to prove a point, I'd lay you out right here." Terry stepped backwards. "But it was simpler than that, wasn't it? You just froze."

"I won't freeze again," said Terry quickly. He looked frightened.

"Too right you won't," said Roy slowly. "Not at this airfield. Never, ever again."

He left Terry standing, bewildered, as a trio of weekend fliers came up at a run, followed by Brian's scabrous Austin car with a towrope. Terry was silent for a moment and then turned and strode, hands on hips, towards the bay a quarter of a mile away.

Sanders emerged from the Austin.

"Best get this straight into the bay, Brian," he said. His voice was one of controlled fury. "Please check every sodding rivet on the skid. Then get it into the hangar. Endorse the logbook. I want Bill Ricketts in tomorrow morning and he's going to go over every inch of that bloody aircraft with a microscope."

"Amen," said Brian. "Don't worry, Sandy."

Sanders turned to Roy. "All right, Roy. Let's hear the worst."

"I'm sorry. He froze on the controls."

"Why didn't you take control?"

"I did. It took a moment. He was locked solid."

Sanders jerked his head towards Terry's receding figure. "What'd he say just now?"

"He told me he'd tried to keep control deliberately, because he knew he could bring it in without me."

"You didn't believe him." Statement of fact.

"No. Not for a moment. He panicked and froze on the controls"

"What did Alan say about him last week?"

"Oh, no natural aptitude – give him two more weeks."

Sanders nodded. "Whad'ya reckon?"

"Well, I used to think this was a club, not an airforce," said Roy slowly. "But this is not safe, for him or us."

Again, Sanders nodded. "I'll tell him straightaway."

"I'll tell him, Sandy."

"I'm chief instructor. I should do it. He can appeal to the committee if he wants to, but..."

They turned and strode after Terry. By the time they caught up with him he was back at the bay, standing with Connie and Steve.

"Breakdown in communication," he was saying to her. "He wasn't *telling* me anything, Connie, I..."

"Private word, Mr. Malcolm?" said Sanders mildly.

"Go on then."

"We'll go to the hangar."

Terry jerked his head towards Roy. "If he's got anything to say to me, he can say it here, can't he?" His eyes were aggressive. Neither Connie nor Steve could see the fear behind them.

Sanders and Roy both could.

"Mr. Malcolm, we both feel..."

"*I* feel," said Roy, cutting in suddenly. "Sandy has agreed to this, but it was my decision, Terry. You're best not in the air, I think."

"Oh, come on, that's bollocks!" Terry panicked.

"It's common sense," said Sanders. "You need two things to learn to fly, Terry. Natural aptitude. Or personal grace. You can only fly professionally with both. If you want to fly just for pleasure, the second is enough to help you learn. You haven't got either."

Terry looked at him for a moment. Then he took his logbook from his pocket and slowly, deliberately, tore it in two. Then he threw it at Sanders's feet.

Sanders nodded with satisfaction.

Terry turned and strode back to his car.

Sanders put his hand across Roy's back and steered him towards the bay's entrance. In the background they could hear Steve and Connie talking.

"Good comeuppance," said Steve easily. "He got me breathalysed last night, you know that?"

"They did me last week," said Connie conversationally. "I think I'm getting off, though."

"I wonder if they eat their young," said Sanders quietly.

"Only with pasta," said Roy.

Sanders chuckled.

From along the runway came the third aircraft, the one they'd left in the hangar to have its skid checked that morning, moving gently along the tarmac behind the remains of the Jaguar, a club member at each wingtip.

"Good show," said Sanders. "He's done his stuff on that skid, then. BRIAN!" he bellowed. "Do us a favour, get Neela out of Number Three. I'm taking Roy up for a check flight."

Roy watched his next pupil, Neela, the nervous secretary, raise herself gloomily out of the cockpit. "Don't worry, Neela," he said. "We'll have two extra flights together today. I'll be back in half an hour."

It was three-quarters. Sanders took the for'd seat as pupil and committed every bog-up in the book. When he had tortured Roy's patience enough they found a thermal, and kept the K7 in the air for another thirty minutes, laughing like maniacs. When they landed, Sanders endorsed Roy's log-book: "Exceptional ability as instructor".

Neela went solo that afternoon.

* * *   * * *   * * *

TERRY'S last offence before leaving the airfield was to swing his car across the grass runway that ran parallel to the tarmac one, blissfully unaware that it *was* a runway, and that the pilot of an ageing Beechcraft was hurriedly shutting down his cockpit check procedure on his sudden appearance. He swept out along the gravel roads on which Bedford one-tonners had carried the quaking nineteen-year-olds bound for the Ruhr nearly half a century earlier; and then he took the long route home, dodging down every country road he could find.

After an hour or so of trying to induce four-wheel drifts around blind bends, saving the council verge-cutters much labour, he felt a little better. He pulled up outside a pub on the Wantage road, where a couple of whiskies improved his mood further; he followed these with a pint or two of beer and would have taken on Joe Louis in his prime.

He started to plan his evening.

There was a phone in the bar and he went to it, to find to his fury that it didn't take phone cards. He begged a fistful of change from the bored barmaid and returned to find that someone was now using it.

He stood close behind the middle-aged man who was talking and moved backwards and forwards scuffing his heels, so that at length the man turned round and said:

"Give us a chance, will you?"

"Well there's only one phone."

"Yeah, and I'm using it."

Terry sat on the back of one of the deep-plush benches nearby and continued to fidget, scuff his heels, clear his throat and occasionally, for good measure, emit a long, soulful sigh. Eventually the man put the phone down and walked out of the bar without giving Terry a second glance.

Terry started to make his calls. To his annoyance, several of his acquaintances were busy that evening. But before long he had a foursome arranged in the city. And he'd persuaded someone else to drive.

"But I was going to watch *West Side Story* this evening," protested Eileen.

"We can video it."

"It's not the same," she said sullenly, avoiding his eyes.

"What's the matter? Don't you want to go out, or what?"

She shrugged and went off to make the tea, broken.

"He's picking us up at seven-thirty," he called after her.

Kevin and his girlfriend turned up just before a quarter to eight. The four of them climbed into the Volkswagen Golf and headed off into the evening sunlight, Eileen clad in tight pants and a tee-shirt with the name of a university on it, Terry in a collarless leather jacket and a new pair of pre-faded jeans. He sat in the front beside Kevin, a rep for a mainframe supplier.

"How did the gliding go today?" asked Kevin as they swept round the roundabout above the bypass.

"I've jacked it in," said Terry.

"Have you?" Eileen was surprised.

Terry ignored this.

"You fed up with it, or what?" asked Kevin.

"Yeah. There's an awful lot of waiting around and I just got bored," said Terry. "I reckon aircraft are the thing, anyway. They've got courses over near Bicester. I'll drop round and see them tomorrow."

"Seems a pity, when you'd got so far with it," said Kevin's girlfriend, Sue.

"Well, I got bored," said Terry, and shrugged.

Later, seated in a restaurant in the city, he expanded on this.

"It's a club for poor sods who can't really afford it," he was saying. "I mean, if you've got the bread, who wants to stand around and push gliders about the airfield and things? I just got fed up. Anyway, there were some really boring people there every week."

"I thought you said they were a nice crowd," said Eileen, not looking at him, toying with her steak.

Terry glared at her over the top of his lager.

"There was one bloke in particular," he went on, "really boring. I knew him at university, in fact. He was so serious about everything, and checking all the controls and that, and he was a real fanatic about it. Mind you, he always did have a bee in his bonnet about something, that guy. He used to be a really hot left-wing Labour supporter at college."

"They're the worst," said Kevin, waving his hand at the waiter for more lagers. "We had them as well. Always talking about socialism and feminism and lots of other isms."

"Well, they all mean something, somewhere along the line," said Sue mildly.

"Yeah, like women screwing each other instead of us," said Terry, accepting the next pint of lager gratefully. "Anyway, as I was saying, this guy was so pernickety... Here, Kevin, don't just have a half!"

"Honest, Terry, it's all I want. I don't want to get nicked," said Kevin earnestly.

"Come on, you're used to it. You can manage at least four pints and still get through," said Terry.

* * *   * * *   * * *

THE police Rover stood at its spot on the top of the motorway bridge. Bob and Tom gazed moodily down through the orange light at the few cars still moving around the bypass.

A car flashed by.

"Tanking on a bit, wasn't it?" said Tom mildly.

"'Spect he's all right, long as he wasn't driving on the verge," said Bob. "What kind of car was it, anyway?"

"Golf GTi," said Tom.

"Then again," said Bob.

Once again the Rover slid swiftly onto the roundabout.

* * *   * * *   * * *

THE front door slammed against the door frame, and, being warped, swung open again. Terry left it, striding to the toilet at the far end of the hall. He snapped on the light and made a half-hearted attempt to close the door, but as usual it swung open against his buttocks.

"For God's sake, Terry, can't you close the door as you're having a piss?" asked Eileen, hurriedly closing the front door as the Golf drove away and the liquid started to fall into the bowl with a heavy beat, a mountain waterfall unfrozen in a sudden spring, a tropical rainstorm cascading off the eaves.

"Stop fussing," said Terry. "Hey, we were bloody lucky, eh? I mean, Kev losing them at the junction like that."

"Kevin was bloody lucky, you mean. And you shouldn't encourage someone to drink so much when you know they're driving you home," she said.

"Oh, nice little law-abiding citizen now are we?" sneered Terry. "Anyway, it's up to him. It's like Steve yesterday. You make the decision about how much you're going to drink yourself, don't you?"

Busy with the coffee, she did not reply.

"Well, you do, don't you?" he said, walking into the kitchen behind her, zipping up his fly. "No-one can make the decision for you."

She still said nothing.

"Come on, what's the matter?"

"I didn't say anything, did I?"

He went into the living room, where he snapped on the television. It was a late-night religious programme. Impatiently he punched the keys, and, finding nothing to his taste, switched it off.

"Don't turn the TV off. There might have been something interesting," she protested, coming through the door with two mugs of instant coffee.

"Stop moaning," he replied. "Always bloody moaning, you are. Christ, do you have to fill the mugs so bloody *full*?"

She shrugged, and sat down on the leather sofa, sipping her hot coffee by sucking it across the rim, a habit that always annoyed him.

"Christ, I don't know why I married you sometimes," he grumbled. "You never even want a screw nowadays, do you?"

She said nothing, but continued to suck. The coffee was hot but there was ice in the pit of her stomach.

"Well, you don't do you? Go on, admit it."

"I've got a problem," she said quietly. "I don't feel well all the time."

"Oh, come on. You'll be telling me you're going though the menopause next," said Terry, his voice raised a little. "What are you? Thirty-two? Thirty-three?"

"I'm going to bed," she said, standing up. She was shaking slightly.

"You haven't answered my bloody question yet."

"What question."

"Don't be thick. Why I can't get my bloody oats."

"I've told you. I don't always feel so good."

"Yeah, but you haven't told me what's wrong with you, have you?"

"It's called cystitis," she replied.

"Well, does that stop you wanting to have a screw?"

"It stops me wanting to."

"Well, then, it's your fault," he said, standing up.

"No it's not." Her voice was still quiet, but a little firmer. "You know why? Because I reckon I caught it off *you*."

"Oh, come *on*," he said, turning sharply towards her. As he did so his shin caught the coffee-table and some of the brown liquid sloshed onto the sofa. They both stared in horror.

"Oh, Christ," she moaned, "get a cloth, quickly]"

"I am, I am," he said, shooting into the kitchen.

"Oh, Christ, our three-piece suite! Twelve hundred pounds," she gasped, "and we've barely paid for it."

Terry rubbed frantically away at the leather, across which rivulets of coffee were running, with a damp cloth.

"No, no, not like that, like this," she said, panicking and seizing the cloth.

"I know what I'm doing," he said roughly, and straightened out suddenly. As he did so he shoved against her, so that she overbalanced and fell backwards across the glass-topped coffee-table. The other mug of coffee slewed onto the carpet.

"Oh, Jesus!" She got up and ran for the door.

"Where the fuck are you going?"

"To the loo," she groaned. "Oh, God, this bloody hurts!"

"You useless cow," said Terry bitterly. "You useless fucking cow."

* * *   * * *   * * *

Roy opened the living-room door and sunlight flooded into his face from the front window. He looked over to where his wife was sitting, her back to him, bent over a pile of exercise books. She turned round, putting her elbow on the back of the chair, and smiled.

"Hallo. Did you have a good day?"

"Fraught," he said grimly, and slung his logbook down on the sofa. "Good in the end, but fraught."

"How's Neela getting on?"

Roy brightened somewhat.

"Got her away today," he said. "Bit rough coming down, but no real probs. I think she's cracked it."

"Oh, that's lovely." She grinned. "I've been wondering about that bottle of Rioja with our supper, you know, the one Liz gave us."

He smiled gently. "You said you'd save that for a special occasion."

"Well, it *is* a special occasion."

"What?"

"It's the 26th."

"What's so special about the 26th?"

"Well, it's the only one this month."

"Okay." He grinned. "I'll open it and let it air."

He went into the kitchen and busied himself with the corkscrew.

"You haven't answered my question," she called out.

"What?"

"Why you had such a fraught day."

"You didn't ask."

"Why did you have such a fraught day, then, ratbag?"

"I've scrubbed someone today. Well, Sandy told me I could, actually. And I wanted to. But it's like he and I always say, we're a club, not an air force. We hate telling people they'll never fly." He came back into the living-room.

"Why did you scrub him?"

"Oh, heavy landing for the umpteenth time, not listening, not taking instructions." He wouldn't tell her about the freeze-up, or the four bolts missing off the skid, or what Sanders had said was a suspect spar. She'd worry then.

"Sounds like Terry Malcolm," she said.

"Right first time. Let's have a drink now."

"Later," she said firmly. "You have one. I can only have a little because of the baby. I'll deal with the spaghetti now. Why were you flying with him anyway? Alan not turn up?"

"He did later." He sat down. "Sissy's had an accident."

"Oh dear. Is she all right?"

"Probably. Some idiot drove past too fast when they were exercising the horses and hers shied. She came off and twisted her knee. She went into the John Radcliffe. She's coming out tonight, but the X-ray shows damage to the ligaments, so she might have a little trouble doing sports now. And she won't walk without sticks for a few months. Alan says it's very painful."

"I'm sorry. Shall we go and see her?"

"He said if we came round tomorrow, he'd give us Sunday lunch. He said they'd all like that."

"Okay."

Roy settled into the remains of the big old armchair with his glass of wine, and thought about Terry Malcolm.

* * *   * * *   * * *

ONE January evening, about ten years before Terry's last gliding lesson, Roy tucked his books under his arm and buttoned his coat. He took a last look around the library before he went, and his gaze fell on a fresh-faced economics student who sat some way away, her long reddish hair falling over her wrists as she scribbled notes about the book she was reading.

God, he thought, I wish I knew you.

She was one of the very few left in the library. Sighing, he went down in the lift and approached the barriers at the entrance.

He plonked four books on the counter. The librarian flipped them open.

"This one's special reserve," she said moodily.

"Nothing like a good port," said Roy.

"This one's special reserve," she repeated.

"I'll bring it back in the morning."

She didn't look up. "You won't forget, will you?"

"Would I do a thing like that?" he asked lightly.

"Probably," she said, pushing a strand of mousey hair away from her mouth with her tongue. "Most of you do."

He shrugged and walked out through the barriers. Outside a bitter wind that had howled through the white concrete canyons of the campus for several days cut into his donkey-jacket and across his neck. He turned up his collar and, head bowed, made his way unsteadily along the snow-covered path.

January. Yeugh. He fretted again about the antifreeze in his car, wondering if there was enough to protect the old engine from the searing cold. He glanced at his watch. No time to eat. The meeting began at eight. He could pick up a pie and a beer in the Union bar and take them in with him.

The campus was near-deserted, just the odd lonely figure scurrying through the bleak winter darkness in the distance. His head felt a little heavy and he wondered if he was getting flu. He thought again about the redhead in the library and felt a pricking in his stomach. Then he thought about the coming meeting and felt boredom settle upon him like a shroud.

It seemed a long way to the Union building. As he pushed open the steel swing door, a cloud of warm air enveloped him and he was grateful for its softness. The ground floor of the building was shaped as a disco-cum-market-place, and the ceiling was three or four floors up, with balconies carrying hexagonal galleries round the space so that drinkers above could watch drinkers and dancers below. It struck Roy, not for the first time, that buildings like this were rather of their time.

He bought himself a pint of beer and elbowed his way through the crush of students to the snack bar, where he chose a steak and kidney pie and chips. Then he made his way to the meeting room on the second floor.

It was crowded, with thirty or forty students taking every available chair and leaning up against the wall. He ate standing up, beer stood between his feet in case someone kicked it by mistake. In the centre of the room three chairs were ranged behind a table. Three people sat in these chairs. A tall, thin girl with a pale face, dark eyes and cropped dark hair sat at one end. At the other was a short young man with curly hair and a mass of pimples. Between them was a nuggety, healthy-looking youth wearing a checked lumber-jacket, his carefully-styled hair waving down onto his shoulders. He stood up, looking taller than he was because of the built-up heels on his cowboy boots, themselves carefully masked by the flared trousers that were mildly spattered with slush from the winter outdoors.

The chairman of the University Labour Club, Terry Malcolm.

"Evening, comrades," he intoned.

There was still some chatter in the room, and he turned and looked in the direction of the voices while continuing to speak. They fell silent. "We've got two main items on the agenda for this evening," he was saying as he did this. "As you all know, we selected all the candidates for the Union sabbatical posts except for one – that of President." He paused. "We'll be doing that one tonight, having, er, failed to reach agreement last time."

Roy sucked a chip and remembered. A rough old meeting, that. It had already been running a long time when they got to the last nomination – candidate for annual sabbatical presidency of the union. Terry had been nominated, and so had the tall, thin woman on his right. Terry had then announced that as it was getting late, the election should be held over for an extraordinary meeting tonight. The motion had been carried, with only a few voting against. Among them Roy, who rarely said anything at meetings and wasn't quite sure why he had lifted his hand that night.

Tonight, however, they didn't start with the election.

"Our first item on the agenda is a motion of support for the Troops Out campaign. I call upon Comrade Michaels to propose the motion," said Terry. "And I must say that it has my support."

He sat down and the tall woman stood.

"The blood-stained history of British imperialism in Ireland must surely be coming to an end," she said, in a slightly halting voice.

Terry lit a cigarette. He was not looking at her.

"It is up to all of us," she continued, "to support the aims of all those who seek to restore the six counties to their rightful owners. We must be wholehearted in opposing Whitehall's fascism and its manipulation of the British mass-media, which..."

Roy glanced at the roneoed sheet in the hand of the student next to him. On it were the words: "The Broad Left deplores the continuing presence of British troops in Northern Ireland and calls on members to support all attempts, of whatever nature, to bring about the withdrawal of those troops."

He sucked another chip thoughtfully.

The door opened and Terry Malcolm flashed a brilliant smile at it. He kept his eyes fixed on the newcomer, thinking longingly of the time after the meeting when he would, once again, home in on her and buy her a drink, carefully excluding those who tried to do likewise. He had had a little success so far; some good dances, some good drinks and one long, lingering, wet, mouth-to-mouth kiss outside her hall of residence which she had given him reluctantly – but then, it had been snowing. He reckoned things were going all right.

Roy glanced up at the door and his stomach turned over. It always did. It was the girl he often saw in the library. She didn't look his way but nodded and smiled at Terry, drawing the door carefully shut behind her. She started to loosen her long woolly scarf and undid the zipper of her jacket, revealing a pair of small, firm breasts underneath her white, thick sweater, clearly visible in outline. Oh, God, thought Roy, they say it's magic being young, but there's black magic and there's white magic, isn't there?

Comrade Michaels continued to speak.

"While we all mourn the loss of innocent life in the Six Counties, we must ask ourselves whether it is sometimes necessary to pay such a price for progress," she said. "The end does sometimes justify the means." She raised her eyes and looked around the room, conscious that her phrase would touch upon a schism that was brewing in the party. "I don't think you have to be a hard-line Marxist to believe that."

Terry nodded and clapped, and numerous other people joined in. Roy did not. God, he thought, I wish I wasn't so damned shy. I'd love to get up on my hind legs right now and say why this is all a load of crap, how all we, and the party nationally, have to do is to go on spewing it and we'll get Thatcher and then ordinary people will just be squeezed, squeezed, squeezed, and... I want to be a teacher. Aren't things already tight enough for teachers?

"And I know we all deplore the capital made out of the victims, by the Capitalist press, of the victims of the unfortunate but necessary operations in support of attempts to end Whitehall's imperialist hegemony." She finished slightly, breathlessly: "I call upon Meeting to support the motion, as written, on the agenda."

She sat down. Roy looked again at the agenda written on the paper. And then looked a third time.

There was scattered applause. Terry stood up. "Please show, all those in favour of the motion."

"Point of order." Roy heard a bold voice. "Shouldn't you ask if anyone wishes to oppose the motion?"

The tall girl frowned. There were one or two mutters. Terry turned towards Roy and his eyes held real malevolence. Roy realised with horror that the voice had been his own.

"Does that mean that you wish to oppose it?"

"Yes," said Roy, his voice a little less confident. His fork, with a cluster of chips, was poised halfway to his mouth. "Yes, I do."

All eyes were turned towards him now. Out of the corner of his own he could see the redheaded girl from the library looking at him in surprise.

Shit, thought Terry. Let's just get this motion through. Get it through, and I'm home and dry.

"You have two minutes," said Terry, looking at his watch.

"I don't think I'll need two minutes," said Roy, still holding his plate of chips. He began to speak, trying to project his voice as best he could without appearing to make an effort. He had never done this before, and he was terrified. His history tutor had sometimes told him, after seminars, that he didn't open his mouth often or wide enough. "It is not a crime to have an opinion, Roy," his tutor had once said, smiling benevolently at him, looking over the top of his glasses. "It is only criminal to spout opinions without due thought. Or to keep silent when a moral issue is being decided, although of course that rarely applies when discussing the, er, somewhat crude antics of the Merovingian monarchs..."

He spoke.

"Comrade Michaels says that we all deplore the continuing presence of British troops in Northern Ireland," he said, rather slowly. Then his voice picked up a little. "Personally, I do. I think it is dangerous to make assumptions, though, because I think there are exceptions, probably within this room, and certainly outside it.

"Secondly, this motion was introduced to us as being in support of the Troops Out movement, but it goes farther than that. It commits us, as it is written – and we have just been told that we are voting on what is written on the agenda..."

"Get on with it," muttered Terry.

"It commits us to support of all attempts to remove those troops, regardless of the form those attempts take. No-one can have failed to hear about the death of a young woman and her child in Derry last night after being caught in a confrontation. And no-one can be unaware that this conflict has claimed the lives of many individuals not involved. If we support the motion as written we support the death and maiming of the uninvolved. I do not wish to oppose support of the Troops Out Movement. I am opposed to continuing military involvement in the conflict. Therefore I do not oppose this motion. Rather, I move that it be referred back. When it has been rephrased, I can't believe anyone here would really object to it."

He fell silent.

The atmosphere in the room was uncertain. The red-haired girl stared at Roy for a moment and then muttered a question to the girl next to her.

"Roy Dickson," came the whispered reply.

"Oh. Showing a bit more spirit than usual tonight, isn't he?"

"That wouldn't be difficult," said her neighbour.

Terry stood up.

"All those in favour of the motion, please show."

To his surprise, only half the hands went in the air.

"All those in favour of referral-back."

Quick counts were done of both.

"The motion has been referred back by twenty-two votes to nineteen," announced Terry.

He sat down. "I kept my side of the bargain," he muttered to the girl on his right.

She didn't answer.

"I now call for nominations for the candidate for sabbatical President of the Union," he said briskly.

"Terry Malcolm," called a voice from the back. It was echoed by several others.

One or two more opened their mouths to speak, but the tall girl eyed them carefully. Looking slightly mutinous, as indeed she did, they kept silent.

"I accept the nomination," said Terry. He stood, and smiled. "Are there any further nominations?"

For a second or so there was silence. Terry opened his mouth to speak again.

"Roy Dickson," said a clear, smooth, well-spoken voice. A woman's voice.

Roy, who had been recovering from his speech, shrinking into the background, looked up in horror. Everyone was looking, not at him, but at the redheaded girl from the library. She herself was wearing a rather shocked expression, as if surprised by the sound of her own voice.

Terry had gone pale. He turned towards Roy.

"Does Comrade Dickson accept the nomination?"

Roy's bowels turned to water. Never mind, he thought, I'm bound to lose. And we are not discussing Merovingian monarchs.

"Yes, I do."

"Then we have a contested election," said Terry slowly. "Comrade Michaels, will you accept the chair?"

"I will."

Terry made a self-deprecating gesture and sat forward, chin resting on hand.

"According to standing orders we allow each comrade five minutes to speak," said Michaels, "for five minutes. Questions will then be permitted afterwards if anyone wishes. Voting will then be by a show of hands. Has anyone any objection? Comrade, er, Dickson?"

"No objection. Who is to speak first?" asked Roy. "Is that covered in standing orders?"

"As I'm ready to speak, perhaps I'd better go first," said Terry, without looking up.

"Do you have any objection?" Michaels asked Roy, giving him a look that suggested any would be unwelcome.

"No," he said coldly. There was a core of anger building up within him.

Terry stood up at this and the other looked at her watch. "Comrades, I am sure you realise that we're at a crucial time in our country's development," he said confidently. "We face the threat of a Fascist government – and that's what it is, comrades, let's be in no doubt about it. Over the next few years, if they are allowed to succeed in their aims, everything that has been built up by working people over the last thirty years will be destroyed. The right of people to organise within their workplaces, the right to free medical treatment and drugs, crucial rights such as abortion on demand will be taken from us by a government elected not by us, but by Fleet Street. The Tories, with the National Front as their vanguard, business as their right hand and the media as their left, are poised to run this country for the benefit of the rich, not ordinary working people. If you want to prevent that you must fight against it.

"Now, more than ever, we as the party on this campus must strengthen our links with grass-roots movements such as the Trades Council, women's groups, the Anti-Nazi League..."

Roy chewed a last, soggy chip.

I've heard all this before, he thought, and I've never liked it and now I'm going to have to answer it. I always hoped that someone would. I've never thought it would be me.

Yet, as Terry spoke, Roy felt his nerves draining away to be replaced, not by anger, but by irritation.

Terry didn't speak for the whole five minutes, but he came quite close to it. Roy was glad that he did. It gave him time to think. Once or twice he saw the redheaded girl glance over in his direction, but she quickly looked away again.

"I've been chairperson of this party now for five months and I believe that I have proved my commitment to the cause of working-class, grass-roots politics. Let me serve for a year as Union President and I know I can strengthen those links with the local people that we so desperately need to forge everywhere if we, as a party nationally, are to win this battle."

There were sporadic outbreaks of applause as he sat down, growing into a proper ovation of a kind. Terry smiled.

"I call upon Comrade Dickson."

He stood up straight.

"What we've just heard," he said slowly, "is what we've heard from just about every campus politician from this party leftwards for the last two years and I'm sick of it."

He sensed the tension in the room, but no-one wanted to express it. He was speaking from the back of the room, but no-one turned round to look at him.

"Even the Liberals, in their desperation to be trendy, have started spouting the language of the campus revolutionary and, in so doing, alienated just about every student who doesn't want to make a hobby out of politics. I'm sorry to be saying these things. There are members of this party in the room today who had to claw their way into this university, because the background they were from was such that it wasn't served to them on a plate. Strange that I hear less talk of revolution and the specialist issues of politics from them; they seem more interested in jobs and schools and hospitals. Funny that."

He paused for a second. He dared a glance around the room. One or two heads were turned towards him now, and one or two faces wore angry expressions.

"We're not thinking straight. Let's dump the rhetoric of class struggle for a minute and consider one of the issues that's in the news right now. The last few weeks, the bin men have been in dispute with local authorities. Their living standards have been held back by the wages policies of their own party. The ordinary man doesn't walk past last week's refuse and think, gosh, what an expression of working-class solidarity against an unfair incomes policy. He says, Christ, look at all that shite in the street, perhaps the other lot *would* get it shifted."

He paused for breath.

"Stop reading the *Sun*," yelled someone, in genuine anger. Terry grinned.

"I only buy it for the crossword," said Roy blandly. "Comrades, our man in the street is absolutely right. The Tories *will* get the crap shifted. They'll simply hand out raises to the public sector, justifying it on the grounds of the law of supply and demand. At the same time, there'll be manning cuts. But people'll put up with it because for each man who loses his job, nine will get more money in their pay-packets. Our job is to persuade them, all of them, that it would be their job next. No-one in this room has thought seriously about how we are going to do that."

"But what about working-class solidarity?" called out someone. "You wouldn't understand that. You're bourgeois."

"Shut up," said someone else. "*That's* rhetoric."

One or two people muttered agreement.

"So let's play a straight game," said Roy. "Let's stop talking about fascism and solidarity. Let's start talking about jobs and schools and hospitals. Let's remind people that because they voted Labour in 1945, they've got free medical care when they need it – and that that's under threat."

He managed a smile.

"And now, let's consider what the President of the Union should be doing besides getting involved in politics – although I do believe he should. Let's talk about the state of the lavatories on the ground floor of this building. Let's talk about the half-hour queue for beer that is driving some people to the University's own bar. Let's –"

"Join the Liberals!" yelled an angry voice.

Roy ploughed on, but only for a minute or two before sitting down. He was exhausted.

There were questions. He barely noticed what they were. Terry answered them confidently enough, but with a touch of surliness. Roy answered more slowly, but briefly.

"I move that we move to a vote," said the redhaired girl.

It was a show of hands. "All those in favour of Comrade Terry Malcolm for Union President candidate," said the tall thin, girl, "please show."

Hands shot into the air. There were seventeen.

"All those in favour of Comrade Dickson, please show."

Another seventeen hands were thrust in the air.

There was silence for a minute. Then Terry, who had gone a little white, said: "What do standing orders say about a tied vote?"

Michaels shrugged. "Not a lot."

"Comrade chairperson," said a rich, well-bred female voice. Everyone turned to face the redhead. "There were a number of abstentions... I move that we vote again by ballot paper."

Michaels shrugged.

"That seems as good a solution as any."

Terry had gone a little whiter.

"We've *never* needed a ballot for anything," he said.

"Well, I think it's the best solution now," said the redhead. "Not everyone wants to be seen changing their allegiance in public."

"You just did," said Terry.

"What makes you so sure?" Her tone was chilly. "Let's have a ballot."

Michaels sighed. "All those in favour."

Most of the arms in the room shot up.

For the first time that evening, Michaels smiled.

"Well, that seems clear enough," she said. She nodded to the redhead. "Since it was your idea, do you want to knock together a ballot-box and some papers? I'll help you."

The girl nodded back.

"Then I move that we adjourn for fifteen minutes," said Michaels. "We'll get everything ready and everyone else may as well go off and get themselves a drink. Okay?"

She sounded almost homely.

Roy stood up, uncertain as to what to do. After a while he went outside with his paper plate and empty glass and made for the bar.

There was a disco going in the marketplace now and he walked straight into a wall of sound. He was glad to let the wall of humanity close behind him, not wanting anyone from that room to talk to him.

When he returned a quarter of an hour later, there was a cardboard box that had once contained crisps standing on the table. Its top had been taped down and a slit cut in the cardboard. When everyone had returned to the room, the redhead and Michaels distributed slips of paper folded in two with the names of the candidates written on them. It didn't take long. Terry and Roy then stood over the shoulders of the two women as they counted. The room was completely silent.

Michaels stood up.

"Ladies and Gentlemen," she said, a smile flickering across her lips, "as the returning officer for this constituency..."

"Don't be bourgeois," hissed Terry.

"Here are the results. Comrade Malcolm, seven votes. Comrade Dickson, thirty-one votes. I hereby..."

There was a roar of amusement. Terry leaned back against the table, and across his face passed a look of what Roy thought was real agony.

The rest of the evening passed in a blur of congratulations during which Roy tried to convince everyone that he had only won the nomination, not the sabbatical presidency; he was looking for the redhead, but she was nowhere to be seen.

Later that night, alone, he walked through the freshly falling snow to his car and cleaned the drift off his windscreen. He hadn't seen Terry much for the rest of that evening, he remembered, although he had still been there.

As he was about to get into his car, a figure passed him, struggling to keep upright in the snow.

"Hey," he called out.

She looked up. "Hello," she said. She unwound the scarf, and smiled.

"Why did you nominate me?"

"I don't know," she said thoughtfully. "Let me give you some advice."

He shrugged. "Please do."

"When it's as cold as this, it's a good idea for a man to zip up his fly. Don't you agree?"

He glanced downwards.

"Oh. Er, oh, well, yes," he said. His fingers flew towards his trousers, then hesitated for a moment. Should he zip up his fly now, or should he wait until the lady was out of sight?

"I mean, you wouldn't want your assets frozen, would you," she said seriously.

"No, er, quite so." His fingers were frozen and he couldn't manipulate the zip.

She laughed. "Good luck – I'll be canvassing for you. I promise!" She turned away.

"Hey," he called out again.

"What?"

"I thought you were going out with Terry Malcolm."

Turning back towards him, she rolled her eyes. "You must be joking. The furthest he ever got with me was to try to kiss me in a drunken stupor. Last week, in fact. It took me about five minutes to push him away." She started to turn away again.

"Hey!"

"What now?" He was still struggling with his fly. Seeing this, she put her hands on her knees and bowed down, laughing. "Jesus, do you want me to do it for you?"

"Might let you if you play your cards right," said Roy sourly. "I just wanted to know your name, that's all."

"Oh, yes. Yes, it's Katy." She turned again. "I'm frozen. I'm going back to hall. Congratulations."

And she disappeared into the swirling snow.

***   ***   ***

"What are you thinking about?"

He looked up. "Eh?"

"You were dreaming." Her fingers were curled round a wineglass now, for she had bowed to temptation; the sunlight reflected off the white wall in the back garden and made a halo round her hair. A gentle breeze lifted the corner of the exercise book she had been marking. "What were you dreaming of?"

"I was remembering a night when my fingers were too cold to do up my fly."

A slow, soft smile spread across her face.

"You haven't mentioned that in years."

"You confused me by nominating me," he remembered. "Because I was already very much in love with you."

"Now you're exaggerating."

"I'm not, you know," he said.

***   ***   ***

The long, hazy dog-days were coming to an end. When they wheeled their bicycles out of the front garden on Sunday morning, it was grey and overcast; deep, gunmetal clouds billowed over the dark green countryside as the two cyclists made their way through village after village in a riot of church bells. They could feel their skins tighten a little as the pressure dropped, feel the muggy air around them, cloying and eddying.

"Slow down, Katy," Roy called out ahead of him. "I'm sweating like a pig."

Alan Ryan lived three or four miles away; it didn't take them long. They turned into his drive through open wrought-iron gates, tall trees shielding the garden from the road. Alan's newish Rover stood in front of the house, which was a Victorian farmhouse in local brick, solid but not too large. Alan opened the door before they reached it, smiling, his eyes anxious.

"Hello, I'm glad you could make it," he said. He was tall and slim with a subtle face, hair receding across the scalp. "Sissy's upstairs still, lying on her bed."

He took them to her room, a teenager's bedroom decorated with horses and pop idols, perhaps a little neater than most. Apart from the bedside table, which was a forest of coffee mugs and pill packets. She looked up at them, her face pale and strained. She was pale anyway, with light, rather thin blonde hair and grey eyes. Her leg was stretched straight, bound with a thick white bandage from the thigh nearly to the ankle, her jeans cut away to accommodate the dressing.

"Not dead yet, then?" said Katy with a grin.

"Not too bad today," said Cecilia with an attempt to smile back. "If I just keep still and don't try to move around much, it doesn't really hurt. And Mum and Dad keep trotting up the stairs with biscuits and papers and things – " she indicated the *Sunday Times* on the bed beside her – "so perhaps I should fall off horses more often!"

"I really don't think so, darling," said Alan. "I'll pop down and see if your mother wants any help with the lunch." He went.

They talked for a while. It did start to rain. For ten minutes or so it did so quite heavily, and then settled down to a heavy drizzle, sending rivulets of water down the pane and softening the light so that Cecilia grew paler and seemed to turn into a sort of bedridden wraith. There were circles around her eyes and, every so often, as she stretched to reach something on the bedside table, she was forced to roll her body slightly; and then she would wince and quickly readjust herself so that her leg was not twisted.

After a while her father bounded up the stairs, two at a time, to tell them that a pre-lunch drink was ready.

"Do you really want to come down, Sissy? It might be easier if you had your lunch up here," he said.

"Oh, no, I'll come," she replied cheerfully. "I can sit on the end of the table and stick my leg out so that it's straight, then I can trip Mum up as she comes in with the dishes."

"All right, then, you little comedienne." Alan leaned down and put his arms under her shoulders to lift her. She closed her eyes as she tried to move her leg forward over the side of the bed.

"Here, wait a minute." Katy put one hand below the shin and the other below the thigh and lifted them carefully so that the bandage didn't catch against the bedclothes. Slowly they moved her upright, like a flotilla of tugs pivoting an oil-rig into place.

Finally she was standing on her own, supporting herself with a pair of crutches. She moved slowly across the room to the door. When she was nearly there, her left foot, dangling uselessly, caught the edge of the carpet. She looked as if she had been shot, the muscles below her eyes pressing the eyelids harder and harder shut.

"Oh, Christ," said Alan, supporting her.

"Daddy," she said quietly.

"Yes, darling?"

"I think I'm going to throw up."

"Let's get her back on the bed. Roy, there's a bowl in the bathroom, can you bring it?"

"Yes, of course."

Alan held it under her chin, but she managed to return to her position on the bed before gagging into the bowl. Nothing much came up.

"If I ever catch him," said Alan later as they sat down to eat, "I'm going to take his leg in my hand and twist it below the knee. I will twist until I hear the ligaments snap and see his eyes age with pain."

* * *   * * *   * * *

EARLY on Monday morning, Terry pushed open the door of John Grieves's office.

"Morning, John," he said cheerfully. "You wanted to say something to me?"

"Certainly did. Take a seat." Grieves indicated the green chair in front of his desk.

Terry took a seat.

"First of all," said Grieves, "congratulations on deciding to join the, er, funny handshake mob." He grinned. "I don't think there'll be any problem. No-one takes all that ritual all that seriously any more, of course, but it does come in useful seeing so many people."

"I'm looking forward to it," said Terry, lighting a cigarette. "Good of them to count me in."

"No problem. And by the way, I, er, would like to invite you to become a partner of Grieves & Son."

Terry's own grin threatened his ears.

"We'll stick on three more grand and I'll get you a 5-series when the new one comes out. We'll sort that out later."

"Well, that's really great. I accept!"

"Good," said Grieves. "In fact, I was thinking, we might get you one of those new carphones, as well. Not sure we really need them, but it's good for prestige."

He paused briefly.

"One final thing. Gather you had a bit of bother with the law, in the car."

That's it, thought Terry miserably. The scheming bastard. He's going to make the whole deal conditional on my licence being kept.

"Well, you needn't worry," said Grieves. He leaned forward across the desk, smiling, his hands clasped. "I had a word with the Super at the lodge meeting. I think everything's sorted out."

III Autumn

The student sat back on the hard chair in Makepeace's study. It was an old chair, a rather hard chair, the sort of chair they had in school dining-rooms in his father's day, and he wondered why a man in Makepeace's position did not furnish his study with something better.

The student shifted in his seat. He was a tall youth of twenty, with a narrow face and black hair that was slicked back from his forehead. His clothes were casual-smart. He looked at his watch. The Master's curt note had summoned him for twelve-fifteen. It was now nearing twelve-thirty. He was not sure why the Master wanted him, although he knew his own tutor was not happy with his progress. Thinking of his tutor, he smiled his contempt for the owl-like face that stared at him with a sort of entreaty in the eyes that blinked at you over the tops of half-moon glasses.

The student glanced out of the gothic-shaped paired windows into the quadrangle below. It was not the largest in the city and was surrounded by flat, rather dull walls into which the same gothic pairs were cut; the odd gargoyle leered at the retreating backs of two dons who strode purposefully across the quad for a Saturday lunchtime drink. Their gowns drifted only a little behind them in the slipstream, for it was a calm October day, one of those one gets just before November strikes, bringing with them a very faint haze reminiscent of August, and china-blue skies; but the haze is from leaves that are about to die and the sun is warming your neck for the last time. This could be the last day of the year on which Samantha and I can drink outside the pub, thought the student with irritation, and looked at his watch again. It had nothing new to tell him so he turned his attention to the inside of the room instead.

It was modest for the master of a college, even a poor one. It was not large; thirty feet at most from door to desk, although the ceiling was high. There was no carpet. The desk itself was a mahogany affair that could have been made at any time in the last century and a half. The walls were white and, for the most part, unadorned; but there was a large black-and-white photograph. There was a bookcase against the wall but it held a hundred books at most. Clearly Makepeace never whiled away the day in second hand-book shops like his peers.

He turned his attention to the photograph. It was old, but black-and-white, not brown-and-white, and of good quality, printed on matt fibre-based paper, so that every tone showed and there was no reflection of the light outside. It showed a group of people in front of a house that could have been Elizabethan; the path itself was of light, clean, even gravel and it was possible to see the mudguard, and half the radiator, of a quality car of a bygone era on the right of the picture. The one visible headlight stood Cyclopean atop a highly-polished mudguard. In the centre of the picture was grouped a family of four, a large man of military bearing, a youth of about the student's own age who bore a strong resemblance to the large man, a thin woman whose hat obscured her face in shadow, and a younger boy who looked a little like a fifteen-year-old version of Makepeace, but who could tell? – the picture was fifty years old, to judge from the garb of the family, the shape of the car and the uniforms of the domestics who surrounded them. But then, such uniforms don't really change much, do they, thought the student. His own parents were too liberated for such antics as domestic staff. Their Hampstead house held only an au pair and a young girl who looked after the kitchen, and a lady who cleaned but didn't live there. Certainly no uniforms.

He looked again at the family in the photograph. The two well-built men looked pleased and proud; the youngest did not, his head down, chin pointing at the gravel, but his eyes looked upwards to face the camera and there was a strange luminosity about them, so that while the eyes of the other people in the picture were not really distinct, the boy's seemed to dominate the space around him.

The student stood a foot or two from the picture, hands in pockets, and half-turned at a light scratching sound like the scraping of branches upon a window-pane. Looking down, he saw that the sound came from the claws of a rough collie on the wooden floor. The dog had trotted into the room, its tail undulating gently, and had curled up on the floor beside the bookcase. It ignored the student, who had missed the master's entry; the man had simply materialised at his desk, behind which he now stood. He looked at the student, who now knew exactly whose eyes had stared out at him from the family group. Makepeace's face was lined and rather severe, the eyes themselves of mid-blue, the hair wiry, strong, grey now of course but complete and slightly curled. He wore a charcoal suit, plain, old, but of excellent cut and quality; his shirt was white and his tie maroon. He was not tall; indeed, rather short.

Neither spoke. They looked at each other for a moment. The student was uncertain of whether or not he should remove his hands from his pockets, so he did not do so. Instead he half-removed them. Eventually Makepeace made a quick gesture with his wrist. The student sat down.

Makepeace also did so. His desk was completely clear; there was not an object on it, not even a piece of paper.

"HOBBES!"

The student nearly jumped out of his skin. The voice was loud and low enough to arouse Hobbes himself from that place where life is nasty, brutish and eternal. The student was unsure of the correct response. Was his knowledge of Hobbes to be tested? He was about to open his mouth when he became aware that Makepeace was not looking at him. The Master sat behind his desk, leaning forward a little, his hands clasped together on its green leather inlay, looking at the floor beside the bookcase.

"Get away from those books, Hobbes, they are three hundred years old," he said quietly. "I do not want you slobbering all over them; it's bad enough when the students do it."

The dog took itself off across the room.

Makepeace sat back and looked at the student with the air of a sewage engineer studying a badly-sited outfall.

"Dr. Elphick tells me that you rarely attend tutorials and that your work appears irregularly and is of limited quality. You made a fearful mess of your Mods. Do you know what" – he named another college – "did at the end of last year?"

The student shook his head. He knew exactly how the dog felt.

"They sent down everybody who was not clearly of upper second standard at the end of the first year. In this college we don't indulge in such perfectionism. I am not even sure if it is within the Statutes. But I am damn sure of what I'm going to do to you if you don't pull your socks up by the end of Hilary term. I am going to have you sent down. I will then give your place to someone whose birth was such that he is surprised to find himself here, and extremely pleased to be. Get out of my office."

The student did so, standing up slowly and walking to the door, his confidence completely evaporated.

Makepeace did not give him a second glance. He reached down to the low bookcase on his left and picked up the receiver of the telephone, and dialled the number of his home in a village some thirty miles away. It rang for a couple of minutes and he could imagine his wife, refusing to be hurried, calmly washing her hands and then wiping them on her apron as she came through the hall. Or perhaps she had been seated cross-legged at her bureau, reading the *Lancet*, or composing, in triplicate, a furious letter to *The Independent* on the amount of paperwork expected of GPs.

"Seven two seven eight."

"Oh, hello, darling. It's Paul."

"Hello."

"I didn't interrupt you doing anything important, did I?"

"No, no. Actually he rang a few minutes ago. I was just going to ring you. He's just got in – some KLM flight, I think, from Amsterdam."

"You mean he's here? Where did he want to be met?"

"Oxford station at two. Can you do that? Have you had lunch?"

"Doesn't he want me to meet him at Heathrow?" asked Makepeace, a slight disappointment in his voice. He ignored the second question.

"He said there was no point. By the time you'd got there he'd have been able to get to the station at Reading. You haven't answered my question."

"Question? Oh, no, I haven't eaten yet, darling, but I don't need anything."

"I'll have something ready for you."

"Thank you. I expect Tim shall want something. What was that piece of music you were talking about last night?"

"What?" His wife was silent for a moment. "Oh, that piece we enjoyed on the car radio on the way back from Wales. It was Schumann's Rhenish Symphony. Why, Paul?"

"I thought I would try to buy the record while I wait for Tim. I'll see you at about three."

"Fine. See you soon."

He replaced the receiver and stood up. He glanced briefly about the room, snapped his fingers at the dog, shut the door and strode off down the stone-floored corridor, past more doors with pointed Gothic stone frames and iron hinges, and down the winding staircase that led into the quad, where he enjoyed the feel of the mild late sunshine. A round, bespectacled figure was hurrying towards him from the main entrance, books tucked under his arm, head bowed against some imaginary storm.

"Elphick!"

"Oh, good afternoon, Master." The owl-like face gave a guilty twitch. "How are you?"

"Very well, thank you. I've just seen that wretch what's-his-name."

Elphick blinked like an animal removed suddenly from a dark cage. "Ah, yes. And – er – what is your view, Master?"

"Oh, I think we'll get rid of him," said Makepeace. "But I'm giving him to the end of Hilary term. Perhaps then I could have your views on his progress."

"Very good, Master." Elphick gave a nervous grin, like a puppy that has just made a mess on the floor and does not understand why he has not been kicked. "I'm glad he's getting a chance. After all, his father was here, and his grandfather, and PPE is really a most challenging degree..."

"We mustn't give anyone an easy ride, Elphick," said the Master. He gave a slight smile. "I trust your new rooms are satisfactory?"

Elphick brightened.

"They're delightful. A fine view over the meadow. Very nice at this time of year. I trust your son arrived back safely last night?"

"No, he was delayed. One of these Third World airlines," replied Makepeace. "But he's just rung. I shall meet him at two. See you on Monday."

They parted. Makepeace marched briskly through the college entrance, greeting a scout in the doorway, and made his way to Oriel Square, where he unlocked the tailgate of a green Triumph 2000 estate car. The dog jumped in and curled up on the floor, satisfied with the long walk he had had around Christchurch Meadow before Makepeace's interview with the student.

Makepeace's route took him up the narrow lane to the High, where he crossed at the pelican light halfway down. He kept up his usual brisk pace as he turned into the Turl. Halfway to Broad Street he turned to his right down the alley which led to the Radcliffe Camera. This took him past a long row of motorcycles parked against the wall, and he looked at them with a certain detached interest – Kawasaki, Honda, Suzuki; they looked of a muchness to him, despite the different names on the petrol tanks. For some reason he found himself wondering when he had last seen anyone ride a Matchless. He wondered why. But the sight of the Radcliffe Camera thrilled him as much as it had done over forty years ago, the dome standing proud against the deep blue October sky.

His walk took him past the dome and down New College Lane. He remembered following the same route from the college to the Turf Tavern – what year was it? – that horrible winter of 1947, barely out of uniform, with his wife-to-be asking him if he thought she was clever enough to study medicine; and he had told her that she was. He hadn't thought or known of what lay ahead for her; the struggle with anatomy, the fraught exams, the days that ran into nights into days for the young hospital doctor, and the years winning the trust of her patients in the villages; the low trill of the phone on the bedside table, the whispered *sshh, don't get up* and the sound of the Ford Consul's tyres scrunching on the gravel or the snow, and the relief he felt when the headlights came back up the drive an hour or two later, lighting the bedroom briefly as she turned the car before the door, *Was everything all right? Yes, I thought we might have a breach birth, the midwife was there though* or *I expect so, I had her taken to Horton General though, just to be sure*, or *Well he was seventy, he was gassed you know, none of them ever were quite the same.* Now and then he knew not to ask but she only cried once, and it was only a snivel really. *You never get used to it, not to that, the young ones. They should have called an ambulance. If they'd just had a spark guard.* After that he didn't ask so often. All that had lain in the future on that February night. The ice in the air had stung their red faces as their footsteps crushed the snow; Catte Street wasn't closed then and the odd car passed by, wheezing along after years on pool spirit. They had passed below the elegant arch of Hertford's Bridge of Sighs, then left into the pub via a tiny alleyway, stretching out frozen hands towards the weak braziers in the yard before cramming into the packed bar for a half of bitter.

Makepeace took the same route today. The braziers were there in the yard, but they weren't lit; there had been a long mild spell. They would be needed in a week or two. The yard was packed with students, some of them of the traditional kind, in sports jackets and slacks with conventional floppy hair, earnestly discussing quantum mechanics; there were the tall, languid ones, not long out of school, still savouring the thrill of a kind of adulthood; there were the rebels with their outlandish clothes, in homage to inner-city streets they had scarcely seen; and there were the foreign research students –

lanky, friendly Americans, enthusiastic Greeks, well-dressed Singaporeans and Malays, courtly Sudanese with razor-creased trousers, all dreaming of the future as they drank. Sometimes Makepeace wondered if much had changed, the more so now that Holywell was largely closed to traffic so that its quietness resembled his own time. But these students were not hungry. They wouldn't go home to a low, smoky fire, cobbled together by the landlady with briquettes made of coal dust and newspaper.

He pushed open the glass door of Blackwell's Music Shop in Holywell and paused for a moment, momentarily confused. Then he made his way down to the basement, wondering where one found Schumann. He could see very few records, apart from a bin of cut-price specials; just miles of cassettes, and something else, thin plastic boxes a little larger than cassettes that he realised must hold compact discs.

"Excuse me?" The cashier looked up from wrapping someone else's purchases. "I'm looking for Schumann's Rhenish Symphony. Where might I find it, please?"

"Did you require a compact disc or a cassette, sir?" asked the assistant. He was polite but busy.

"Neither. Actually I want a record."

"I'm afraid we don't carry very many, sir, not nowadays," said the assistant. He waved his hands towards the rack. "That's all we have, but you might find what you want there. Otherwise, I'm afraid we can't help you."

"Thank you."

Frowning, Makepeace flicked his way through the few surviving records. They were mostly compilations of Christmas carols or Gregorian chants or mediaeval plainsong or suchlike. He abandoned the quest.

Still frowning, he hurried down Holywell and across into Broad Street. More students were drinking outside the King's Arms on the corner. As he passed Blackwell's main bookshop he wondered for how long they would still sell books, and when one would have to buy Hegel's *Philosophy of Right* on a disk that you slipped into your computer.

At Boswell's he turned left and found himself dragged from gown to town. This was the city, thronged with thousands of Saturday shoppers. Many had children with them. Pedestrians spilled out into the roadway; no cars were permitted there, but commercial traffic was, and the buses floated quietly through the crowd like airships, mothers hauling their offspring out of the way at the last minute. The sheer prosperity of the place hit Makepeace like a hammer; he rarely came here on a Saturday. Everyone looked smart, and carried plastic bags from clothes shops and electrical retailers. He remembered that there was a record shop on the other side of Cornmarket and he went into it, but his luck was no better. Coming out, he noticed a sign on the entrance to the church opposite and remembered that his wife had told him there was a sale in the crypt on certain days of the week; he looked at his watch. One-fifteen. Ample time to have a look and get back to Oriel Square to collect his car.

The church had a dark, grimy frontage and was surrounded by a cemetery on one side, and a rather dark garden on the other. Makepeace descended a narrow stairway and was relieved of fifty pence at its end, before being shown into the crypt. The large room was fairly busy, and there were several boxes bursting with records.

Ten minutes later Makepeace emerged, smiling, with the Schumann under his arm, having paid less than a pound for a fifteen-year-old recording by Karajan.

* * *   * * *   * * *

WHEN Tim came off the train, Makepeace was at first alarmed by his appearance. The man, his middle child and youngest son, was in his early thirties but looked several years older now. He was a little taller than his father; his eyes were softer, and his hair straight and dark. Perhaps it's my imagination, thought Makepeace, but I think he's thinning out on top. His face, like his father's, was fairly broad; it too had aged five years in the two since they'd seen him last, and both face and body were thin. He was dressed in a denim jacket and jeans.

When he saw his father, he smiled, and strode towards him with a crispness that belied his appearance.

"Dad! You look well," he said, his voice well-bred but with a slight provincial inflexion that was hard to identify. They shook hands firmly. "Thank you for coming to meet me."

"I was in college anyway. But really, you should have rung me. I could have collected you from Heathrow."

"I didn't want to bring you anywhere near Heathrow," said Tim cheerfully. "The place is a nightmare. Look I'm sorry I... Oh, Dad, I can carry own bags, really... I'm sorry I'm a day late, the plane landed to refuel at Kingston and they had no foreign exchange for aviation spirit. And then they ran out of booze on the plane. Christ, I'm glad they transferred us to KLM."

Makepeace laughed. "Two years in the jungle and then they run out of booze on the way home. Listen, you look as if you've been unwell."

"Oh, no, not really, it's been much easier this time, only a couple of shots of malaria. And I haven't even had the shits much," his son replied. "For Heaven's sake let me carry that bag, Dad...Oh, good, you've still got the car!"

Makepeace smiled slowly. "Still going strong. Well, I like it, Tim, and I really wouldn't get much for it if I sold it now. Say hello to Hobbes."

Makepeace drove with measured manner, keeping well behind the cars in front but going quickly when he could. His son looked around him with pleasure, seeing the October countryside as if he never had before; in a sense, he felt, he hadn't.

"How long will you be home for this time?"

"I don't know, Dad. Certainly a week and then I must go to Geneva."

"Do you know where they're sending you next?"

"They haven't said but there are mutterings about Africa again."

"Not back to Central America?"

"No." His son sighed. "I don't think so and anyway, two years is enough for now."

"But you must speak Spanish well now?"

"Not bad. How is everyone? Has Mum said when she's going to retire? And how about you?"

"Me soon," said his father, pulling out to overtake a Mini. "I'll be sixty-four. I can go on until sixty-seven if I really want to, but I don't think I shall. Your mother is only taking a couple of surgeries a week now and I think she'll stop next year as well."

"What are you going to do?"

"Me?"

His son glanced at him. "Well, you won't be gardening all day, will you?"

Makepeace shrugged. "I'll find plenty of ways to stay out of mischief. There's a book I want to write putting Hobbes and Locke into their social contexts. I've been thinking about it for years but I've always been too busy. And your mother wants to travel a bit. I don't see why not, although I suppose the novelty's worn off for you."

"Yes, it has," said Tim. "All I do is stay in one place with one lot of refugees for two years, trying to persuade hostile locals to give us enough fuel and food for them. Dad, Mum said something on the phone about James giving everyone a big surprise, whatever that might mean."

Makepeace kept his eyes on the road. "Yes, he's got married."

"He's what? That's a bit sudden, isn't it?"

"Somewhat."

"Oh." Tim frowned. "When?"

"About two weeks ago. I haven't seen them since the wedding," said his father, glancing in the mirror before steering into a side turning at an oblique angle.

"Was it totally unexpected?"

"Yes."

"Who is she?"

"Her name is Tamsin," said Makepeace, accelerating away down a long, straight country road. "She's some kind of actress."

"You've met her?"

"Once or twice."

He said nothing more, so Tim prompted him: "What's she like?"

Makepeace was silent for half a minute. Then he said:

"Frankly I think she's unsuitable."

"That probably means," said Tim, "that she suits James very well."

Makepeace glanced at his son. "Yes, well, you can judge for yourself. They're travelling to Scotland and asked if they might stay overnight, so you should meet your new sister-in-law in an hour or two."

"What does Mum think about all this?"

"She wishes them luck. As do I."

"Yes, of course," said Tim. "Sorry. What about Liz?"

"Your little sister has not told me what she thinks for years."

"Oh. What was the wedding like?"

"I really wouldn't know. They went off to Amsterdam and did it there one weekend for some reason. Your mother and I didn't know about it until afterwards."

Tim grunted. He reached into his pocket. "Do you mind if I smoke?"

"No, of course not."

"Would you like one?"

"Not while I'm driving." Tim lit one of his duty-free Kents and opened the window a slit to let the smoke out. They were passing through undulating countryside now, Makepeace driving quite quickly, as he usually did when the road was clear. The car ran strongly, the six-cylinder engine smooth and quiet, though after fifteen years the suspension could no longer prevent the car from heaving and swaying a little on corners. They passed a farm at a crossroads, slurry hissing beneath the wheels, and rossed a major road; and then found themselves twisting and turning, climbing and diving among some attractive small hills. Makepeace had decided to take his son the rural way so that he could see the October gold that he had missed the last four or five years in succession. Tim appreciated it.

"Liz is still at home then?"

"Yes. I'm not too happy about that. She's 18 now. Though she's been down to see James this week."

"So she didn't get into university?"

"She didn't get the As. Anyway, she wants to go to drama school. She seems most reluctant to do anything else."

Tim made a sound of irritation.

They fell silent for a while. The car crossed the northwest corner of Oxfordshire and joined a quiet main road. They passed the Warwickshire border and as they did so, the road surface changed slightly. At the same time a subtle change came over the landscape.

Tim remembered this and relished it. It was clearest during the summer, when the bright sunlight cast a haze over the fields, and that haze seemed to intensify on the grass as you passed into the Midland county; the trees to grow larger and yet seem farther away, and a sort of slow mystery settle on everything you saw. He remembered exploring on his bicycle as a child, and the day he had ridden into a meadow past a tree-lined hedge to see a huge Elizabethan mansion rise in front of him. It did not need huge imagination to see Shakespeare as a young man, poaching deer. Go into the cities and it was lost; but look again at the faces of stonemasons working on a church in, say, Stratford or Kineton, and there was something ancient in those faces, an angularity, a light in the tone of the flesh that mirrored the hazy magic landscape.

They were nearly home now. For the first time Tim did feel a slight anticipation. He had been on leave from his last posting, but had not wanted to travel all the way home. Instead he had headed north to the colour and cheer of Mexico then returned to his duty station feeling empty, as if he should have gone somewhere where he could be reminded, if only for a week, of who he really was.

Makepeace drove them into a village of red-brown brick, and

round a green. The church was ahead of them and, to its right, a shoulder-high hedge beyond which lay the house. It was a Victorian rectory, not large by the standards of its time, but not small today. Its roof rose in twin inverted vees on either side of a thick oak front door; the eaves were painted a startling white.

"Welcome home," said Makepeace, his face broadening slowly into a smile. "I've been looking forward to saying that."

"I've been looking forward to hearing it."

They took his bags from the car. Makepeace pushed open the small white gate and led him up the garden path to the front door where a tall, slim woman in her sixties, conservatively dressed in tweed skirt and white blouse, stood smiling. Her face was lined, her eyes were strong and bright; her gunmetal hair was held in a permanent wave.

"Hello, Mum," said Tim, hugging her, "I've come to eat everything in the house."

"Well, there's a big ham ready for you tonight." She squeezed him tightly. "And your room's ready. Are you well?" She held him back and studied his face. "You look very pale, darling. Have you been ill again?"

"Only plague and polio."

"Darling, will you be serious?" Her voice was low and had a slight West Country tinge to it. She took him by the arm and led him through the white-painted hall. "What have you got this time?"

"Not a lot." He turned to her, still smiling. "I've had a couple of mild bouts of malaria, that's all."

"Tummy all right?"

"Not bad."

"I'll take a stool test tomorrow and we can run a blood sample up to the lab on Monday. Have you got enough malaria prophylaxis?"

"Dear God, Mother, you make me sound like a walking germ-warfare laboratory," said Tim, frowning.

"Well, when you got hepatitis in Ethiopia, you never told either of us. We'd have been worried sick if we'd known."

"Of course we would, Christine," said Makepeace. He shut the heavy oak front door. "That's why he didn't tell us. Let's have some tea."

"Yes, of course," she said, leading her son into the kitchen, "and then he can have a little while on his own to rest and unpack. Darling, do you like Hobbes?"

"He's an awfully healthy-looking dog, isn't he?"

"He's incredibly clever. Daddy bought him from a farmer in Shropshire. Sit down, we've got Jaffa cakes."

"Jaffa cakes!"

Christine Makepeace brought tea in a huge silver pot, one that he remembered was rarely used, only on special occasions, and usually in the front room, which was not much lived in during the day. He preferred the kitchen, a rambling semi-rustic mess complete with Aga, not bought in an antique shop but in place since the 1940s. The room was spotlessly clean and completely unplanned, having evolved as it was used, and was furnished with big oak cupboards and a table that was probably Victorian.

"So," said Tim as she sat down at the table. "Has my dear brother arrived?"

"No," said Makepeace shortly.

"We expect him about six," said his mother.

"He'll be late," said Makepeace.

"And he's bringing this whatshisname?"

"Your sister-in-law, dear," said his mother, a little reprovingly. "Supper will be at eight." She looked at Tim. "Are you hungry now? I've got some salad ready, and I can make some soup."

"No, no, I had some sandwiches on the plane, and a snack on the train. What's for supper? Ham?"

"Ham and white sauce. And a spinach tart for Tamsin."

"A what?"

"She doesn't eat any meat," explained his mother.

"Or eggs. Or fish," rumbled Makepeace.

"Your brother says she's a Vegan."

"Does that mean she's from the planet Vega?" asked Tim.

"God knows. Most of these theatrical types are on damn strange," said Makepeace.

"Well, I'd like to make an appeal," said his wife, halting her teacup on its way to her lips and speaking over its rim. She looked a little worried. "If you find her a little silly, Tim, you must remember she's your sister-in-law. And try not to scrap with your brother. He's done very well for himself, even if he's different from you."

"Don't worry, Mother. If she really annoys me I can always shove a ham sandwich down her throat, I suppose."

"No you won't," his father said, and stood, and stretched. "I'm going to take your bags to your room and then you can have a good rest before they come. They'll be gone tomorrow."

"Sure, Dad."

He stood up and collected his bags before his father could lift them.

* * *   * * *   * * *

THE bed, the same one he had slept on as a teenager, felt soft but supportive; the air cool and fresh, the ceiling above him looked brilliantly white. He stared at it and was reassured to see the same hairline cracks in the plaster that he remembered from two years ago.

He imagined his body as a ship. A ship that had just entered port and tied up. Perhaps a warship. The armourers had gone ashore, pleased to be in friendly territory. Around his body, engineers, armed with clipboards, marched from one bay to another shutting down generators and checking oil levels. He smiled with pleasure as he heard yet another winch cough and decline into silence. Bunkering and essential maintenance. Shore leave. Then slow steaming to Geneva. It's going be the Horn of Africa, he thought, irritated. Why can't they send me to Thailand, then at least I can go to Bangkok on my local leaves and drink lots and eat as much as I like. He thought he could hear his father clicking bottles together in the drawing-room below and smiled. I'll have a drink tonight before Mum gets her hands on my stool sample and announces that I need a two-week course of Flagel. Who *needs* solid shit?

He reached over and took his plastic digital watch from the table beside the bed. Just past five. Before long his brother would be here, bringing his new wife with him. Also Liz, Tim's sister, a very late afterthought by her parents that had damn near killed her mother. Liz had, as her mother put it, "gone up to town" to meet Tamsin the previous week and had stayed with them. His parents had not said so, but he sensed they'd rather she hadn't.

He put the watch back on the table. Another hour of peace, then.

The light was fading. Above him as he lay on his back, the white ceiling turned a darker white and then slowly into grey as the rectangle of orange sunlight cast from the window, broken into diamonds by the fake leaded lights, the idea of some nineteenth-century rector, retreated slowly towards the outer wall. He associated this view of the ceiling with something in his childhood, and tried to remember what it was. Then he had it: flu. Lying there with a fever would be the only time he lay in bed all day, usually in winter when the virus was strong, his joints aching, his head thick with the frustrated will to sleep.

Fever. The last had been the worst and it had struck him suddenly; they had been travelling to the border, he leading in the Land Cruiser, the big white one with air-conditioning and a stereo and nice soft seats. That morning he had supervised the assembly of the convoy that would take 300 refugees back to the border. They had all signed voluntary repatriation papers. It was about 100 kilometres. As the refugees had been herded into the blue Mercedes lorries, he had looked at their faces; round Indian faces, blank, expressionless, listless, just as they all seemed to be. Over the previous month he had sometimes sat with the protection officer as she interviewed them one by one. Why, she was asking them, did they wish to be repatriated? The answer, delivered in a monotone mixture of their own dialect and mainstream Spanish, was always the same. What, gringo, is the point in doing anything else?

The fumes from the Mercedes diesels turned the air acrid. He looked skyward. There were a few clouds, not too many; it looked hopeful. The day before yesterday it had rained. Together he and the station head from the capital, an intense Asian, had argued bitterly. We need a day, Tim told him. We need a day because if we go tomorrow, the roads will be sodden and it could take us three days from here to the border.

"Then take food."

"We'll need another lorry."

"We don't have one."

"I know," said Tim stiffly. "I am supposed to be logistics officer as you know."

"And if I allow you to delay another day?"

"We go on Thursday."

"And if it rains again on Wednesday?"

"Then we do not go on Thursday."

"And if it rains again on Thursday?"

"Then we do not go on Friday."

"And what will the refugees say to that?" asked the section head, sitting back in his leather chair and crossing his arms and smiling with self-satisfaction.

"Very little," said Tim. "They never say much about anything. Haven't you noticed?"

The satisfied smile vanished.

"All right, go on Thursday. And go to hell."

Tim shrugged and left the room.

On Thursday morning he had scanned the sky anxiously, and had seen no rainclouds. But it was useless, because he knew that it would come later in the day. Now, at three in the afternoon, he sat in the left-hand seat of the Land-Cruiser, bracing himself as his driver flicked the car in and out of all-wheel drive and slewed and skidded through deep ruts that had already been full of water. It was then that the fever had come, quite suddenly, just as he remembered it had in

Africa; it was as if the pressure to his vital pumps and valves had fallen off so that the human machinery became soggy and unresponsive to his commands, like an aircraft when the air is too thin for its wings. Glumly he stared out through the windscreen, which ran thick with jets of tropical rain; the wipers flashed back and forth in a vain attempt to keep up.

Three long, deep blasts of a Mercedes horn sounded behind them. It was a prearranged signal. He motioned to the driver to stop. The latter did so, and then sat there motionless, having made no attempt to position the vehicle so that it could be easily restarted.

Tim opened the door. This itself seemed to consume most of his strength. They were on the crest of a hill; below them and to the right, he could see the outlines of a few adobe houses, blurred in the driving rain.

He turned and squelched a few yards back to where the three Mercedes lorries had stopped. The middle one was stuck at a crazy angle, front buried sump-deep in mud, rear sticking up so that the driving wheels, although touching the ground, could obtain no purchase, for there was no weight on them.

He went up to the transport officer, a young American, ex-Peace Corps, checked shirt, close-cropped hair.

"What's your prognosis?" he asked gloomily.

The American shrugged. "We got a stuck truck."

"Yes, I know, but it's the fifth time today. How many more miles are we going to do before nightfall?"

"Search me. Tim, I don't know if we're going to shift this mother right now."

"No, of course not. I'm sorry."

The other looked up from the back bumper of the lead lorry, where he had been supervising the tying of a towrope. "Yeah. We got water?"

"Not enough for twenty-four hours of this. There's a village of some kind down there. I'll suss it out."

"Okay. You don't look so healthy yourself, Tim boy."

"I'll be OK. See you shortly."

"Ciao."

Tim turned and walked away. As he did so he glanced at the lorries. Here and there a chicken's head twisted back and forth amid the bodies. The refugees crouched down on the flatbeds, their hats pulled down against the torrent. They didn't appear to have changed their expressions at all, thought Tim. Christ, you bastards, why don't you get down from that sodding lorry and push and then maybe we'll get to that violent shithole of a country you all agreed to return to.

He walked forward to the Army jeep that was parked ahead of the Land-Cruiser. Three soldiers sat on the back, dressed in fatigues. All had machine-pistols. And sunglasses. One of them was trying to find some music on a transistor radio which he held to his ear. The others simply sat there, sodden. Standing orders, thought Tim, but Christ, I could do without these clowns.

Tim jerked his head towards the village.

"*No hay bastante agua,*" he said, cursing his Spanish. "*Por eso, vamos a ver los pueblos allá.*"

The soldiers looked back at him blankly.

"*Vámonos,*" he said, as firmly as he could.

"*Bueno,*" muttered one of the soldiers. Two of them followed him unenthusiastically. Their Army boots squelched through the puddles.

They approached the village down a narrow track that led off the road. The village was made up of a few squat, dark houses; a few chickens scratched about, as they always did. The rain had eased off slightly. A man with a broad Indian face looked at him uneasily from the first doorway.

"*Buenos días,*" said Tim. He felt unsteady on his feet and the fever was thickening in his head.

"*Buenos días.*" The villager was looking at the soldiers, who had unslung their machine-pistols. He seemed very tense. He was powerfully-built by local standards. Tim guessed that he was quite young, but his face was a thousand years old.

Tim gestured at the weapons, glancing at the soldiers. "*No es necesario*," he said wearily.

"*Si, Señor Makepiss*," said one of the soldiers. He was standing with his legs slightly apart, his face blank.

Tim shrugged, and turned back to the villager. "*¿Cómo está usted?*"

"*Regular.*" The villager spoke slowly. One or two faces looked from the other low houses. "*¿Qué deseas?*"

"*Agua.*" Tim gestured with head towards the nearby convoy. "*¿No hay bastante agua en los coches. Tiene agua?*"

"*Sí, la tenemos.*"

"*¿Es limpia?*" asked Tim, the long list of Geneva guidelines about the cleanliness of water flashing through his head. He swayed slightly. The villager noticed. He saw Tim's white face and smiled slightly.

"*No es limpia,*" he said slowly. "*Ya sabe que en todos los pueblos de nuestro país no se puede beber el agua limpia. Es solamente para los refugiados.*"

"He say," said one of the soldiers, "no-one 'ave good water except *refugiados*."

He spat, and then looked in the direction of the convoy.

"*No es importante,*" said Tim. His voice faltered a little, his head felt like lead, and the sweat that always poured off him in this God-forsaken country seemed to be flowing in buckets, draining crucial fluids from the brain. "*Pero el agua es necessaria, por favor, señor. ¿Dónde está el agua?*"

One of the soldiers fingered his machine-pistol.

The villager shrugged, and gestured to Tim to follow him. Together they walked through the mud of the village, and in the middle distance Tim could see a handpump, of a sort that he had seen in every country in which he had worked.

Above the horizon beyond the standpipe, the sky was lightening rapidly from grey to a sort of yellow, thin and limpid. By the tap knelt a female figure, her back to the approaching party. She lifted a pail of water onto her head, stood and turned. Tim saw that she was young, perhaps fourteen. She stood with grace, her arms above her head in the manner of a maiden on a Greek vase, steadying the pail. Her body was slim, although her hips were wide enough to offset the shape of her young girl's waist; she wore a ragged skirt that ended just below her knee. The waist was bare, a sleeveless shirt covering her torso, stretched tightly across young breasts. Then the clouds parted, releasing a shaft of sunlight that lanced into her face and lit her round cheeks and large round brown eyes; so huge, so round, round eyes, round cheeks, and then she smiled, and the corners of her enormous mouth creased into a moonscape of small, firm muscles.

Tim fainted, hitting the ground before her with a thud and a little jet of muddy water, and the world disintegrated; and the mud took the weight of his head from his neck and he thought, Christ, free at last.

* * *   * * *   * * *

YES, but you weren't, were you, thought Tim, looking up at the ceiling where the patch of orange from the setting sun had finally receded towards the windowpane. The American had revived him with water and then with oral rehydration salts and injected him with 150 milligrammes of chloroquine and he half-sat, half-lay in the seat of the Land-Cruiser for another twenty-four hours until they reached the river that marked the border, and he had watched as the boats took the refugees, still with their blank expressionless faces, across to whatever awaited them on the other side. Then they let him rest.

He sat up slowly, and swung his legs over the edge of the bed. He lit one of the Kents and smoked it slowly, looking out of the window at the last traces of autumn daylight. Beyond the village he could see ploughed fields and hedgerows disappearing under a veil of autumn mist, so that the world moved seamlessly from dark land to the silvery-blue canopy of the sky, a few stars now visible. Tim remembered walking home along the lanes and across the fields on such nights as a boy, and thinking how the very quality of the light seemed to disintegrate and the essence of matter decay, as if the generator that ran the world was shutting down, quietly, revs dropping a few hundred a minute so that existence, cancelled, was run down slowly. He remembered a night when his father had taken him fishing and, encumbered with rods, they had walked home in the twilight round the edge of a ploughed field and Makepeace had recited Thomas Hardy to him as the thick heavy scents of the season had closed around them.

Only a man harrowing clods
In a slow silent walk
With an old horse that stumbles and nods

In the distance, Tim saw two small pools of light appear in the mist. They approached steadily and formed themselves into a car's headlights and then the car itself appeared, the last light catching its silver roof and bonnet. It was a Porsche, one of the modern water-cooled, front-engined types. It passed the little white gate that led to the front door and turned into the drive at the side of the house, wheels noisily compressing the gravel. What a car, thought Tim; it looked like a squashed torpedo. It had a long, wide bonnet and the hatch at the rear had a wide expanse of glass. Inside, he could see through the window a pool of light from the instrument panel, his brother's hands silhouetted on the wheel.

The lights dimmed, and as they did so the headlamps could be seen retracting into the bonnet; then the engine stopped and the panel lights went off. He heard the front door open, and half-expected to see his mother walk forward in ear-protectors with a pair of ping-pong bats to guide the taxiing projectile into position.

The doors of the car were open now and James was walking around the front of the bonnet. Although it was Saturday, he was wearing a dark suit. He was tall and broad, with short, smooth blond hair, a few years older than Tim; 35, but he looked a little younger.

From the passenger door came a blonde woman, also fairly tall, and the figure of his small sister wriggled out from the back seat. It was too dark to make out her face.

A last rim of red showed on the horizon. In the gloom the fields had retreated to grey-blue and there was nothing more to be seen. He heard the front door close with a heavy click. Turning away from the window, he drew the curtains and looked in the mirror.

I suppose I'd better shave, he thought.

Ten minutes later, the three-day growth shaved off his chin, he came slowly down the stairs; he still had his jeans on but had found himself a clean shirt and, after some thought, a tie. He pushed open the door to the front room, which was furnished in a rather comfortable old-fashioned, style; there was a suite of two old, thickly padded, low armchairs and a sofa. The walls were cream. There was a television in one corner and a stereo in the other; both were twenty years old. There was a thick fitted carpet which was rather newer.

His father was in one armchair, his brother in the other; his mother was in the kitchen. James's short blond hair was parted at the side; his face was square, his eyes pale blue. He was still wearing the dark suit. Elizabeth was curled on the sofa, small, thin, with dark, short brown hair, a round mouth and huge dark eyes.

"Ah, Tim." His brother rose and crossed the floor to meet him.

"James. You're looking well."

"Quite. You look dreadful," said his brother. He had a deep and rather booming voice. He shook Tim's hand warmly. "I trust you've brought back hordes of native women with you for my delectation?"

"No," said Tim. "How's the advertising business?"

"Splendid. We've just had our little sister staying with us for a few days. Say hello to bro, Liz, if you remember him."

Tim turned. His sister didn't rise and he bent down to give her a peck on the cheek.

"Hello. Mum says you've been ill again," she said. Her voice was oddly low for one so small.

"Only the usual stuff," he said, and lowered himself down onto the sofa beside her. "James, where's my sister-in-law?"

"Tam? Oh, she's gone to the bog," said James cheerfully. "She'll be out in a minute."

"Good wedding was it?"

"Short and sweet."

"How long have you known her?"

"God, everyone's asking the same question," said James, frowning slightly. "Three months."

"Ah. Well, nice to see you again," he said, and turned to his sister. "Dad said something about you wanting to go to drama school."

"I hope I'm going to."

"Have they accepted you?"

"No, but Tamsin says she thinks I should get in."

"Oh. Good for Tamsin."

There was silence for a moment. Then Makepeace himself spoke.

"I'll get you all a drink," he said. "Elizabeth, darling, would you please go and ask Mummy what she'd like?"

"She'll have a sweet sherry," replied the girl. "She always does."

"I'll ask her," said Tim. Standing up and opening the door, he found himself facing a tall, slim girl with long, very light-blonde hair and a rather pale face with regular features. She was wearing a leather jacket and leather jeans. He looked her up and down.

"Hello. Going parachuting?" he asked.

"Eh?"

"Never mind. You must be my sister-in-law."

"Then you're Tim," she said, reaching for a smile.

"Indeed. Lovely to see you. Excuse me, I must ask my mother if she'll have a sweet sherry, as she always does," said Tim. He went off down the corridor.

"Ah, Tamsin." Makepeace turned away from the sideboard, a bottle of Scotch in his hand. "Please excuse James's brother. His manners get worse every time he gets home. What will you have to drink?"

"It's the witch-doctors," said James gravely.

"Scotch, please," said Tamsin. Her accent was hard to place. Makepeace thought that she was probably a Londoner. "You what, Jimbo?"

"The witch-doctors," said James. "He trains witch-doctors. It's part of an income-generating scheme the UN are running for refugees."

"Ha ha," she replied. "Hey, what a lovely old toilet! It's one of those big ceramic ones, you know, with a deep bowl and a chrome flush. Did you get it from one of those specialist dealers, Mr. Makepeace? You know, the ones that do house-demolitions?"

"Er, no," said Makepeace, looking a little confused, "as a matter of fact we put it in new when the house was renovated. About the time Tim was born, I suppose. I can't really remember. Never really thought about it, to tell you the truth."

Tim, who was standing hands-in-pockets outside the door, smiled to himself and resumed his journey down the passage. He turned in through the kitchen door.

"Hi Mum," he said. His mother was sampling some white sauce from a pot, using a long wooden spoon. "Did you know we had an antique bog?"

"I beg your pardon, dear?" She didn't look round.

"Nothing. I say, Tamsin's come down, she's finished spraying her trousers on."

His mother smiled. "Oh, you've met. I hope you're going to behave yourself tonight."

"Mother! Would I ever do anything else?"

"Well, yes, as a matter of fact you might," she said. "I'll have a sweet sherry – I assume that's what you came in to ask. Darling, do you think it's wise for you to drink anything before I've done your samples?"

"Of course it's wise," he replied.

He returned to the front room and took his place on the sofa, his mother coming in just behind him.

"Tim," said Tamsin from her perch on the arm of her husband's chair, "your brother has just been trying to tell me that you train witch-doctors."

"Yes, I do, in a manner of speaking," said Tim, taking a Scotch from his father. "Thanks, Dad. Yes, I'm not doing it at the moment, but in Africa we used to give them small-business loans, you know, like the Enterprise Allowance scheme. In fact a couple of local councils here are showing an interest."

Tamsin looked at him warily. "Are you serious?"

"Deadly serious. We had one bloke who used to put curses on people so that their skins turned inside out. We got him to stop and gave him a grant to clean up the camp's water supply. And what do you do?" He put his glass to his lips and drank. She looked back, a little confused.

"I – er, I'm an actress," she said.

"And a damned good one too," rumbled James.

"What sort of acting?"

"Well, I've done a couple of commercials," she said cautiously.

"I thought I'd seen you before somewhere," said Tim, nodding sagely. "That deodorant ad, isn't it?"

"No," she said seriously.

"Oh, I do beg your pardon."

"I've done tampons, though."

"Oh, really?" he smiled. "That must be an, er, sanitary experience."

"Tim, do shut up and drink your Scotch. If you must drink Scotch before the meal instead of after it," said Makepeace.

"Yes Dad," said Tim. His father was frowning, but he thought he could see a smile flickering around the corners of his mother's mouth.

"For the money," said Tamsin, "I really didn't mind. And it kept me in tampons for six months."

"Do you enjoy that sort of work, Tamsin?" asked his father politely. "It sounds rather glamorous."

"Oh, it isn't glamorous," she said, flicking a strand of hair away from her cheek. "It's work. But it can be fun. It depends what you're doing, really."

"Sometimes people like Tamsin spend hours standing in the rain in ploughed fields and that sort of thing," said Liz. "She was telling me about it."

Tim produced a rather crushed packet of duty-free and offered it to his father, who took one with a grunt of thanks, and to Tamsin.

"No thanks. I don't smoke," she said, chin tilted upwards.

"Quite right," said James. "Revolting habit. Hasn't Mum been telling you two about the dangers of passive smoking?"

"Yes, but I prefer active smoking myself," said Tim, lighting up. "Still got the De Luxe Filters account, James?"

"We lost it to another agency," said James, a little coldly.

"I nearly forgot," said Makepeace quickly. "Darling, do you remember that piece you liked so much when we heard it on the car radio, coming back from Wales?"

"Oh, the Schumann? Yes, what about it?"

"I found the record in Oxford today." He stood up and went over to the sideboard, taking the record out from underneath and putting it onto the turntable of the old stereo. "I thought you'd like it."

"Oh, how nice," and she smiled with genuine pleasure as he flicked the switch to turn on the turntable and the old stereo came to life. Carefully he lowered the needle on to the second movement.

"It's crackling a bit," said James.

"Well, it's a secondhand record," said Makepeace, turning round. "Blackwell's don't seem to have records any more, it's all cassettes and these compact disc things. Quite extraordinary."

"No-one really buys records anymore, do they, Jimbo?" asked Tamsin, turning to her husband. "I haven't since I was about 15."

"There's no point anymore."

Schumann interrupted with the lyrical opening to the second movement of his Rhenish Symphony. There was silence for a moment. Makepeace sat down.

"Oh, that's delightful," said his wife.

"Isn't it?" replied Tim, "I'll record that onto a cassette and take it back overseas with me."

"Are you definitely going back overseas, Tim?" asked his brother.

"Eh? Oh, I should think so. I've got to go to Geneva at the end of next week, probably, and get my marching orders."

"Have they said where?"

"Not for certain but there's a rumour of Somalia," replied Tim.

"That sounds a bit awful," said James.

"I can't quite visualise where it is," said Tamsin.

"They're terribly proud people," said Makepeace. "I remember your mother's uncle, just before the war..."

"It's in Africa," said Tim.

"Dreadful dysentry he had..."

"I know *that*."

"You could get a proper job, in London..."

"The pointy bit that sticks out on the right..."

"Mum, Tamsin thinks I can..."

"It *is* a proper..."

"Does she really?"

"Near Ethiopia then?"

"Tim's got a diplomatic passport, you know."

"I suppose you get the shits quite a lot, Tim?"

"Jimbo, don't be disgusting."

"I'd like to do adverts too.."

"Was that the one with two native..."

"No, that was Daddy's uncle..."

"I find flat Pepsi does the trick..."

"That's right, it was. Everyone thought it was awful, but he said they all did it."

"Tam got the runs in Minorca..."

"Jimbo, do belt up."

"Can you eat spinach souffle, Tamsin?"

"It's not cooked with any fats, is it? I mean, butter or anything?"

"You're Vegan, aren't you? Where *is* Vega?"

"That second movement is divine."
"They don't eat meat on Vega, then?"
"No, no, vegetable oil."
"Lovely leather jeans they make on Vega."
"Let's have dinner," said his mother.

        * * *   * * *   * * *

AT THAT time of year, a clear night is a cold night, even when it has been warm all day. Now a crisp, clean breeze blew off the fields and in through the open side of Tim's bedroom window. The curtain, billowed towards him as he sat at the desk. It irritated him and he drew it back. It was chilly, and he felt the old-fashioned iron radiator below the window to see if it was on; it was. He pulled a chair that was against it an inch or two away from the metal to prevent it from being damaged by the heat, and then looked again at the pile of forms on the table in front of him. They did not inspire him; he could write his report tomorrow, he decided.

The table was lit only by a small anglepoise on the dresser beside it; there was no other light on in the room, and Tim could clearly see the stars in the sky outside. He thought he could see the Milky Way. The stars seemed every bit as bright as they did in lower latitudes. The window faced west, and, in the distance, he could see a faint glow on the horizon that he knew was Stratford-upon-Avon.

He lit a cigarette, took a few puffs and then blew a lungful of thick smoke out of the window, where it billowed solidly in the cold night air. He glanced at his watch; it was after midnight. He supposed he should sleep, but thought better of it and reached for a small bottle of duty-free Bell's on the dresser; he poured a small amount into the bottom of a glass, added a little water from the jug, swilled it about and then sniffed it appreciatively.

There was a knock on the door. It was a soft, diffident knock. He wondered who would knock like that. His mother would rap sharply. His father would probably call him. James would walk straight in although he might head-butt the door first out of politeness. "Come in," he called in a low voice, so as not to wake the household, although in truth the Victorian walls would have stopped a tornado.

The door opened and Tamsin came in. She stopped just inside the doorway and pushed the door closed, very softly, and stood on the threshold.

"Hallo," she said. "I hope I'm not disturbing you. Jimbo says that you're an insomniac and usually stay up half the night."

"I used to, yes," said Tim. He looked round, arm on back of chair.

"I – well, I just thought I'd pop in and say goodnight." She smiled uncertainly. "We're leaving quite early in the morning, you know. Jim wants to try and reach Scotland before dark."

"Oh, yes. Yes, of course."

Neither said anything for a few seconds, and then Tim volunteered:

"Fancy a nightcap?"

"Yeah. Go on then," she said. "Shall I use your toothmug?" She indicated an upturned glass on the edge of the sink.

"Yes, do."

She brought it over, and sat on the windowsill, feet dangling. He pushed the chair towards her.

"Footrest."

"Ta. This radiator's lovely and warm."

"Hmm." He poured her a third of the tumbler of Scotch and picked up the water-jug. He raised his eyebrows.

"No. I'll have it straight."

"Quite right. Thou shalt not commit adultery," said Tim. "I once poured Pepsi into my Scotch when I was visiting a missionary camp. The Scots priest damn near killed me."

"Quite right too. Cheers."

"Good health. Congratulations on the marriage."

"Do you mean that?" She looked down from her perch on the windowsill. He noticed that her eyes were large, grey and rather liquid.

"Oddly enough, I do," he replied.

"I wanted to tell you something," she said, putting her glass down. "These leather jeans."

"Mmm, yes," said Tim, looking at them. "Jimbo bought me them. What would you do, Tim, tell him to take them back?"

He thought for a moment. "No, I don't suppose I would. Sorry, I'm blowing smoke all over you." He reached for the ashtray.

She stretched her hand out towards his and guided it away. "Don't worry. It's Jim who can't stand it, not me. He goes wild when I light up."

He grinned suddenly. "I thought you didn't smoke."

She smiled back. "Not when he's around. Give us a fag, then."

He leaned back as she took the cigarette and lit it. She kicked off a shoe and waggled her toes in the stocking. "Mmm, that's better. You gave us a hard time tonight, you know. Especially me."

"Well, what do you expect?" asked Tim. "Bloody Jim, preaching against smoking and shifting cigs through his ad agency. And what he sticks up his nose is nobody's business."

"Yeah, I do that too," she said. "Be fair, though. That's not like regular smoking. He's just a recreational drug user. We both are."

"There's no such thing," said Tim with a gentleness that surprised him. "Look, the cocaine trade is violent and dirty. You can't boycott South African goods because of apartheid but use cocaine. You can't object to smoking and then use something that threatens your health just as directly. You can't reject meat and then live complacently in a society which is massively wasteful of resources. It's just as bad as the hypocrisy of earlier generations. It's the Perrier paradox. That's why Jim gets up my nose, if you'll forgive the phrase."

"Well, that's not my fault, is it?"

"Nope. But why in God's name do you have to swan off to Amsterdam to get married then come back and tell Mum and Dad about it after the event? It's a bit off, isn't it?"

"No, it isn't. Not really." She tipped a bit of ash off her cigarette and then rolled her cigarette thoughtfully against the glass of the ashtray. "Look, Jim and I aren't terribly serious people. Neither of us are. Sometimes Jim thinks he is. But we're not. At any rate, we'll never be what your parents probably think we should be. Do you see what I mean? God, I'm not expressing myself very well."

"No, I know what you mean," said Tim.

"I want to say something else as well," she went on, her voice a little stronger now. "Which is worse, wearing leather and not eating meat, or doing both? Or, come to that, sticking cocaine up your nose but not smoking cigarettes – or doing both? Do you see what I mean?"

"Yep." He shrugged. "I suppose so. It's just that I can't get away with that sort of compromise. Not doing what I do and seeing what I see."

"Ah. Now I think I understand you." Tamsin leaned over and grasped the bottle. "'Scuse me while I top up my Scotch. It's quite toothsome, really, Bell's, isn't it? Anyway. Back you come from the pure and holy crusade amongst the starving millions and in trots your big bro with his new Porsche and matching bimbo. And..."

"And I explode with self-righteousness like Vesuvius erupting red-hot lava all over Pompeii," said Tim. He grinned.

She was looking directly down at him from the windowsill. "Just see us as ourselves, all right?"

She stretched out her foot and planted it in Tim's stomach. Tim was leaning his chair backwards on two legs and she pushed him so that he nearly fell over. "Get the message?"

"I got it. Mercy, sister," he groaned, hands in the air.

"Good," – and she withdrew her foot, and put her hands together in an attitude of prayer, turning her eyes to the ceiling. "Here endeth the first lesson."

"Amen," said Tim. "Pass the Scotch."

"Gladly. Do you know what Jimbo said just now as he stuck a tube up his nose?"

"Go on."

"He said, 'I didn't know my brother was such a bastard. I'm going to offer him a job in the agency'."

"God. What would happen if I took him up on it?"

Her expression turned more serious. "You'd probably do rather well. His billings are well up. It might even be a good idea for you, Tim. Try another lifestyle for a while."

He shook his head. "No, I wouldn't enjoy it and he can find people who understand the business better. Tell me something, Tamsin. You had Liz staying with you for how long? Three or four days?"

"Mmm, 'bout that."

"You haven't been letting her at the cocaine, have you?"

She shook her head at once. "No. Even we have enough common sense not to do that, Tim."

He nodded. "Good stuff. Are you serious about this drama school business?"

Once again she shook her head. "No, Tim. She might get in, and I wanted to encourage her because I think she should try if she wants to. But I don't think it's the best thing for her. She should try and go to art school."

He raised his eyebrows. "Art school? Why?"

"Because she does quite extraordinary watercolours," said Tamsin. "But you must know that."

"No, I didn't," replied Tim, surprised. "She always did quite nice sketches, mind you."

"Well, I think she's quite original. She's been doing these pictures of scrapheaps."

"What?"

"Scrapheaps. It *sounds* stupid, doesn't it?"

"Not necessarily," said Tim slowly. "Is she going to be here a few days?"

"So far as I know. Why don't you ask her that?"

"Yes, I will. Tomorrow."

"Good." She swallowed what was left in her glass, stubbed out her cigarette, stretched, and stood up. "Will you come down and see us before you go away?"

"If my brother lets me."

She laughed.

"He'll let you. Now I'd better get back or he'll start getting paranoid about what I'm doing with you."

She leaned down and put her arms around his shoulders. Her long hair trailed in his face as she pressed her cheek against his.

"See you in a few days, then. Goodnight, Tim."

He watched the door as it clicked softly shut.

A moment later the curtains flickered as the wind, a little stronger now, stirred the clouds of cigarette-smoke in the bedroom; and somehow the cold air wasn't refreshing now, but bleak.

* * *   * * *   * * *

CHRISTINE Makepeace leaned against the doorframe of her husband's study, arms crossed.

"Is that really what you want to do?" she asked him. He was seated at his desk in front of the window.

"Yes, I'm afraid so." He had been staring out of the window, but now he turned and looked at her. "It's quite clear, darling. If you're really not in any doubt as to what it was."

"I'm in no doubt," she replied. "What I question is what you propose to do about it. I would far rather go and see James in London when he gets back from Scotland, and explain to him how we feel about it."

"No. I'm not having that in my house," said Makepeace. He turned back to face the window.

"Well, then, go on." She shrugged.

There was a moment's silence.

"Either way, church is in half an hour," she said, more gently.

He nodded without turning round.

"Yes, all right, dear. I'll be ready."

Any moment now, the bells would start ringing for morning service, he realised. He looked through the glass at the bright orange leaves of the oaks that bordered the garden, standing out against the pale clear sky; a few hundred yards away the blunt square tower of the Norman church rose grey against blue.

He took from his drawer a writing-pad. Opening it, he flipped over the blotting-paper at the front; then he took a pen from the drawer. He unscrewed the top of a bottle of black Stevens ink and then took the upper body off the pen, an old grey one that he had had for many years. The plastic bladder inside was empty. He was about to dip the nib in the ink when it occurred to him that the plastic might be split or rotten. He screwed the body back on and flicked a lever out on its side. When the nib was in the ink he pushed it slowly back into position. The pen made a greedy, sucking sound. He buffed off the top of the nib with a piece of blotting-paper and wrote some gibberish on the margin of the *Sunday Times*. The *Times*, being newsprint, absorbed the ink and he watched it spread with irritation. He repeated the exercise on a piece of proper writing-paper, and gave a grunt of satisfaction as he felt the nib glide smoothly across the surface.

Next he pulled the writing-pad towards him, wrote out the addresses and the date and then, in slow, regular hand that was almost copperplate, he began.

Dear James,

It was nice to see you and Tamsin here yesterday, and I hope that your journey to Scotland was satisfactory.

Unfortunately, while clearing your room this morning, your mother found traces of a white powder that she identifies as cocaine. I am informed that this is what is sometimes called a 'recreational drug', inducing a feeling of well-being.

Frankly I cannot accept that there is any such thing as a 'recreational drug', particularly one which I understand may in some cases cause cardiovascular troubles that can lead to death. I am aware that attitudes to such matters may vary from generation to generation, but nonetheless I feel it would be better if you and Tamsin did not come here for the time being.

Regarding Elizabeth, she is of course nearly 19 now and may do as she wishes, but I would be obliged if you did not encourage her to visit you.

I regret this decision and am sorry that it should be necessary. With best wishes,
Your Father.

Makepeace studied the letter for a moment, blotted it, and pushed the top onto the pen, which he put in the drawer. Then he folded the letter and put it into a white envelope, which he sealed. He put it into his inside pocket. Then he sat for a minute, stock-still, as the church bells began to ring.

The past may be summoned by bells, or by any other commonplace. But Makepeace did not understand why the bells should have reminded him, today, of a long-dead afternoon, when they had rung outside his study window a thousand times and brought to mind nothing in particular. Then he thought of the sky. It was that shade of blueness, common in autumn but not in summer, that recalled for him an afternoon when a July light had caught the sky in such a way instead of refracting it in the summer haze. Perhaps it had rained that morning, but the grass felt dry enough as he walked across it to take up his position, dressed in cricket whites, head bowed to the grass where daisies sometimes grew or, more often, were crushed beneath the iron roller that the groundsmen sometimes brought that way.

Certainly it must have rained at some stage that month, for the grass was an almost violent emerald. Between grass and sky was a line of bucolic oaks, thick leaves billowing upwards into the gentle warmth of the summer's afternoon. Beneath the trees stood Hood's decrepit little car, the tracks made by its narrow tyres stretching back from the whitewashed pavilion by which it stood, towards the far-off quadrangle with its red-brick Victorian school buildings. White-clad boys sprawled in front of the pavilion; the next two in to bat sat, padded-up, on the running-board of the car. One of them plucked idly at the dull spokes of the spare wheel so that they gave a faint ping.

Makepeace turned and stood facing the batsman. On the whole, he did not mind fielding, provided the ball did not come his way; if it didn't, the only disturbance would be the change of overs which had just occurred. He was happy that it had, having just dropped a catch because he had been facing into the sun; now he had a slightly better chance. Not that facing the sun had protected him from Hood's tongue-lashing when he had dropped the catch. When he had pleaded the sun in mitigation he had drawn from Hood the stinging comment that as the sun did not appear to have affected anyone else's catching, and what did he want, for the game to be played in winter, above the Arctic Circle? This had drawn chuckles from the others, who had made squinting gestures at him whenever Hood, who was also his housemaster, wasn't looking.

He could see Hamlyn, the bowler, walking back from the crease flexing his muscles and stretching his arms. He watched the batsman as Hamlyn ran back towards the crease in what always seemed to Makepeace to be an affected manner before the ball was loosed off towards his opponent.

There was a hard, summery sound, somewhere between a click and a thud, of leather upon willow and the ball sailed into the sky, bright red against the blue. It took Makepeace a few seconds to appreciate that it was coming in his direction and that he really ought to try and catch it. He ran forward a few yards and stretched his hands towards the descending orb, paralysed with fear lest it break his fingers. As a result, it slipped through them, and rolled onto the ground.

There were ironic cheers.

"How could you, Dwarf?"

"Silly little man!"

Makepeace threw the ball back to the bowler underarm and it rolled slowly back along the ground.

"I say, can't you chuck that pill a bit harder?" called Hamlyn.

Makepeace did not reply.

"Dwarf does it again," said someone.

"Shut up," said Hood. "Makepeace Minor, get off. Someone from the batting side can replace you."

Makepeace showed no obvious reaction as he walked off the pitch.

"Where are you going?"

Unsure if the question was meant for him, he half-turned.

"Answer me when I speak to you. Where do you think you're going?"

"To the changing-rooms, sir."

"I told you to get off," said Hood coldly, hands behind his back. "I never said that you could go. Go into the pavilion and wait there until the bell."

"Yes, sir."

He turned and made for the pavilion. On the pitch, the game resumed, a bowled-out batsman having taken Makepeace's place. The entrance to the little whitewashed pavilion was behind the car. The entrance was blocked by two other fourteen-year-olds, one of them plump and spotty, the other tall and athletic.

"Where do you think you're going, Dwarf?"

"Into the pavilion."

"You can't go into the pavilion."

"Why not?"

"'Cos I say so," said the tall, athletic one.

"'Cos we say so," said the fat spotty one.

"Mr. Hood said to go into the pav."

"Tough luck. No dwarves in the pav," said the tall one.

Makepeace put his head down and tried to push his way into the little white pavilion. Instantly they had him on the grass and were pinning him down, the fat one sitting on his chest and the tall one on his legs. The latter took his wrists and started to twist them.

"What are you doing to my little brother?" came a voice from above. It was a deep, amused voice. The three looked up to see Makepeace Major standing above them, dressed in flannels and carrying a book under his arm. His straw boater was in his hand. He was a giant to them; eighteen years old, and tall anyway, over six feet.

"Sorry, Makepeace Major. He dropped a catch," said the tall one respectfully.

"Oh, did he. Well nonetheless, try not to kill him, would you?" said Major. "Get up, Paul. Why are your whites in such a mess? They're not white, they're green."

"I've just been on the grass," said Paul sullenly.

"Well, you shouldn't go round dropping catches, should you, you silly little man?" He turned and strode off.

The fat one aimed a kick at Paul's shins.

Later he stood in Hood's study. The sun was going down; it would not be dark for quite a while, though, as it was only half-past seven. The sun slanted in through the windows and cast a yellow pool on the walls behind him. Hood himself was sitting at his desk, fiddling with his pipe. The floor of the study was of bare boards, but there was a square carpet immediately in front of the housemaster's desk. Paul was, quite literally, on the carpet.

Hood himself, a thickset man with lowering, bushy eyebrows that nearly joined in the middle, sat beneath a college oar; below the oar was a group photograph of youths in cricket whites, Hood at the front with the arms of a cable knit sweater tied loosely round his neck. For some reason Paul kept seeing the backs of Hood's hands as they curled around his pipe; they were quite impossibly hairy.

"Hmm."

The housemaster started to make a series of sucking noises. There was a slight bubbling sound and the tobacco in the pipe started to take. Wisps of smoke flew up from the bowl like Indian signals, in time with the housemaster's sucking. They drifted over to Paul, who found the smell quite pleasant, but was trying not to sneeze. There was silence in the room, apart from the sucking and blowing; but outside, as if from a great distance through the thick walls, came the sounds of boys shouting at each other and the catcalls and thunks from an impromptu cricket match in the quad below.

Hood leaned back and looked at his pupil.

"It is as well that school breaks up tomorrow," he said coldly. "I have no idea what to do with you."

Paul said nothing.

"I still have had no satisfactory explanation as to why your clothes were stained bright green when the bell rang before supper."

Still Paul kept his counsel.

"Dammit, boy, you looked like a creation of Mr. H. G. Wells. Why?"

"I fell over, sir."

"How can you fall onto the grass when you're in the pavilion?"

"I wasn't in the Pav., sir."

"Why not?"

Paul didn't answer this, either.

"Well, did I tell you to go into the pavilion or didn't I?"

"You did, sir."

"Then why weren't you in it?"

Once again, he said nothing.

"Good God, boy, I asked you a question."

The phrase 'deafening silence' is not an idle one. To Paul it seemed like two great walls in the haunted tomb of a Pharaoh that one might see in a horror film, the walls moving slowly in to crush you, your lungs bursting because you did not dare breathe.

"I am wondering whether or not to beat the answer out of you," said Hood. "I should do. When you have just let the side down by missing a perfectly easy catch, you should go in and face the people you have just let down. Life is a team effort. That is what we try to teach you here."

He looked at Paul.

"I am not going to beat you because I have already done so three times this term and it does not appear to have made one iota of difference."

He sat up and took a sheet of paper from the side of his desk. Then a pot of ink appeared, and a pen. Paul stood in silence, not watching the master; instead he was looking out of the window, watching the others run across the quad, catching and laughing. The sounds of their game were far away. All he could hear clearly was the scratching of the housemaster's pen upon the thick white paper.

It took Hood some minutes to write the letter. Finally he addressed the envelope and left the two together on his desk. Then he looked up.

"I have written a letter to your father that I shall ask Makepeace Major to deliver," he said. "In it I am asking your father to impress upon you the fact that the school was not built for your benefit."

If it occurred to Paul to ask for whose benefit it had, in fact, been constructed, he kept his peace.

"When you return in September I hope your attitude will have changed. If it has not, your continued presence in the school must be called into question. Get out of my study."

Paul turned and left the room. He went into prep, aware of the others making squinting gestures at him as he walked to his desk.

Later that night he lay on his back in his iron bed. Everyone appeared to be asleep, only the occasional sound of footsteps in the corridor outside betraying the fact that the prefects were still around. Two beds away, someone's alarm clock ticked loudly. It was a sound he had never been able to stand, but attempts to get its owner to cover it or put it in his bedside cabinet had always ended in conflict. There was no need for an alarm clock anyway; anyone left in bed when the prefects went through the dormitory in the morning would be swiftly roused, often having his bed upended.

In the distance, Paul heard the clock in the tower above the chapel chime eleven.

He turned over. He still could not sleep, but the assorted snores from the other thirty beds in the room indicated that he was alone in this.

He moved his fingers round under the counterpane so that they were between the sheets and the mattress, on the side of the bed; and pulled the sheets up so that he could slip his legs quietly down onto the floor. He found his slippers and dressing gown and put them on;

then he walked to the door of the dormitory, moving now and then from left to right to avoid the creaky floorboards he knew were there. The oak door with its iron fittings opened slowly, but mercifully without a squeak or a groan. He juggled his body through the narrow gap that was all he dared leave between door and jamb, lest the electric light from the corridor flood the dormitory and wake somebody. Then he was away, moving silently down narrow corridors that bent to left and right, lined with wooden doors behind which prefects passed the last hour or so of their evening; distant murmurs reached him of cricket and holidays.

"Hey! Where on earth do you think you're going?"

He recognised the voice as that of one of the prefects and neither stopped nor looked back. Instead, he ran on down the corridor and then turned right down a wide, shallow flight of worn stone stairs until he reached a corridor that was wider than the others, and ran around the inner quadrangle of the building. Sprinting now, he passed an endless row of gothic windows to his left; to his right, the doors to the staff room and the masters' studies, punctuated by noticeboards from which hung small pieces of paper, mostly forgotten, that swayed in the rush of air as he passed by: a batting order, a summons for the members of a school society to come to a meeting, its ink run where raindrops had fallen on it as its author brought it across the quad. Ahead of him was the entrance to the chapel, the staircase dark and welcoming.

He did not know whether his pursuer had followed him this far, but he leaped up the stairs nonetheless; once again, they were shallow and wide, the centres of the steps worn an inch or so below the sides and awaiting repair. The staircase turned a corner and he found himself in the darkness of the chapel.

Here he paused, listening for the sound of steps below him. Once he heard a creak, but could not be sure. He leaned against the cold stone of the Chapel wall, closed his eyes and let a flood of breath from his lungs.

Although the lamps in here had long been shut off for the night, it was far from pitch-black. There was a moon, and the silver-yellow light allowed Paul to distinguish the individual pews in front of him and the shadowy altar fitments, as well as the fake-mediaeval Victorian beams high above. Between pews and altar and offset to the right was the lectern on which the Bible was laid for the reading of the lesson. The Bible sat upon a brass eagle with outstretched wings, assiduously polished by Padre's acolytes so that it glinted dully in the moonlight. Paul could have sworn he saw a glint in its eye. Collecting his thoughts, he instinctively genuflected towards the altar and then cast his gaze around him while he considered his position.

The sound of shoes upon the main staircase came to him slowly; their owner was not in a hurry, knowing full well that there was no way out of the Chapel that avoided the staircase. But did that person know for sure that he was here?

At the back of the chapel was a door which, Paul knew, almost certainly led into the bell-tower. He tried the black-painted iron handle and it operated smoothly, lifting the latch with a barely audible click. Once again, he slipped through the door, opening it as little as possible. He pulled it to, and found himself climbing a stone spiral staircase.

There was little light here. What there was, came from the windows that were cut into the wall after every complete revolution so that every now and then there was a section which was completely dark. Once his foot failed to find the edge of a step, simply touching it with the toe; he slipped, and barked his knee, but quickly pulled himself up. Before long he was in the loft itself. Beside him were the bell-pulls, gyrating slowly in the breeze that came through the slats from the outside world. Just above him, the bells themselves could be seen in faint outline, the rims shining in the moonlight; little more was visible. It was cooler than he would have expected, and he gave a slight shiver as he bent towards the slats and looked out.

He could just see the sky. The moon sat in a patch of clear space, but clouds had built up around it now and pressed towards it, their edges lit with a strange glow so that their contours were thrown into relief like an alien coast. They moved steadily in the wind. Below, the school buildings cast shadows across the tarmac as if it were day, while the countryside beyond was clearly visible, the fields a weird aquamarine, the trees black against the ground.

Paul sat down on the chill flagstones and put his head in his hands. He heard the sound of heels on stone far below him and knew before he heard the door open in the chapel that he was going to be found. The metallic clicks of the prefect climbing the stairs reached him as if through a veil, unconnected, irrelevant, part of the same world as the clouds that sailed across the moon; he could do nothing about either.

"Get up, you snivelling little swine."

He uncovered his face and stood, but he had not been crying. The eighteen-year-old gripped his upper arm and propelled him down the stairs; he retraced his route through the chapel and down the main staircase to the corridor that ran around the quad, every small detail clear now, the grey stone pillars in the corridor, the maroon tiles on the floor, the bare light bulb and the harsh shadow cast by an open door; then up a smaller staircase, of wood this time, with metal strips inlaid on the steps to prevent wear, strips which cut into the soft soles of his slippers. Then a bare corridor where the floorboards squeaked as they made their wordless way to the study.

The study was small and cramped and alive with boots and trunks and coffee-mugs. Paul thought he caught the whiff of cigarette-smoke as he was pushed into the room. His brother, seated on his wooden chair with its leather seat, was reading *Esquire*. He glanced up briefly as the two of them entered the room.

"Where did you find him?"

"In the bell-tower."

"How extraordinary."

Makepeace Major returned to his perusal of the magazine; Paul stood still as the prefect eased himself into his own chair.

"What were you doing in the tower?"

"Nothing."

"That's no sort of answer, is it? What were you doing out of your dormitory after lights-out?"

"I went out for air."

"Why? Had some wicked ogre siphoned all the air out of the dormitory, I wonder?"

"No."

"Then why did you need to go outside for air?"

"I couldn't sleep."

"Everyone else seems to be able to."

Paul said nothing.

"No-one else seems to feel the need to wander around after lights-out, do they?"

Still Paul had nothing to add. He stood rigidly on the floorboards, his hands by his side.

"This is dumb insolence," said the prefect. He tipped his chair back on its rear legs. He turned to Makepeace Major, who was calmly reading his magazine.

"Out after lights-out, one," he said. "In the bell-tower, two. No-one's supposed to go up there. And three, dumb insolence. What do you think I should do with him, Makkers?"

"Oh, give him a whacking," said Makepeace Major, without looking up.

"I think five would be jolly good, don't you?"

"Eh?" Makepeace Major swivelled round in his seat. "Well, actually I think three would do it, one for each crime. Have you got your cane?"

"No, dammit, I broke it on Jones the other day," said the other, in a tone that conveyed that this was exactly what he had done. "May I borrow yours?"

"Yes, of course," replied Makepeace Major, and returned his attention to the magazine.

"Thanks." His roommate leaned over to the corner near Major's desk and extracted the thin, fairly short cane from behind the radiator. He stood up, turned his chair around and indicated the back of it to Paul. "Lean over this and take your trousers down, Makepeace."

Paul didn't move.

"Well, get on with it," said the prefect impatiently.

"Why?" asked Paul.

"What on earth do you mean, why?"

"I mean, what do you want from me? All of you?"

Makepeace Major looked up. His younger brother's voice wasn't angry, or fearful; if anything it was puzzled. Both the older boys looked at Paul, vexed.

"Makepeace, if you don't get those pants down in five seconds you'll get two extra stripes, for cheek," said the prefect.

Paul looked at him. He seemed to be slowly shaking his head back and forth, more in confusion than anything else.

"Oh, for Heaven's sake," said Makepeace Major. He stood, jerked his brother onto the back of the chair and pulled the pants down. The cord around the waist stuck slightly over the hips before the pyjama-bottoms collapsed around Paul's ankles in a little heap of linen. The cane came down one, two, three times. It stung badly, but did not break the flesh.

"That'll do," said Makepeace as his roommate brought the cane up for a fourth blow. "He's in trouble when he gets home anyway. Paul, go to bed."

So Paul had gone to bed.

The following afternoon he was standing on a platform in a station somewhere in the West Country. Once again the day was fine; clouds had crossed the sun a little earlier but had drifted away. It was mid-afternoon. Once or twice it crossed his mind to wonder what was awaiting him when his father saw Hood's letter, but he didn't think about it that hard; instead, the question dissolved into a sort of greyness in which it joined his painful, stinging thigh. He looked blankly at the town across the tracks, outside the station. Beyond the station was a road; beyond the road were a few small warehouses and a pub with advertising hoardings extolling the virtues of Oxo, Fry's Chocolate and someone's summer sale. Behind him stood a pile of brass-bound blue tin trunks, initials stencilled across their tops, their spring-loaded clips closed and leather straps lashed around them for good measure; assorted bits of bric-a-brac were piled atop them – a straw hat, a book, a tennis racquet. Makepeace Major was a few yards away. He was reading an orange-and-white Penguin paperback; every now and then he would tire of this and reach into his pocket for a cricket ball, nearly forgotten that morning and stuffed hastily into the pocket of his grey flannels. He would toss this around for a few minutes and then stuff it back into the pocket; it stuck out slightly, red leather contrasting with grey cloth. Once again he would concentrate for a minute or so on his paperback, before closing it with a dull thump, looking up and down the line and saying:

"Gosh, it would be today that it's late. What a bore!" When this drew no reply from his younger brother he opened the cream-and-brown door of the booking office and strode over to the timetable. It merely confirmed what he knew already so he strode out again and caught up with a porter.

"I say, what's happened to the 4.30 to Southcombe?"

"I think it'll be here at four-thirty, sir," said the porter.

"Isn't it four-thirty yet? It must be!" The porter took his watch from his waistcoat pocket and looked at it studiously for a minute before replying:

"One minute to go, sir!" At which point Paul, a few yards away, realised that he could see a plume of smoke a mile away down the line. It approached slowly, the plume drifting white and grey in the still air, wheezes, hisses and whistles slowly separating themselves from the clatter of the traffic in the road outside. Then the round, clock-like smokebox of the little tank-engine crawled into view and the green blocks of the tank itself could be seen, and the grimy face of the capped driver who leaned out of the window. Finally, the smell of sulphur hit them and the short train drew up; barely had it stopped before the porter opened the doors and lifted their luggage into the compartment, heaving the cases into the luggage racks where their hard corners stuck down through the netting. He hastened to the guard's van with the trunks.

"Good, now we'll be home for dinner. Paul, do cheer up. Try and look as if you're going home for the holidays, not trooping into a Latin lesson."

The door thunked shut behind them and the latch clicked into place. The carriage had a smoky, sleepy atmosphere, and the train did not run fast; it pulled away from the station with a peasant-like caution and made its way slowly upwards towards the moors that lay inland, crossing a river here, a road there. Once it turned tightly and crossed a river bridge, then turned again and ran beside the riverside road through a forest that broke the afternoon sunlight and spattered it on the ground; beside them, for a minute, ran a swallow-tailed charabanc full of cheerful men in flannels and open-necked white shirts whose collars spread over their lapels like counterpanes. They were mostly smiling and there was a crate of beer in the aisle. Then the road bent away and here and there a lump of granite would break the surface of the earth in the wood and then the trees disappeared, and there was a dry stone wall between them and a field of grass so green that it startled the eye, while away beyond it hills rose, covered with stones and ferns and strange, rocky outcrops that erupted mid-grey against a thickly blue afternoon sky.

"God, this place is boring," said Makepeace Major, glancing up from his paperback.

Paul was looking out of the window, his cheek pressed against the glass, the tired leather strap of the window blind dangling in his hair. He could see the faint outline of the engine as it rounded a bend, encased in smoke; then the breeze whipped the veil away, and he could see the stone wall beside the railway line end, and the wooden platform begin, with its small booking hall and waiting room with its tattered posters.

The train ground to a halt, brakes squealing, and hissed out steam. Paul flung open the door, dropped his suitcases onto the platform and ran towards the guard's van.

Makepeace Major exited in a more dignified fashion.

"I say," he called towards the porter, "would you give us a hand with these cases?"

The porter brought a luggage-cart. Together they emerged from the station; in the lane outside stood a green Crossley.

"Ah, Williams," intoned Makepeace Major to his father's driver and handyman, who had advanced to meet him. "Splendid to see you."

"And you, I'm sure, Master. Did you have a good journey?"

"Not bad, thank you. Paul, give Williams a hand with the luggage, will you?"

"Thank you, Master Paul, I can manage." Williams, thin and fifty, set about strapping the luggage to the rack.

The hills rose around them as the car droned through the lanes, although the high hedges meant that they could see little. Much of the road was of gravel, spraying upwards into the underside of the car's mudguard and running boards. It was warm, and Williams gripped the T-handle and pushed the windscreen open a few inches so that a cooling breeze came into the car; with it came the scents of wildflowers and grass and occasionally cowpats. Sweeping over the brow of a low hill, they saw the house set into the back of a wooded slope ahead, its Elizabethan granite indistinguishable from that of the rocks that littered the fields around them. They passed through the village a mile or so before the house, passing the church, half-hidden by trees, as was the vicarage towards which Paul glanced for a minute to see if there was any sign of life. There was none.

"I'll give this letter to Father directly," said Makepeace Major suddenly.

"Yes, of course," said Paul. He looked at his older brother, but the latter was not looking at him. For a moment he wondered if Makepeace Major was being officious. He wasn't sure. Perhaps his brother thought Paul would have preferred it if the letter could wait but if he did, he was wrong.

He thought little of the matter as he stood in his bedroom, hands in pockets, staring out of the window. Perhaps his father would beat him, but he didn't think so. At Easter, arraigned for some transgression, he had been curtly told that as he was too old to be beaten, he would lose his pocket-money instead. He hoped that his father would not punish him by forbidding him to visit the vicarage instead. It worried him, but there was little he could do about it. Suddenly he was conscious that he had been far more frightened at Easter. He wondered why.

There was a brief knock on the door.

"Come," he called softly. The latch was pulled up with a piece of leather that ran through a hole in the door, which somewhat predated doorknobs. He heard it click now and the maid entered. He had already seen her in the hall.

"Begging your pardon, Master Paul, but your father would like to see you in his study before supper."

"Thank you."

As the door closed he went over to the washstand and poured cold, clean water from the earthenware jug. He splashed his face and wrists. Then he looked out of the window a last time before going downstairs.

A few minutes later he was once more standing on the carpet, this time side-on to a west-facing window so that the evening sun streamed in on him, leaving his father, behind his desk, largely in shadow. His father, tall, broad, fifty and faintly choleric, had Hood's letter open upon his desk.

"The trouble is," his father said loudly, "I can't see what you can do with your life. I really can't see you following your brother into the Army. Even if the regiment would have you, I doubt if you would cope. You would plainly be unable to go to Oxford. That much Hood has made clear. You could not do the work. That means that the colonies are also out of the question, at least in an official capacity." He sighed, and looked out of the window, but the sun was too strong for him and he blinked and turned back towards Paul. "The only solution I can think of at the moment is to find you a position with some commercial concern trading overseas. It does seem a pity after all the opportunities that have been given to you in life, doesn't it?"

There was no obvious reply to this, so Paul did not attempt one.

"Well, doesn't it?"

"I don't know, Father."

"What do you mean, you don't know?"

"I've another two years at least at school, Father."

"Yes, but what are you going to do with them?" His father raised his eyebrows. "More of the same, eh? Mark my words, if you don't pull your socks up I'm going to have to arrange a crammer for you. Go and get ready for dinner."

He sat through dinner half-listening to his brother chattering loudly about the term just passed. His mother, tall and rather bony, said little to Paul other than to tell him to remove his elbows from the table. On the whole he was happy to be left in peace.

"I suppose you will be going over to the vicarage tomorrow, Paul," she said suddenly, halfway through the sweet.

"Well, yes, I expect so."

"He'll spend the whole summer with Christine, stealing birds' eggs or catching minnows or something," said Makepeace Major. He burped.

"Do try not to do that at table, dear," said his mother. She picked up the water-jug and turned to the maid, who had just appeared through the dining-room door. "Ellen, why is this water such a disgusting colour? It looks as if someone has crumbled earth in it."

"Beg pardon, Mum, they're having some trouble with peat in the water."

"They certainly are," said Mrs. Makepeace. "Can't you have a word with them, darling?"

"I expect so," said her husband, digging into his stewed apple. "Paul, don't you think it's about time you stopped spending your summers in the woods like a Red Indian?"

"He'll grow up as wild as that wretched girl. And her father gets more and more eccentric every day. Have you seen his motorcycle?"

"Gosh, has the Vicar got a motorcycle?" said Paul's elder brother.

"How spiffing. Perhaps he'll take me on the back."

"Well, I think it's perfectly dreadful," said his mother firmly. "I told the Bishop about it."

"What did he say?" asked her husband.

"He asked what kind it was. Well, I didn't know but I said I thought it was a Matchless and he said 'Oh, jolly good' or something and wandered off."

"Darling, I'm sure the Vicar won't start flirting with nonconformism because he rides a motorcycle," said her husband, his eyes on his stewed apple.

"It seems a trifle undignified for a man of the cloth, though, I must say."

"Yes, it does. Paul, do stop fidgeting, boy."

The next morning Paul wheeled his bicycle out of the shed next to the stables and stood it in the yard. He polished it quickly and cheerfully, and pumped up the tyres. The front one wouldn't harden; he pumped and pumped, and grew hot, for it was a close summer's day. Clouds covered most of the sky, but the sun itself was free and the grey of the clouds was a bright gunmetal fringed with white; here and there triangles of blue broke the pattern.

"Damn it," he muttered, standing back. He put his forefinger to the tip of his tongue and then dabbed the saliva over the valve of the front tyre and, sure enough, a small bubble appeared, grew and broke.

"Damn it," he repeated.

He opened the saddlebag that hung over the rear wheel and found a tube of valve-rubber. Hoping it wasn't rotten, he tore a little off using his thumbnail as a knife and unscrewed the valve, letting the rest of the air out with a satisfying *whoosh*. Then he worked the rubber down over the thin shaft of metal at the base of the valve, rolling and unrolling it so that it stayed flat, and screwed the valve back in. It wasn't rotten and this time the tyre stayed hard when he pumped it. The chain looked slack, so he turned the machine over on its saddle and adjusted the screws capping the rear forks until the wheel was straight. Next, a little oil on the chain, and a little more on the brake rods so that they slid smoothly in their channels.

He rode down the lane towards the village. This stretch of road was unmade, and he bounced over the stones in its surface; as he did so, his weight compressed the leather saddle and the vents in it closed, nipping his rear. The high hedges, over his head, were topped with wildflowers that shone in the sunlight against the grey patches of cloud and, every now and then, the long grass on the hedges rustled and parted as some small animal dived for cover.

The first few cottages in the village flashed by, ancient whitewashed walls buttressed out of the lane, grey thatch and tiny windows; up ahead, the war memorial rose from the dust and he spun round it and up to the lych-gate outside the church. The bicycle settled into the grassy bank, rear wheel whirring, as he jumped onto the granite block in the gate, which was meant for coffins, and hauled himself irreverently into the churchyard on the other side. The gate leading to the vicarage was just ahead.

Before he even got there he could hear the sound of music on a gramophone scratching out from between the plane trees that guarded the entrance to the vicarage. Opening the little gate through the hedge, he could see that the front door was open.

He entered cautiously, knowing that the door usually was open in summer, but feeling it wrong to enter the house uninvited. The music seemed quite loud from here; classical, and quite heavy, with a strident theme. It was coming from the second door on the right. This was where the Vicar sometimes worked, but 'study' was the wrong description, somehow, for the chaos one saw within. The Vicar himself liked to call it the 'mess', and this was more appropriate. Books lined the walls but had also taken over the chair and the desk, the low table and the floor; papers were scattered, unidentifiable bits of machinery and tools, watercolours of plants; a jacket or two jostled for space with unfinished sermons, illustrated magazines and inkwells. An atlas lay open on the floor, at the page covering the United States. Christine had asked at breakfast that morning where Minneapolis was and the Vicar, being somewhat at a loss on that point, had seized the volume from the shelf; and, being unable to move all the books on his chair quickly enough, had simply knelt down on the threadbare carpet instead.

The Vicar wasn't there; instead his daughter sat, legs curled, on the floor. Her head was turned away and all he could see was a helmet of smooth red shoulder-length hair.

"Hello, Christine," he said uncertainly.

She swung round and stood up and marched across the room, a large grin, dark blue eyes and a mass of freckles that threatened to join up and turn her speckled face to brown.

"I knew it! I knew you'd come today, I saw the car and you were both sitting in it and wearing your silly wing collars and I met your brother this morning and isn't he a pompous ass! and you've grown and you've had your hair cut and you haven't written me once this term which I think is simply GHASTLY!" she said, and plunged both her strong hands onto his waist and tickled him until he sank to the floor, pleading for mercy. "And I've got a new bicycle and I bet I can go faster than you can now bet you anything you like race you to the river so THERE," And she planted her knee on his stomach,

"Oof," replied Paul. He looked up at the round, smiling, freckly face with its huge eyes and grinned back. "Get your knee off my breakfast or I'll sick it up all over the carpet."

"Oh, Daddy wouldn't notice," she said, and dug her knee deeper into his guts. "I'll let you get up when you tell me what this music is."

"I can't," gasped Paul. "It's stopped." A series of whirrs and clicks emanated from the gramophone on the sideboard.

"Well, that's your fault because you weren't listening," she said. Nonetheless she got up and walked towards the sideboard. He raised himself up on his elbows and wondered why the movement of her rear end below her slim waist interested him; then he decided that it didn't. "It was the fifth symphony of Tchaikovsky," she was saying in her clear, open voice. She lifted the arm off the record and parked it; the huge horn of the gramophone poked over her shoulder and made it look as if she was playing the tuba. "How is school?"

"Dreadful."

"More dreadful than at Easter?"

"Yes, much more."

She took the record off the turntable and slotted it into the brown paper sleeve. It was quite heavy, and fell into the sleeve with a thump; a little shiny shellac could be seen beyond the record sleeve where the paper had begun to split.

"Oh dear. Daddy hates me doing that."

She came back across the room and knelt beside him on the carpet. "Why is it more dreadful?"

"It just is."

"Tell me why."

"How's your school?"

"It wasn't too bad this term," she said, flicking her hair back off her cheek with her fingers. "Really quite jolly, in fact. 'Cept they say I'm going to have to work much harder if I'm going to study medicine."

"I think you're mad, anyway," said Paul. "Women aren't doctors."

"Only because people say they're not, silly."

"Oh. Well, maybe." He thought for a minute.

"What is it about school that's so bad?"

"I can't say. Not really."

"You look so miserable. You did at Easter. And at Christmas. I do so wish you'd tell me."

"You wouldn't understand," he said.

"Of course I'd understand, you great oaf."

He looked at her, and she back. They looked at each other for a minute or two and he studied her face with more interest than he had before, mapping the freckles and the round nose and the big gash of a mouth that wouldn't stay still, and the eyelashes which were reddish-orange.

In the distance, a noise began. It started as a low hum and then grew slowly, catching a rough note; and she scrambled to her feet and ran to the window. He followed, and stood beside her. The road down from the moors could be clearly seen, stretching three or four miles into the distance, and a smudge on the horizon turned into a dust-devil that swirled its way between the high hedges to a point where the road ran straight towards them, and then they could see a black dot leading the devil at a cracking pace. Slowly it formed itself into a man on a motorcycle and grew larger and larger until it vanished behind the trees. She led him out into the drive, pulling him by the hand; and then it came towards them through the gates, a giant headlamp and slim, curved chromium handlebars, the Vicar encased in goggles and a leather helmet whose straps drooped down beyond his jawbones so that he resembled some strange potentate from Mongolia or Tibet.

The Vicar fiddled with the controls and the engine stopped. Propping up his machine, he removed the Tibetan helmet and stood, all six foot four of him, before them.

"Ah, Paul." He gripped the boy's hand warmly. "I heard you were back. I trust you'll be staying to lunch?"

Paul muttered his acceptance.

"Good. I'll telephone your house and tell them. I don't expect lunch will be long. Do come inside. I've just been to see Mrs. Oakes. Splendid lady, Mrs. Oakes." He strode into the house ahead of them. "She will insist on writing these sermons for me on the evils of Bolshevism. If she's not careful I'll use one of them. Mrs. Early! Mrs. Early!" And he disappeared into the recesses of the house to tell the housekeeper that there would be one extra for lunch.

"And how is school?" he asked later as he marched into battle against a pork chop. The Vicar appeared to have no qualms about speaking with his mouth full.

"It's much the same, Reverend," said Paul respectfully.

"He says it's dreadful," said Christine.

"That sounds more likely."

"He won't tell me why."

"I've just spoken to your father on the telephone," said the Vicar. He removed a piece of bone from his mouth. "Hmm. Yes, he rumbled on about what a lazy little bounder you were and how he despairs of your doing anything useful when you finish school, if you ever do."

"I'm not very good at work," volunteered Paul.

"Why not? I'm sure you're brighter than that horrid thick brother of yours," said Christine.

"Don't be rude, darling," her father admonished her. "Just because he used to tease you about your freckles."

"I like your freckles," said Paul.

"I like you," said Christine.

They grinned at each other.

"Why aren't you good at work, Paul?" asked the Vicar. "The question must be answered, you know, or you won't be able to go into the Army and slaughter people with your brother."

"I can't concentrate," said Paul.

"No, people who aren't happy can never concentrate. That's why complete dolts do better at public schools than people like you." The Vicar forked up a huge potato and propelled it into his mouth. "Do they tease you about your size?"

"Daddy," said Christine, shocked.

"Yes," said Paul.

"I'm not surprised," said the Vicar. "There was a boy at my school who had a crooked finger." He pushed his plate aside with a grunt of satisfaction. "They teased him mercilessly about it because they couldn't find anything else. Of course, you know what wild animals do."

"I beg your pardon, sir?" ventured Paul, puzzled.

"They attack any member of the pack that is not identical."

"Oh." Paul thought for a moment. "They do like to encourage team spirit, sir."

"Oh, do they? Is that a good thing, Paul?"

"Well, of course, sir." Paul looked a little more puzzled.

"Why is it a good thing?" asked the Vicar. He looked up at Paul suddenly and raised his bushy eyebrows.

"Well, it just is. I mean... Team spirit's necessary, isn't it, sir?"

"Is it?" The Vicar sat back heavily in his seat, which jerked and groaned as a result. "Paul, a man must defend any statement that he makes, especially when he is defending something that seems to be causing him an awful lot of trouble. Why should team spirit be a good thing?"

"It's a good thing because..." Paul cast around for a moment. "Because if you drop a catch at cricket, the whole team suffers."

"So it loses the match. Oh, custard, splendid. Thank you, Mrs. Early. I understand your father has threatened you with the crammer, Paul."

"Well, yes, as a matter of fact he has, sir," said Paul.

"Good. Then we won't have any more of this team spirit nonsense from you. Why should the team not lose the game, Paul?"

"It doesn't want to, sir."

"If you're good at cricket and popular in the team, no, you don't want to. If you're awful at the game and not in your heart part of the team, you shouldn't care less. Could you care a brass farthing whether or not the team loses at cricket, Paul?"

"If they do, I always get the blame, sir."

"That, Paul," said the Vicar, grasping the spoon before him, "is entirely beside the point. Unless a victory is of direct benefit to all of you. If it is of direct benefit to only a few then it is probably of indirect benefit to only a few as well, unless there is some very concrete reason to the contrary. Otherwise there is no reason for you to play and there is probably some other activity in which you could indulge for the common good."

"Like going to a crammer, Daddy?" asked Christine.

"An excellent place to start. Split the team into its constituent parts and as individuals, they will probably add up to more than they did before. And that, Paul, is why I have just suggested to your father that you be removed to a crammer forthwith; preferably one where you will be treated with some imagination."

"But if I have to leave the school, I'll be letting everyone down," said Paul, alarmed.

"That's what I've just been trying to explain to you," said the Vicar. "You won't."

He sat back in his chair again and closed his eyes. Paul's alarm increased.

"He's going to quote some poetry," said Christine, undiverted from her custard. "He always does that before reciting *Hiawatha* or Genesis or something."

Her father ignored her.

"The worth of a State," he commenced,

> *in the long run, is the worth of the individuals composing it;... A State which dwarfs its men, in order that they may be more docile instruments in its hands* EVEN FOR BENEFICIAL PURPOSES – ("My emphasis, Paul.") ...*Will find that with small men no great thing can really be accomplished; and that the perfection of machinery to which it has sacrificed everything will in the end avail it nothing.*

He opened his eyes again.

"The closing phrases," he intoned, "of Mill's *On Liberty*."

"Let me see," said Paul. "What you are saying, sir, is that we should all do whatever on earth we like, and the devil take the hindmost?"

"No, Mill did *not* say that," said the Vicar. "Read the book, boy. Get stuck into Hobbes and Locke and Rousseau while you're at it. What are you two doing this afternoon?"

"Eh? Oh, Christine thought that we should go down to the river," said Paul, momentarily confused.

"Oh. Good. Yes. Go and play Red Indians," said the Vicar cheerfully. "I must rush down to the Linton's, old George is still not well.

"...Yes, go and play Red Indians. You may not be able to for much longer. The way things are, none of us will."

Repairing to the drive, he transformed himself once more into a Tibetan. They heard the Matchless roar and crackle its way out of the drive; then it pulled away down the lane, and the sound of the exhaust hammered against the high stone banks.

So they went down to the river. It was a mile or two there and they did race, Christine winning after riding over the gravel with a recklessness that Paul dared not emulate. Then they scrambled over the dry-stone wall and half-walked, half-ran to the river, panting for breath when they arrived at its banks. It flowed quickly here, at the base of a deep combe, the other side of which was heavily wooded; the water was some yards wide.

They stepped from stone to stone to the rocks in the middle. In the part near the bank it was shallow and clear, with fine yellow-brown sand on the riverbed; the rocks in midstream were dark and mossy, and the water, nowhere deep, cascaded between rocks across beds of moss. Ahead of them was a wide, shallow pool. Above it, there was the darkness of the wooded bank where the river curved to the left, and in front of the bank the insects caught the light as they played above the water. For several minutes they sat, leaning back-to-back, on the widest rock and then Christine said:

"You're wrong, you know."

"What about?" Paul's eyes were closed; as he breathed out he could feel her breathe in, so that their backs moved against each other like bellows. The rushing of the water filled his ears and he felt as if the world had stopped, pulled up, switched off, cooled down.

"To say that I wouldn't understand."

"Understand what?" He opened his eyes. The white clouds drifted slowly across the blue above.

"About school. About other boys being horrid to you all the time."

"Well, boys *are* horrid," he said. "That's what you don't understand. They're different from girls."

"No, they're not," she said. "No-one is. Not unless they're made to be. That's what *you* don't understand."

"But it's the holidays now," said Paul after a moment, "so it doesn't matter."

"No," she replied. "Only we matter."

So they turned towards each other and put their heads on each other's shoulders. He could feel her breath very softly on his cheek. His eyes closed again. Still the bells continued, becoming more and more insistent until eventually she said:

"Would you rather go to evensong, dear? I can't, I'm on call, but I really don't mind..."

"Eh?" He opened his eyes, and turned. She was standing at the door of his study, coat on and ready. "No, I'll come. I'm sorry, I was miles away."

"Yes, you were, weren't you?"

She smiled, and then closed her own eyes as a herd of elephants hurtled up the stairs.

"I see our son has lost none of his energy to malaria," she said softly.

"Yes. Pity about the other one."

"I still think you're over-reacting."

He shrugged and stood.

Upstairs, Tim stopped in front of one of the doors on the landing and rapped it with his knuckles.

"What," said a sleepy voice from inside the room.

"Are you not getting up, Liz?"

"When I feel like it," his sister replied sleepily.

"Well, can I come in?"

"If you want to."

Tim did. His sister was curled up in bed, nose and eyes just visible above the counterpane. He sat down on the chair opposite, ignoring the items of underwear strewn all over it that made a cushion.

"I've borrowed Dad's car," he announced.

"Bully for you," she replied drowsily.

"And I thought we'd go out for a drink before lunch."

"What's the time?"

"Coming on for eleven. But Mum says we needn't eat before two. They're going to church, anyway, so we can go to the pub. Where are these pictures?"

"What pictures?"

"Tamsin told me about them. She says you're into sketching scrapyards."

"Tamsin told you? I thought you weren't into Tamsin."

"We buried the hatchet."

"I'm amazed she even talked to you."

"Well, some women like to be treated a bit rough," he said, flexing the muscles in one of his arms.

"Oh, shut up," she said, opening her eyes a little wider. "You're such a silly bastard."

He frowned. "You know, if I believed everything I said, then I suppose I would be."

Liz watched him as he stood up and went over to another chair, in the corner, where a large artist's pad was leaning against the chair-back. He took it, sat down on her bed, and started leafing through it.

He came upon what looked, at first, like an array of multi-coloured French loaves leaning against each other at crazy angles. Slowly they formed themselves into the half-crushed shells of cars, bits of bodywork pressed out to form sharp angles, windows distorted in shape and round stubs of axles with brake-drums hanging in the air. The composition had been done in the form of a vertical oval with white space around it. On the next page, set in a similar vignette, a car stood, more or less complete but with its headlamps removed, its bumper askew and its bonnet slightly open; then a stretch of open land scattered with bits of machinery, behind which a mound of wrecks rose towards a grey, gusty skyline.

The last picture arrested him at once. In the centre stood a lonely figure, seen from the back; he was on a pathway that led between hillocks of scrapped vehicles, and on the hillocks grew trees. The hillocks stretched for miles, and the man had a small dog on a lead.

They were all watercolours. They were mostly in pastel shades, but now and then bright flashes of primary colours caught the eye. Each picture had been carelessly leaved back into the pad.

"Where did you do these?"

"Here."

"Not at the yard?"

"They chased me away. I was taking photographs."

"Didn't you ask if you could stay and sketch?"

"I didn't have a chance. The man had a dog and he said he'd turn it loose."

"Did he really say that?"

"No, well. What he said was 'I got guard dogs – you oughta be a bit careful before you come sneakin' round 'ere'."

"Oh." Tim put the pad carefully onto the desk. "Did you try to get permission to sketch?"

"No! As I said, he chased me away."

"Well, perhaps you could take these along and ask them. I'll come with you."

"It doesn't matter," she said. She sat up, stretched and yawned. "They're only pictures of bits of rubbish."

"I disagree. I think they're rather original."

"Well, it's a rather funny thing to do. I'm not surprised I was chased away, really. Are we going out for a drink, then?"

"Yes, when you're dressed and ready." He stood up and opened the door. "I'll go and read the papers while you wash."

He was a little surprised that it didn't take her long. But in less than twenty minutes she came into the living room with a slightly shy air, dressed in jeans and an old coat and a big long scarf that dangled to her waist.

"Where are Mum and Dad?" she asked.

"They've gone to church."

"Oh. Of course."

"Well, don't they usually?"

"Two Sundays out of three. Where's Hobbes?"

"He's quite happy. I've shut him in the kitchen."

"Come on then. I bet you're driving hasn't improved."

"It's still pretty horrible." He locked the front door behind them. "I always had a driver in Central America. I usually did when I was in Africa, but now and then I drove myself."

"Don't you prefer that?"

"No. I like to sleep or look at the scenery, and sometimes my driver popped out and did my shopping."

"How very feudal," she said, as the car drew away. "Having a driver."

"Well, not really. I'd be lost without him."

They left the village. After the clear night, it was a much colder day, but the world was clean and bright, and Tim loved it. He handled the old car with care, concentrating hard to keep on the left-hand side of the road. He enjoyed the damp tarmac that sparkled in the sunlight, and the greenness of the fields.

"Let's go to the White Hart," he said suddenly.

"We'll go right past the scrapyard then," replied Liz.

"Good. We can stop."

"I'm not sure I want to."

"Why not? I'll go up and tell the Rottweilers that you're sketching the scrapyard as a metaphor for post-industrial society."

"Do you think they'd buy it?" asked Liz.

"No, not really," said Tim, taking a sharp right turn. "Rottweilers don't like post-modernism."

"Oh," said his sister. "I think these were giant poodles."

"Ah," said Tim, winding down the window a little. "Maybe they're classically trained then."

They reached the scrapyard after a mile or two on a flat, straight road. The mounds of scrapped cars could be seen rising above the hedge that bordered the yard; on the road, there was a shack or two, and behind them a small house, perhaps forty or fifty years old. Tim pulled up in a lay-by immediately opposite the house, reluctant to park too close lest the crusher come down and claim the old car for the fate it had so far outwitted.

"Well, this is it, then, Liz."

"Can't see any sign of life."

"Nope."

"Shall we push on to the pub then?"

"Let's get out and see if there's anyone around," replied her brother. "We may as well."

He got out of the car, bringing with him the big A3 pad with the watercolours leaved into it, and led her across the road. She followed him reluctantly. As they approached the door of the house there was a sudden barking and a dog came scampering out to meet them; it stopped a few feet short and stood there barking, but wagging its tail. It was a sort of rough collie, black and white and obviously old.

"A collie," whispered Tim. "Try Landseer."

They did not need to knock on the door. Behind the dog a man appeared, middle-aged, with a slight beer-belly but not really fat; his sandy hair was thinning and he wore an old windcheater. His face was open; cautious, but not unfriendly.

"Morning."

"Morning to you," said Tim cheerfully.

"I recognise you," he said to Liz, a bit suspiciously. "Didn't I chase you out of here last week?"

"Yes, you did."

"Hanging around with a camera in there. What do you want?"

"She's an artist," said Tim quickly. "She was doing some sketching from pictures she took in your yard."

The man thought for a minute.

"Funny sort of a place to go sketching. Quiet, boy."

The dog fell silent.

"Well, it is a bit," said Tim, when Liz said nothing.

"Thing is, I guess she should have had permission before she went into that place."

"Could say that," said the man. He viewed Tim as if undecided as to what to do with him.

"Well, we wondered if you'd mind her popping in every now and then. Just to do a bit of drawing and maybe take one or two pictures."

The man regarded Liz for a moment and then said:

"Why would anyone want to make pictures of a scrapyard?"

"Forms and shapes," she said hesitantly. "And colours."

"Oh."

After a few seconds more of silence Tim took up the sketchbook. "Here they are," he said. "Want to have a look?"

"Go on then."

Tim opened the pad for him and the man regarded the first picture with the same suspicion, the second with a flicker of interest, and at the third he frowned.

"Funny sort of subject for an artist," he said thoughtfully. "Mind you, they're better than a lot of the crap you see nowadays. Least there's an idea, like, and you can see what it's of."

"That's right," said Liz, relaxing a bit. "Thing is, everyone knows what a car looks like. But look, it's the little details. Like that headlamp hanging off by a wire, see. And the way that door hangs when it's open. What I wanted to do was do, well, six or seven, and try to get them exhibited."

Suddenly the man laughed. "Well, what the hell. I'll tell you what I'll do. You give me one of 'em when it's done, and I'll let you sketch away in here to your heart's content, if that's what you want to do."

Liz grinned.

"Good stuff. My name's Liz."

"Mine's Derek," he said. "Come in and we'll take a walk round the yard, just to show you what's what. But mind you don't get the dogs set on you. They're not all like this old boy. He wouldn't hurt a fly. The others would, so you always come and see me when you arrive."

"Amen," muttered Tim.

They could hear dogs barking in the distance as they walked into the scrapyard, but they must have been penned up. Slowly they picked their way over a litter of old exhaust pipes and axles; once they saw a differential and two wheels still linked to it by half-shafts, like dumbbells. They walked between two large mounds of car-bodies, then between another two, along a path, like some weird metallic heaven where the hills had changed into an automotive Valhalla; and Tim saw at once where the idea for the painting with the trees had come from.

At the end of the pathway they came to a large hut with a corrugated-iron roof. "This is where we keep bits and pieces," explained Derek, pushing open the door. "We don't do house-clearances but we do take bits and pieces of junk. If someone gives us an old car he quite often shoves something else he wants to get rid of in the boot. Sometimes we don't find it 'till later, when we go through the car to see if there's a jack or a wheel we can sell."

The light in the shed was dim, coming as it did from a window that was dirty and cobwebbed. Jumbled around the room were a hundred and one household objects; an old spade, a garden seat with a cracked leg, and a big old jug of the type that used to be seen in people's bedrooms, usually resting on a washstand. There was the frame of an old bicycle, minus its wheels.

"Couldn't one do something with that?" asked Tim, pointing to it.

"Yes, I think we probably can," replied Derek. "Trouble is, so many bits are missing, I'm waiting till someone brings in another old bike that's been involved in an accident. Then we can strip off the rod brakes and callipers and make a whole bike. Look at this."

There was pride in his voice as he pointed to the bench in the corner. On it was an old gramophone, complete with its heavy, bulbous arm – and a huge horn that rose above his head as he stood before it. "My Mum and Dad used to have one like that."

"Good grief," said Tim. He went to have a look at it. "What are you going to do with it?"

"Clean it up and then we'll try to auction it," said Derek. He shrugged. "Be honest, I don't really know whether it's worth anything. I shan't leave it to chance, though."

"It reminds me of the HMV record label," said Tim. Arms crossed, he turned to Derek and smiled at him. "Do you remember the dog, looking into the horn?"

"His Master's Voice. HMV," said Derek, "Yes, I do. That's the trouble with my job. Like, you keep seeing bits of your own past recycled and you remember how bloody old you're getting!"

He laughed and winked at the old collie, which was standing at the door, forepaws on the threshold, regarding them with interest.

"Tim, come and have a look at this," called Liz. He turned, and saw her crouching on the floor and studying what looked, from a distance, like a large wooden box, about the same size as a cardboard crate in which drinks might arrive at the supermarket. Its surface looked as if it might once have been polished, but was now dull and cracked, and covered with dust.

He crouched down beside her and lifted what looked like a lid. Underneath was a turntable, padded in felt, with a thick playing arm of brown Bakelite.

"Christ!" he said. "It's a very, very old radiogram."

"Where's the radio bit?" asked Liz.

"There, down the front, look," said Derek. He bent down to join them. "You got your control knobs along here, tuning, on/off and volume, and then there's this window which shows you the stations."

"I can't see the window," said Tim.

"Ah, I can." Liz rubbed the dust off with her fingers. "What do these words mean, Tim?"

"Athlone. Motala," read Tim. "Helsinki. Helsinki? Prague. They're European cities with radio stations. Look." He started turning the tuning knob gently and the line across the screen moved on to the names. "Here, the Home Service. Remember the Home Service?"

"I do," said Derek, "but I doubt if she does."

"Nope. Pass," said Liz. "Does it work, Derek?"

"Dunno. Be honest, I'd be amazed," replied Derek. "It runs on valves that sometimes go – no transistors then. And you couldn't get the valves now."

"It'd make quite a smart booze cabinet," said Tim thoughtfully. "That box is quite deep enough to hold a Scotch bottle. And with a bit of careful polishing, that wood will look quite smart."

"You want it, you help yourself," offered Derek cheerfully. "These things aren't worth much, not in that sort of condition."

"Can we? I'd love to take it home," said Liz.

So they did. Tim was still not strong and he took a few minutes to get it into the car, huffing and straining and trying not to trip over bits of deceased motor-car on the way; the radiogram released a cloud of dust as he pushed it into the boot of the Triumph.

Ten minutes later, he and Liz were sitting on iron-legged stools in front of a small fire that flickered warmingly in the saloon bar of a pub a couple of miles away. Tim cradled a pint of bitter, Liz held a half. The pub was nearly empty; the time was only just past twelve.

"I'd forgotten how much I liked pubs," said Tim.

He looked around him at the comfortable seats and tables, the beer-pumps with their hunting scenes, and the standard horse-brasses arranged above the fireplace. There was nothing very original about the pub's interior; like most, it had been refurbished, but was none the worse for that. The beer had a rich, satisfying taste and he swallowed it greedily.

"So." He put his beer down on the floor. "What are you going to do with your life, then?"

"I want to go to drama school."

"I know. Why?"

"Because there's just nothing I want to do more than act."

"Why?"

"Why does anyone want to make a career out of acting?" she asked, shrugging.

"I wouldn't know," replied Tim, "because I'm one of the ninety-nine percent of the population that doesn't want to. The remaining one percent seem to assume that the rest of us can answer rhetorical questions like that."

She looked up at him, puzzled.

"What are you saying?"

"Well, it's a grossly egocentric job to want to do, for a start. I nearly said profession."

"Come on." She reached for her glass. "Now you're just being aggravating, like you were last night."

"If getting aggravated makes you think, then I'm all for it."

"Who are you to say?" She sipped some beer, swallowed it and exhaled. "If someone doesn't want to be aggravated, who asked you to judge whether or not they need to be?"

"Now you're going round in circles," said her brother crisply. "Tell me, in straight terms, why you want to be a bloody actress."

"Because I want people to share my interpretation of a role, an emotion..."

"Exactly. Pure egocentricity."

"All art is."

"I disagree. But that's a side issue. Why should you pick on such a self-indulgent career when you're obviously very good at something completely different?"

"I'm not that good at it. Look, Tim, you can't accuse people of being self-indulgent. You fly off to some jungle somewhere, spend two years scratching the surface of a problem then come bouncing back like a tourist with a warm glow in your heart and twenty thousand dollars stashed in the Chase Manhattan or whatever foreign bank you use. If that's not self-indulgent, what is?"

"There's no way I'm self-indulgent," said Tim, rather slowly. "Some of the things I must do are hard. Anyway, even if I personally was self-indulgent, the job isn't."

"Isn't it, Tim? Have you ever sat back and tried to justify what you do to yourself, in the way that you want me to?"

"I don't have to. The richest third world countries, like Malaysia, have a per capita income a quarter of ours and the poorest, like Sudan and Bangladesh, a tenth of theirs. That's all the justification I need. Whether or not I get a nice warm glow out of what I do is irrelevant."

"Okay. It's irrelevant. But answer me honestly – do you get a nice warm glow, etc.?"

He laughed, and shook his head. "No, Liz. I'm part of too many cock-ups for that. That's what it's really like."

She nodded. "It's funny, Tim. Don't you think we're just like each other in some ways? Sort of... Well, we're just sort of bloody awkward really, aren't we."

He grinned. They looked at each other for a minute. Then she said:

"It's academic anyway. I'm not going to drama school. I'm not going to art school. I've got one poxy A-level."

"So go back and get some more," he said, softly. "What are you, 18, 19? So much time. Anything you really want to do, you have a much better chance than you think."

* * *   * * *   * * *

IN HIS study in the Victorian rectory, Makepeace was staring out of the window at the orange leaves of the oak that guarded the entrance to the garden, searching his mind for something that had come briefly to light and then eluded him. Leaving church that morning, he had had a distinct sense of *déjà vu*. It seemed it might be a previous occasion when he had left church with Christine, and there had been autumn in the air; much earlier in the season, but still with a feeling of things passing that he could not place.

"Are Tim and Liz back yet, dear?"

"Eh?" Hands in pockets, he half-turned towards the door. "No, they're not; not yet. They will be any minute, I expect."

He had been walking up the path from the church after the service and the Vicar was ahead of him, vestments flowing. Yes, that was it. That was the key. The Vicar had left before them and made briskly for the gate. Were there bells? Yes, he thought there were bells.

He turned to Christine. She grinned slyly.

"We're free. We can escape. I'll race you to the river."

"We can't today."

"Why not?"

"I don't know. I say, Father seems rather agitated."

Crack. It was gone, as if someone had flicked a switch and he was aware of the garden gate opening. Liz staggered in with Tim; between them they carried a large dark object that trailed a cable, plugless, like a tail, splayed at the end where the separate leads came from the cover. They were laughing and giggling as they came in and Makepeace thought he smelled beer.

"Dad! Dad! We've got a new piece of furniture for your study."

"What on earth is that?"

"It's a booze cabinet," said Liz breathlessly. "Here, can we put it on this shelf beside the mantelpiece?"

"Good God, it's heavy," said Tim, chuckling. Liz looked slightly flushed. Obviously a good Sunday lunchtime drink.

They plonked it down. A little dust rose in the air as Tim stood back, clap-cleaning his hands. "Splendid," he said expansively. "Now, what shall we listen to? The Home Service? Henry Hall? *In Town Tonight*?" He bent down to look at the grimy screen. "Or we could pick up the latest from Athlone, or Helsinki, or Motala..." He spun round, and straightened an imaginary bow tie. "This is the news from London, and this is Alvar Liddell reading it."

Christine nodded. "Yes, your father does seem a little strange." Paul's father had run quickly up the aisle and caught Christine's by the shoulder: "I say, Vicar, you have a radio set."

"Well, yes, I have." The Vicar glanced at his wristwatch. "We'd better hurry, Colonel. It takes a minute to warm up and we haven't got much time. Come on, Christine dear."

Puzzled, they followed him. Over the threshold of the vicarage came the Vicar, his daughter, the Colonel, his wife, their children, Mrs. Early, the domestic staff and numerous others of the village who had issued forth from the service in their wake. They all crowded into the study where, a few weeks earlier, Paul had lain back with Christine's knee on his stomach. The Vicar bent down and switched on the mains; then with a *snick* the power was turned on.

It took a little while to warm up, as the Vicar had warned; and they were a little late. From the background, the sound of a man's voice, well-bred, perhaps a little effete, began to grow louder. Paul stared at the front panel of the radio set, which glowed a little in the shadow of its corner despite the bright outside, and read the names on it, Athlone, Helsinki, Motala; and now the man's voice could be clearly heard, droning something about Poland.

Everyone in the room had frozen. Mrs. Early stood rigid with her hands clasped so tightly together that the blood was driven from them. Paul saw his elder brother fighting to keep a look of exultation from his eyes; the muscles round his mouth hardened and pulled the skin taut, but not as taut as it would be when the dry desert wind shrank it as he stuck out lifeless and eyeless from the turret of his burnt-out tank before Benghazi two years later. And Paul would feel the sand of Silesia between his toes as he stared through the barbed wire at the endless pines that surrounded his prisoner-of-war camp.

Outside, in the Vicar's garden, the first leaf, a freak perhaps, detached itself weeks early and fluttered its way to the ground like the fragments of a letter that Paul took from his pocket on a sunny Sunday fifty years later and tore into strips, then smaller strips, then smaller yet until nothing of its substance could be divined.